coming up roses

STACI HART

Cover design by **Quirky Bird**

Editing by **Unforeseen Editing** and **Love N Books**

Book design by **Inkstain Design Studio**

coming
up
roses

To those of you searching for home:
Sink your roots into the earth.
Stretch your leaves up to the sky.
Because home is where you are.

A Good Groping

LUKE

Not a single thing had changed in five years.

Not the little bell on the door that rang entries into my family's flower shop. Not the ancient oak barrels, stuffed to the brim with petals and greenery. Not the smell, that mixture of earth and sweet perfume only made by hundreds of varieties of flowers in the same room.

That smell meant one thing: I was home.

I scanned the shop for activity—and my family, who was never far from here—but found none. So deeper into the room I went, running a hand over the timeworn wood of the counter as I passed.

But all I saw was stillness, and all I heard was music playing somewhere in the back.

I followed the sound, past a table littered with stems and scissors, twine and twigs, floral putty and pin frogs, a vase stuffed with a vivid array of poppies. But when I turned the corner where a row of humming coolers stood, I found one thing that *had* changed.

Before I'd left Manhattan five years ago for Los Angeles, Ivy and I'd fooled around on the regular—no strings, no relationship, just a reliable supply of flirting and flings. Her ass—which had always been the shape and firmness of a ripe, juicy peach—had filled in, rounded to utter perfection. She was hinged at the waist, reaching back into the cooler for something a little too far for comfort. A burst of desire shot through me like a lightning bolt, from the bottom of my spine to the top, inspiring my mouth to water, triggering a hard swallow.

Ivy Parker, my old fling. And I knew just how to greet her. I could already hear her giggling my name—after the year I'd had, the comfort of a familiar smile sounded like exactly what I needed.

I didn't remember Ivy's hair being so dark a shade of red, nor did I remember the delectable thickness of her thighs, which were pressed together. My eyes dragged up the seam and to her ass again, bouncing between her jeans pockets before sliding up the curve of her small waist.

"Shit," she swore from inside the cooler, leaning in a little more.

I wet my lips, which tilted into a smirk. I slipped my hands into the curve of that little waist in the same moment I fitted my hips to her ass, pulling her into me.

"Miss me?" I asked as she went stiff as a ruler.

A squeal and a yelp sounded as she bolted up, slamming her head on the grate above her. Vases teetered, and my hands shot out to catch one but not quickly enough. It toppled over with a thunk and a splash, knocking over another, then another, like bowling pins full of water.

Water that spilled all over the girl caged in the cooler by my hips.

The girl who was not Ivy Parker.

Tess Monroe bucked, huffing and squealing, and I stepped back with my face shot open and stuck there like I'd just laid eyes on Medusa and she'd made marble out of me.

She backed out, standing with deliberate slowness and absolute fury as she turned to face me, the physical incarnation of Medusa herself, ready to blast me into oblivion with nothing more than a murderous glare.

My mortification was marked by a wildly inappropriate laugh, stifled at the very last second. She looked like a cat that'd been dunked in a bucket, rage wafting off her, riding every controlled breath. Limp auburn hair stuck to her face, strands of deep red against the pale of her skin. Smudged half-moons of mascara ringed her eyes, set ablaze with fury. And her fitted white T-shirt clung to every bend and swell of her body, tucked into high-waisted jeans that hugged those curves I'd just been salivating over like a second skin.

I realized then that the water must have been very cold. And her bra must be very thin.

"Tess?" I said stupidly. "You look…different. I thought—"

Her hands fisted by her sides, and I braced myself to catch one if she swung at me. But she didn't. No, she stood there, unmoving, with water dripping off her in a steady *pat, pat, pat* on the polished concrete floor.

"And you haven't changed at all," she shot with her smart little mouth. "Still the same degenerate you always were. I'll have to update the sign. We've gone eighteen hundred twenty-five days without anyone getting groped in the greenhouse. Should have erased it the second I heard you were coming back."

I laughed. "Admit it. I give an excellent grope."

She made a noise somewhere between a squeak and a growl, her jaw bolted shut as she stormed past. But I hooked her arm, chuckling.

"Hang on, Tess. I'm sorry—I really am. I thought you were Ivy," I admitted.

Instead of looking forgiving like I'd hoped, she seethed. "Well, sorry to disappoint," she ground out.

"Who said I was disappointed?"

I stepped into her before she could speak, and she froze when I cupped her face. The first taste of her skin against my palm was cool, warming immediately as her cheeks flamed with a brilliant flush. I couldn't tell if it was an angry flush or not.

But I didn't hesitate to consider it as I inspected her, turning her head so I could check it for bangs or cuts.

"You hit your head pretty good," I said gently. "I wouldn't have grabbed you like that if I'd realized it was you. You okay?"

"I'm fine," she snapped, removing herself from my grip.

She turned on her heel, blowing past the table and to the back where we kept the cleaning supplies.

I followed her like an asshole. "I'm looking for Mom. Have you seen her?"

Tess swiped a scratchy white towel off a stack and blotted her face. "She's at home, waiting for you. You should go. Now."

"Oh, you're not getting off so easy." One of my brows rose with one corner of my mouth.

She rolled her eyes so hard, I was pretty sure she saw Bleeker Street. "Go away, Luke."

My smile slipped, and I glanced back at the coolers. "I mean it. At least let me clean up the mess."

"I've got it," she fired because surely her mouth was a weapon.

"I insist," I said with velvety persistence, reaching around her for a couple of towels. "Let me try to make it right."

She froze but for her eyes, which tracked my hand like it was a goddamn cobra.

"You know," I started with what I hoped was a reassuring smile. Her eyes cut to me with a flash. "I don't bite."

"That's not what Ivy said," she countered.

That bought her a full-blown laugh. "Fair enough. But I haven't nibbled on Ivy in half a decade." I turned for the coolers. "Where's

4

she at?"

"She's off," Tess said, toweling off her hair. When she thought I was out of earshot, she let out a heavy sigh.

I propped open the cooler door and knelt down, towel in hand as I inspected the damage. Nothing had broken, though some of the flowers had been smashed in the fall. I pushed up to stand with a sigh of my own and began hauling the damaged arrangements out of the cooler, fixing them up as best I could.

Tess scowled at me from across the room. I smirked back at her, unfazed, if not a little guilty.

Really, very little could faze me. It happened to be one of my special gifts along with the unfastening of a bra with two fingers, making a woman orgasm in under two minutes, and generally getting my way by sheer force of charm.

One of the few women immune to that charm was Tess Monroe.

Tess had been working for my mother since high school. Of course, that was back when we'd had half a dozen flower shops spread over lower Manhattan before the slow choke that brought on a retreat that left us with only the flagship store. Where Ivy was always up for a flirt, a laugh, and a subsequent romp behind the banana plants, Tess was her unamused, disapproving opposite. One of my particular joys in life was making her uncomfortable in the hopes she'd reveal a crack in the wall or the flesh of her soft little underbelly. I knew it was there—I'd seen her light and laughing and kind with literally everyone else. Once upon a time, we'd even been friends.

But now? My presence alone shot her hackles off her back faster than you could say *Pass the peonies*. And that drove me just a little bit crazy.

As I set the last vase on the table and turned for the cooler once more, I resolved to give grown-up Tess all of my grown-up charm.

While I mopped up the water, she worked behind me, the snap

and click as she rearranged what I'd already arranged sharp and irritated. It was always like this with her, an impatient, intolerable sharing of space.

She was the literal worst person on earth for me to have inadvertently groped, and I had a feeling I'd be paying for that infraction for a good long while.

Tess didn't let anything go easy.

When I finished with the cooler, I tossed the soaked towels in one of the waste buckets and wandered into the shop to gather the flowers needed to fix the bouquets. A few stems of sweet pea. A handful of lavender astilbe spires. Chestnut pods, green and furry. A bunch of craspedia, round and the color of sunshine. Dahlias, pink— no, peach—and white. And then I made my way back to her as she fussed over the vases.

Her eyes narrowed as she cataloged my wares—looking for a mistake, no doubt. When she didn't find one, she let out a huff.

"Thank you," she mumbled, picking up the sweet peas and submerging them in the bowl of water next to her to trim the stems.

"Hey, that's my line," I said with a sideways smile. I picked up a dahlia, measuring it to the vase before doing the same.

"You really don't have to do this," she said quietly, tightly.

"I owe you one, Tess. And honestly, I don't mind. I've been doing it for Mom since I was little."

She huffed a laugh. "So much for Hot Wheels and frogs."

"Hot Wheels and frogs were why I was cutting flowers. You think I wanted to be making bouquets at eight? Mom nearly broke her neck on a car show I'd set up behind her table, and the frog came in a shipment of plants and lived in my pocket until it kamikazed into her lap. I arranged funeral lilies for a week."

Another impatient laugh, coupled with the shake of her head. She hadn't met my eyes. "So you *have* been a menace since conception."

"As the youngest of five, it's my birthright."

Her cheeks flushed when she laughed again. Her eyes were rich and brown, like fresh-turned earth, her lips dusky rose to match her cheeks.

God, she was pretty. I could still remember the girl I'd known, the one who'd been my friend so many years ago. I couldn't seem to recall what went wrong, where that friendship fell apart and turned into whatever this was.

"You know, there's something I can't figure out," I said blithely.

"Why you're so insufferable?"

"Why you don't like me, Tess. *Everybody* loves me," I joked.

Her face flattened, and she finally looked up at me. "Really? You can't think of a single reason why someone wouldn't—*don't touch my scissors.*"

I lifted my hands like she'd pointed a gun at me. "Ever stop to think it's not me who's insufferable?"

"Nope, never. Not once." She snatched the scissors I'd tried to use on the craspedia and pointed them at me. "You're the most arrogant, ridiculous man I have ever met, and you just happen to be the very last man I'd ever entertain."

"In the bedroom?"

"In the hemisphere."

A laugh burst out of me. "Don't worry, Tess. There's plenty of time to change your mind about what latitude you can tolerate me in. We'll be seeing a lot of each other now that I'm home."

Her face bent in a frown, the point of the scissors dropping a hair. "What do you mean?"

"I mean I'll be working here. Every day. Right over there." I nodded to the counter. "Meet your new counter attendant and delivery boy."

She sucked in a breath through her nose that threatened to seal her nostrils. "No."

"All hands on deck if we're going to save the shop from ruin. I didn't think you'd balk at the help."

"Well, you aren't just any help, Luke Bennet. You are trouble, and you always have been." She jabbed the scissors in my direction.

But before I could argue, my mom walked in, and as always, the universe tilted in her direction.

The moment I drew her into my arms, I was truly home.

And not one thing had changed.

Poison Ivy

TESS

Everyone hates parts of their job.

Maybe it's the paperwork. Maybe it's the day-to-day grind. Maybe it's that client who never knows what they want, or the guy who always cooks fish in the microwave.

But not me. I loved every corner of that store, every flower, every petal, every stem. I loved the greenhouse. I loved Mrs. Bennet. I loved creating, and I loved making something beautiful.

I didn't hate anything at all.

Except for Luke Fucking Bennet.

There were many adjectives to describe how I felt in that moment. Furious was paramount, followed closely by defensive and bewildered, touched with a hint of unease and a healthy helping of attraction, which was a noun, but also an undeniable fact between Luke and me.

He lit up like a lighthouse when he saw his mother, pulling her into a hug with arms like tree trunks. She squealed like a girl when he picked her up and spun her around wildly.

Wild. That was perhaps the best adjective to describe him. His hair, dark as sin, disheveled and untamed. His eyes, crisp and bright, a shade of blue so electric, so luminescent, it defied logic. Golden skin, kissed by the California sun that had shone on him the last five years. His smile told a tale of lust, loose and easy, given without thought or care. And though he didn't have the discipline of a predator, his body moved with the ease and grace of a great black cat.

His lips said he'd come home to help save the shop, but his history said otherwise. I'd believe he ran out of money. Or that he was running from Wendy Westham, their marriage come unraveled, just like we'd all known it would. I'd believe just about anything beyond altruism.

Luke Bennet had come home to wreck everything he touched, just like he always did. And the saddest thing? He didn't even have a clue. Not one.

He was feral, a thing unbridled, without rules or constraint. He went where he wanted, did what he chose. Never, not in a million years, would he be called responsible or dependable. And he hadn't changed a bit in five years, but for the slight crinkle at the corners of his eyes.

Should have worn sunscreen. Irresponsible asshole.

My teeth ground together with a squeak, and my eyes followed my hands as I *snip, snip, snipped* stems, imagining they were Luke's neck.

I realized I sounded like the insufferable one, like he'd said. But ten years of being ignored by Luke Bennet would do that to a girl.

Maybe ignored was the wrong word. Forgotten. Rejected. Disregarded.

Because Luke didn't *ignore* anybody. In fact, he had a knack for making every person he came across feel special and important to him. As such, every girl in a thirty-block radius—including yours truly—had, at some point, had a massive crush on the handsome, cavalier charmer. Regardless of the fact that he systematically snakebit every woman he came across and exploited every little crush to the fullest extent.

The worst part? He didn't do it with a single malicious intention. He just gave and took and moved right along.

I almost couldn't be mad at him.

Almost.

Except I couldn't forgive him for the night he'd forgotten. He didn't remember that kiss, touched with whiskey and fire. It had branded me like a red-hot iron, but it'd meant so little to him, he didn't seem to have a flicker of a memory of the moment. And the next day, when I saw him at work, he treated me as if it had never happened.

Worse—he'd brushed right past me on his way to manhandle my best friend, Ivy.

"Lucas Bennet!" Mrs. Bennet said in that fond way a mother scolds her child. "Let me get a good look at you."

He set her down, standing proudly, smiling softly. If he wasn't a beast, he'd look like a boy.

Mrs. Bennet lifted her hands to his face, her gnarled fingers brushing his cheeks. My heart lurched at the sight.

Rheumatoid arthritis had twisted her hands, limited her mobility, ceased her passion. I'd been her hands for years, my mentor, my surrogate mother. She'd taught me everything I knew, inspired my own passion. I'd found my calling, thanks to her.

I'd found a place to belong, thanks to her.

And now, Luke had returned with his stupid, perfect ass and his pizza bod. You know the kind—broad shoulders, narrow waist that pointed to some spicy pepperoni you'd just love to get in or around your mouth. Even through his T-shirt, I could make out the landscape of his back—hills and valleys, ridges and rolling bulges, like alluvia drawn by water running through sand.

My life as I knew it had officially been flung into a meat grinder, and Luke Bennet's hand rested firmly on the crank.

Snip, snip, snip, I cut, so mad that I saw everything behind a curtain of fuchsia. I barely even noticed Brutus, the shop's cat and premier rat hunter, had taken a seat on the table next to me, watching me with detached curiosity, golden eyes knowing and dark fur gleaming.

I had known Luke was coming home—the rest of the Bennets had just arrived, and per the usual, he was late. Really, I should have assumed he'd be working here. What else would he do? The whole point of their return was to help with the shop, and everyone had a job to do. Even Luke. Though the extent of his skillset consisted of making a joke out of everything, seducing unsuspecting women, and being a nuisance. Working the counter seemed to be the only thing he *could* do.

It was here where we'd first met, here where he'd worked every summer until he graduated high school. And then he gallivanted off, never going to college, never planning for anything. Instead, he traipsed around the city without a care in the world, working a hundred jobs in a handful of years. Then, he met Wendy, and off they went to California by way of a Vegas courthouse. Two months—that was the length of their courtship.

Seriously, she could have been a serial killer for all he knew.

No one thought Luke would ever get married, but if I'd had to pair him with someone, it would have been Wendy. They were equally vain, vapid, and vacuous, thus making them perfect for each other.

No one had been shocked when he caught her riding a Hollywood producer like a pony.

I'd heard she'd laughed. I'd heard she'd mocked him. I'd heard she'd left him because she learned the flower shop was failing, thus depleting Luke's trust and income by way of his share in the store.

I'd heard a lot of things, though who knew how many of them were true? Because everyone loved Luke, and as far as they were concerned, he could do no wrong. The way Mrs. Bennet spoke of Wendy, she was an evil thing with no other desire but to ruin Luke's life and happiness. Luke's brother Kash had softer things to say, but they still painted her as a user and abuser of sweet, innocent Luke.

Some days, it seemed I was the only one who thought he was a louse. I could fill a notebook with infractions to prove my case, if I were so inclined. There may or may not have been such a notebook somewhere in the recesses of my room, but I'd never admit, even with a gun to my temple.

I was shivering, I realized, my fingers numb in the cold water, my wet shirt freezing, my hair dripping in icy rivulets down my back.

"Oh, to have all my babies under one roof," Mrs. Bennet crooned, her eyes misty.

"Except Marcus," Luke amended. "He wouldn't deign himself to live at home, Mr. Independently Wealthy."

Mrs. Bennet tsked. "He lives two doors down. Deny it all he wants, but he likes being home just as much as any of you." She turned to me, beaming. "Can you believe it, Tess? Can you believe he's home for good?"

"No, I really can't," I said, snipping another stem with more force than was necessary.

Her smile fell as she assessed me. "Why on earth are you all wet?"

"Funny story, that." I filled up my lungs to tell her that her son had humped me in the cooler, deciding to leave out the way his very large, very strong hands had felt clamped on my waist or the delectable feel of his hips nestled into my ass. My official statement was: groping and a possible concussion with some mild to moderate shaming to really lay it on thick.

But he cut me off. "It was my fault. I scared Tess, and she hit her head. I would have come up sooner, but I was helping clean up."

Her face softened, opening up like she was looking at a box of kittens instead of her grownass lying liar of a son. "That's my Lucas, always willing to help."

I rolled my eyes when she wasn't looking. Luke caught the motion and smirked.

Stupid bastard.

I dropped my scissors on the table with a clunk and wiped my hands on a towel next to the bowl. "Excuse me. I'm just going to go get cleaned up."

"Okay, honey," Mrs. Bennet said with a smile. "Come on, Lucas." She threaded her arm in his and towed him toward the door. "Come get settled in."

"Oh, I will," he said to his mother, though he was looking at me with that outrageous smile of his tilting his lips. "I'm in for the long haul. So don't you worry. I'm not going anywhere."

The Brood

LUKE

Mom hadn't stopped talking, but I didn't hear a word she'd said. I hummed like an engine, my skin sparked with electricity, and every thought in my head was of Tess Monroe.

I remembered her as a sixteen-year-old kid with eyes too big for her face and hair like a shiny penny. We met here at the shop, though we lived a block away from each other, the Bennets went to private school, and Ivy and Tess went to the local public school. Once upon a time, we had been friends—summers spent working together in the shop, pizza and video games at her place, sneaking into the greenhouse after hours with booze my sister had bought for us. The occasional rabble-rousing with Ivy, Tess on our heels, hissing warnings that we'd get in trouble.

And though I was a shameless flirt, it never went anywhere with Tess. But somewhere along the way, something changed. I always chalked it up to the loss of her mom since the events happened within a few weeks of each other. After that, Tess locked it down like

Fort Knox, complete with an armored guard and automatic weapons.

Didn't stop me from trying though my efforts seemed to piss her off even more.

Mostly, I exercised my impulses on Ivy, who in turn exercised hers on me. We were never a thing, not really. Friends, sure. Hookups? Absolutely. But never anything more. I hadn't seen her in five years.

Tess either, and my, what a pleasant surprise that had turned out to be.

I'd always been averse to the word no—respectfully, of course. With Tess, it was more of an itch I couldn't stop scratching. I wanted her to like me. I wanted her to want me. I could count the people who didn't like me on two hands, and Tess occupied the right hand, index finger.

And that was something I decided to rectify.

As the youngest of five, I'd learned early how to get my way, a skill that proven useful in life and lust. Not so much in love. In that department, I'd failed miserably.

Sadly, I seemed to be the only one who was surprised.

I pushed open the door, chiming the bell to mark our exit from the store, and around the sidewalk we went, to the grand stoop next to the shop that marked the Bennet family home.

The Longbourne Flower Shop had been a staple of Greenwich Village since the nineteenth century when my industrious British ancestors purchased a handful of buildings and made it their home and business. Greenhouses were built on the roof and spanned the backyards of all five properties—the shop, our home, and three tenant buildings which had been sold in the 90s to fund Longbourne's expansion. It was our claim to fame, our draw. We were the largest greenhouse in Manhattan, and that we provided our own flowers rather than the Chelsea market or Long Island made us famous. Once, at least.

Home was a modest word for the building we occupied. Nearly

five thousand square feet of Victorian brownstone stood proudly on Bleeker, our home passed down through five generations and grandfathered in by New York's generous laws and codes. Six bedrooms, two parlors, servants' quarters, a library. And as we passed through the grand doorway, the house seemed to be untouched by time, just like the flower shop. Although, rather than roller skates and skateboards and backpacks like when we had been kids, the entryway was littered with a jumbled pile of shoes, gym bags and purses, coats and scarves in the dead heat of July.

Laughter and chatter floated through the walls and doorways, the chaos of the house as familiar as Mom's arms around me and the scent of the flower shop.

I'd always hated the quiet. Wendy hated that I couldn't sit in silence. There was always music going, no matter the time of day or what I was doing. Even when I slept, I slept with white noise. It used to drive her crazy.

Then again, everything drove Wendy crazy.

It was just that the Bennet home was never quiet, nor was it clean despite a crew of three women who came weekly to try to manage the mess. Really, it consisted of them moving piles of things from one place to another in an effort to clean around them.

Mom and I headed into the dining room, which brimmed with raven-haired Bennets.

Our mother had an odd—and for some of the Bennet brood, inconvenient—taste for Roman names. The eldest was Julius, who went strictly by Jett. Calling him Julius would result in one of several reactions—a black eye, a popped nose, or a fat lip. Once, I'd earned all three along with an atomic wedgie. His twin sister was younger by three minutes. Elaine—Laney, which was our grandmother's name—was as irreverent as she was headstrong and opinionated, a Bennet gene that streaked strong and loud. And then there was Marcus, who lounged at one end of the table in his suit with a newspaper in hand like some relic from the past—no one other than Dad read newspapers anymore. But there he sat with his nose in the crease like the dork he always was. At his side stood Kassius, my twin by Irish standards. Kash and I had been born eleven months apart and shared a room until I left for LA.

By all accounts, he was my best friend on the planet.

At the other end of the table sat our father, and though his expression was closed, his eyes shone bright and brilliantly blue— another Bennet trademark. As was typical, his shirt was smudged with greenhouse dirt, the beds of his nails always packed with soil, no matter how well he'd washed them. His hair was the color of freshly fallen snow, and his lips quirked at the corner like they held back some secret they'd never let go of.

Their faces turned to us, coupled with a bawdy burst of noise, and before I could say hello, they were out of their seats and swarming me.

Jett hooked me around the neck and pulled me, twisting me into an awkward hold. "Hey, little brother. Had enough tofu and bikinis?"

"Never," I said, twisting out of his grip.

Laney flung herself at me, wrapping her slender arms around my chest. "I love that he calls you little when you're taller than all of them."

I wrapped her up in a hug, laughing. "He's just jealous. It's hard being this beautiful."

Marcus wore a sideways smile as easily as his Italian suit, offering a hand for a shake. God forbid his shirt get wrinkled. "Good to see you, kid."

I rolled my eyes, keeping Laney in my grip with one arm when I took his hand. "You're two years older than me."

"That's dog years in maturity."

Before he could argue, Kash busted into the mix like a puppy, making a sandwich out of Laney, who squealed between us like a giggling piglet. Kash laughed into my ear, clapping my back.

"Missed you, man."

"You missed me being your wingman," I corrected.

"Please—if anybody was the wingman, it was me," he said with a smirk, shoving me in the shoulder when he let me go.

Dad nodded, his sideways smile firmly in place and his hands in the pockets of his scuffed-up pants.

"Look, Mr. Bennet," Mom said proudly. "He's here! California's too far. Always said it was, didn't I?"

"Glad you're home, son. Hopefully the lack of miles between you and your mother will serve you as well as it will her."

"Oh, you," she huffed playfully, swatting at his chest. "It'll suit him just fine. It'll suit all of them, won't it?"

We offered our agreement to appease her, as we always did. Truth was, four out of five grown Bennet kids moving home had been born out of necessity rather than desire. Though not our own necessity— that of our mother's.

It was the only way we were going to save the flower shop, and it would take all of us to do it.

"Come sit down, Lukie," Laney said, pulling me toward the table. "How was your flight?"

"Long, but the flight attendant had a crush on me."

Marcus rolled his eyes as he sat. "You think everybody has a crush on you."

"Well, with bone structure like this, who wouldn't?" I asked with a shrug. "Besides, I'm never turning down free drinks."

"You are girl crazy, Lucas Bennet," Mom said with a tsk and a smile.

"I can't help it. I got all your charm and good looks. I was doomed from the start." I jerked my chin at Laney, who sat next to me. "When'd you get in?"

"Yesterday. God, I missed New York."

"What, Dallas wasn't kicking it for you anymore?"

"Oh, it was kicking something. More shit than anything, judging by the percentage of cowboy boots worn in that city." She chuckled at her own joke along with the chorus of our laughter. "Honestly, I was looking for a reason to get out of there. I missed the city."

"You say that like there aren't a couple million people there," Marcus argued.

"But it's not *New York*," she said, as if that explained everything. "It wasn't hard to walk away from my corporate job, not even a little."

"What, you didn't get turned on doing social media for a computer company?" Kash asked with a brow up.

"Nope," Laney said. "Now, if it'd been Apple, you'd have had to drag me back kicking and screaming."

Mom laughed a little too loud. "You didn't all have to come home. Really, we were doing okay, weren't we, dear?"

Dad cleared his throat. "Okay being a relative term? Sure."

"See?" Mom said, gesturing to Dad in confirmation.

Marcus's face flattened.

But when he opened his mouth to speak, Mom cut him off. "Now, we appreciate you kids coming home to help out, but don't you dare feel obligated. Your father and I will be just fine. Don't you worry about us."

Jett cast a glance around the table at us before covering Mom's hand with his. "We're happy to help out, Mom. Anyway, it's not like we had anything else going on, did we?"

We echoed our affirmatives in solidarity, which were, of course, lies.

Laney had a great job with a stable, growing company. Jett managed a bookstore on the Upper West but had taken a leave of absence to come home. I'd been living on the other side of the country, not that I had any real roots there or any long-term prospects to speak of. Not that I did long-term either. But if I *did*, I still would have dropped it all to come home.

Kash had never left though. Instead, he took to the greenhouses to help Dad, who wasn't getting any younger. If anyone was going to take over the shop that'd been in our family for generations, it'd be Kash.

And Marcus … well, after making a relative fortune in hedge funds, he'd bailed to day trade. And then to buy the shop—and its substantial debt—with the sole intention of turning the business around.

The honest truth? Mom was perfectly content making pretty things and ignoring ugly ones, and Dad was happier in the dirt than the paperwork. When business was booming, Longbourn had taken care of itself. But when times got tough, no one possessed the acumen to patch up the holes in the boat. And it had almost sunk.

I only hoped we would get it back on the water. With our bullheaded bunch, I had no doubt we'd get it moving again, if powered by nothing more than dog-paddling and sheer will.

"You starting at the shop tomorrow?" Kash asked, kicking my boot under the table.

"I dunno. Mom?"

"If you're ready. Not that we have much business these days, but we always do more in the summers, especially when you're on the counter," she said, patting my shoulder.

Laney snickered.

"Yeah," Kash said. "I'd be willing to bet Cougar Judy orders a couple of bouquets once she hears you're behind the counter."

Mom's smile fell. "Judy always was one of our best customers. I wonder if she's been getting her arrangements from Bower Bouquets."

A collective chorus of derisive noise filled the room. Bower was the name on the company dartboard. They'd come in with a corporate swoop that put an end to almost every other shop in Manhattan. Ours had only survived this long because Longbourne provided wholesale flowers to neighboring shops and existed as a monument, a cornerstone of the neighborhood, and the only greenhouse of this size in Manhattan. The hip little boutiques and the big chains had driven everyone else out, and even the boutiques had to fight for scraps, what with Greenwich Village rent and the convenience of ordering flowers on 1-800-Roses4U.

"You know," she started, "at garden club last week, Evangeline Bower was on her high horse about the new stores they just opened. She looked down her long nose at me through her whole humblebragging speech. She thinks I'm crass? Well, I think she's a snob, plain and simple."

"Maybe her French twist is too tight," Laney joked.

"Judy's not going to Bower," Jett soothed. "She just *loves* Luke."

Laney laughed. "We can put his pretty face in the front of the store and watch the ladies roll in."

Mom softened, laughing when I framed my face and batted my lashes at her.

"Maybe we should put him in a sandwich board out front," Laney joked.

"We can write *Plant one on me* on the front." Jett smirked.

"Only if he's naked," Kash added.

"With a bell," Marcus insisted.

"I mean, I wouldn't say no," I said with a shrug.

"You always were the one I couldn't get to wear pants when you were little," Mom said. "And by the fifth baby in six years, I found it hard to be bothered to care."

"We cultivate many things," Dad said. "Roses, poppies, and a penchant for exhibition."

Mom laughed again, beaming at us as we volleyed. "All of the Bennets under one roof. It's just a dream to have you home again."

"Not all," Marcus corrected.

Mom gave him a look. "Marcus Bennet, you are here every single night for dinner, and you do your laundry in my mud room. Do not pretend you don't love it here, or I will call you a liar."

He glanced at the ceiling and shook out his newspaper, but a ghost of a smile flickered across his lips.

As I scanned the faces of my family, I had to admit, I found my own sense of peace along with a shift I had yet to place. It'd been years since all of us were able to get home for a holiday, years more since we were in permanent residence. And now we were home, banded together with a sole purpose—save Longbourne.

I had the feeling it would take everything in us to do it. But if I had faith in one thing in the world, it was the Bennets' ability to tackle every obstacle in our path like the feral, determined dogs we were.

And we wouldn't give up the fight until we won.

Let Her Be Wild

TESS

"**D**addy, I'm home!"

The door closed with a snick, and I flicked on the light in the apartment where I'd grown up.

There was the same old couch, the same dated table. The same old wallpaper Mom had loved so much and the same faded curtains that matched said wallpaper so exactly, you could barely tell where one stopped and the other began. It was a time capsule, left unchanged for fear we'd lose another piece of her to memory.

I dropped my bag by the door and made my way through the living room, setting my flowers on the kitchen table as I passed. "Daddy? You here?"

"Back here, baby," he said, his voice dulled by walls and a hallway.

I wandered down the hall and into his office where I found him sitting at his table under the harsh light of a lamp, painting a tiny soldier under a magnifying glass.

He smiled up at me, his eyes warm over the top of his reading glasses. "Heya, Pigeon. How was work?"

I sighed, stepping into him to press a kiss to his forehead. "Terrible," I said cheerily. "Luke Bennet showed up at the flower shop and made a mess."

"Nothin' new there." He frowned, the effect wrinkling his forehead and echoing his days as a sergeant. His sergeant face was the kind that scared boys off and made men prepare for a long, painful set of push-ups.

I flopped down in an armchair with another sigh. "He's working the counter and deliveries. Came back from California to help save the shop. Fat lot of good he'll do. He's such a train wreck. I wouldn't put it past him to accidentally set the place on fire."

At that, Dad smirked. "Well, I knew the boy was good-looking, but I didn't think he was so handsome he could combust."

"Oh no—it'd be from setting off Black Cats in a bucket or mixing something dangerous with the fertilizer."

He made a noncommittal sound and turned to dab paint on the soldier in his hand. "Just keep your head down and ignore him."

"That happens to be my specialty, but I'm a little out of practice after five years," I huffed like a brat, and annoyed with myself, I changed the subject. "Did you eat dinner?"

"No, not yet. I've been snacking." He nodded to a bag of trail mix on the corner of the table. "I didn't realize how late it was. Nothing makes me lose time like assembling an army."

I chuckled, hauling myself out of the chair. "Come on. Let's get you fed."

"Yes, ma'am," he said, leaning back in his wheelchair as I grabbed the handles.

He hated when I pushed his wheelchair but accepted my doting as the affection it was.

He'd lost his legs in Afghanistan, third tour, IED. And he was the lucky one, the only one in his unit to survive. We moved to New York just after that, into an apartment left to my mother by her mother. Four years later, Mom was gone. It'd been me and Dad ever since.

By the time they'd found her cancer, it had spread to her lymph nodes and bladder. Chemo slowed it down but couldn't stop it. One year from her diagnosis, and she slipped away from us. Before she'd died, she'd made me get genetic testing—I always assumed to ease her mind, make it easier to let me go. The results were good, although she still put me on preventative birth control and helped me organize a plan for my doctors, including regular screenings to be insisted on, no matter my age.

I hadn't been the only planner in the family.

Much of the last year of her life she had spent teaching me how to adult, preparing me for what would come next as best she could. *By failing to prepare, you prepare to fail*, she'd quote Benjamin Franklin with a smile. Grocery shopping. Managing bills. Budgeting. She showed me the best way to clean around a faucet and how to get out every imaginable stain from laundry. I learned how to help Dad when he needed it—though not through practice. He was so hell-bent on the idea that he didn't need help, it inspired a level of independence not always seen in people who had lost so much freedom. Never had I heard him complain. Never had he asked me for help.

I was always there to offer it anyway. And on occasion, he even let me.

Like when it came to cooking. His recipe repertoire was limited to cereal, hot dogs, and chili, but Mom had left me recipes on recipes, all written in her hand and housed in a box my father had made her when I was a baby.

I pushed him up to his spot at the table, the space with the missing chair, and pressed a kiss to the top of his head.

"What do you think tonight? Betsy's famous beef Stroganoff or Meatballs à la Betsy?"

"Stroganoff. I've been dying for that sauce for what feels like ages."

I chuckled, heading over to the recipe box. My fingers lingered as I flipped through the cards, the corners curled and soft, some speckled with grease or sauce. I found the one I had been looking for and set it on the counter even though I knew every word by heart.

"What'd you bring home today?" he asked to the sound of crinkling paper as he picked up my flowers.

"Bells of Ireland, love-in-a-mist, Iceland poppies. Nimbus sweet peas. Ranunculus."

"Those the big orange ones?"

"Mmhmm," I hummed with a smile as I moved supplies from the fridge to the counter.

"These should photograph nicely."

"I hope so. The color combination is going to get me a load of likes on Instagram. I'm so glad Mrs. Bennet lets me bring home the flowers bloomed too far to sell."

"So am I," he admitted. "There's nothing so inspiring as to have such fresh beauty delivered daily. Makes the house feel alive."

I smiled at him over my shoulder. "Our house looks like a crazy plant lady lives here."

"Well, one does." He smirked at me before sticking his nose in the flowers.

It wasn't a lie. Our house was full of plants, every corner teeming with broad leaves. Pots of ivy hung above, the vines led across the ceiling by hooks. They were Mom's, and I'd kept them alive all this time. I had a recurring nightmare that I came home one day and they were all dead, crisp and brown and withered.

"It's genetic, I suppose. Can you imagine what your mother

would think if she could see Matilda now?"

I glanced at the biggest of the ivy plants, which spilled out of its pot like a waterfall. A few years ago, it'd grown so heavy, I had to bolt the hook into a beam to keep it hanging.

"She'd probably tease me for living in a virtual jungle and tell me to get out my pruning shears."

He chuckled. "You'd never do it."

"Not in a million years would I trim that beast back. Let her be wild."

"It's good advice, Tess. You could stand for a little more wild in your life."

"Hey, I can be wild," I said, dumping the steak into the pan with a sizzle.

He made a teasing noise.

"What?" I asked as I grabbed the big pot and filled it with water for noodles.

"You're about as wild as a goldfish."

"I'll have you know that wild goldfish can take over a river within a year. They are a force to be reckoned with."

"I'm just saying, it wouldn't kill you to go out every once in a while."

"I go out," I insisted. "Last week, Ivy and I went to dinner."

"You were home by nine-thirty."

I shrugged. "I'm just saying. I do things."

"The same things."

"I like when things are the same. Predictable. Is that so wrong?"

"No, I suppose not. We all crave the predictable. It's just a little easy, that's all. A little adventure wouldn't kill you, you know."

"Some adventure could. Like skydiving. Or shark diving."

"A date wouldn't."

I sighed, smiling as I turned for the table while dinner simmered. "Maybe I'm happiest when you're the only man in my life."

He watched me pick up the flowers and move to the island. "Tess, if the only man in your life is an old one with no legs, you might need to reevaluate your priorities."

He was teasing me. I didn't think it was particularly funny, but I laughed it off anyway, spreading my fare out on the island and reaching into a cabinet for the vase I wanted.

"And where would I meet someone?" I asked, convinced there was no answer.

"One of those apps. Bundle or Timber?"

"Bumble and Tinder," I corrected on a chuckle. "I don't know. It just seems so … random. And unnecessarily risky. I'd rather meet someone in real life and forge a connection than pick someone from a stable like a horse."

"That'd require you to actually get out of the house."

I frowned down at my hands as I trimmed stems. "You sound awfully judgy tonight, Dad."

A sigh, heavy and full. "Sometimes, I worry I'm holding you back," he admitted openly, as was his way. As was mine.

But I shook my head, eyes on the flowers, heart in my throat. "You're not holding me back, Daddy. You're holding me steady."

A pause, long and pregnant. "Come here," he said gently.

For a moment, I didn't move. But there was no denying him, not of one single thing he wished. When I met his eyes, they were sad and deep. I didn't know when he'd gotten so old. In my mind, he was still young and smiling, his face smooth and hair thick and shaggy. But in moments like this, his life was etched in the lines of his face like a story on stone.

He took my hand. "I love you, Tess. And I want you to make me a promise."

"Anything, Daddy," I said softly.

"Be wild. Because life is lived in the moments you don't see coming.

Not in the comfort of predictability, but in the thrill of the unknown."

My heart folded in on itself at the thought. "But I … I don't know if I know how."

But he smiled. "Then that's what you should figure out. Do one thing this week that scares you. Just one. And if you can't think of anything, ask Ivy. I'm pretty sure she has a running list."

At that, I laughed, the sound catching in my throat, tightened from emotion.

I couldn't deny him. But I didn't know how to honor the request.

The acrid smell of meat a little overdone hit my nose, and his too.

"Better get that," he suggested, effectively letting me off the hook for an answer.

I hurried to the stove and grabbed the pan, picking it up to cool it a little as I salvaged dinner and digested what he'd said.

He wasn't wrong, which was perhaps the most bitter taste left once I'd swallowed his words. I hadn't been on a date in an unspeakable amount of time, and since Ivy had landed herself a bun in the oven and a serious boyfriend—fiancé soon, if I had to bet—we'd barely gone out at all. Not that we'd gone out much before. I was as bland as my father had suggested. There wasn't much time to party when you were up at four every morning and at the flower shop at five, six days a week. By nine, I was toast, crispy and rough and in desperate need of some buttering up.

I wanted more out of life, I did. Someday, I hoped for the dream—a doting husband, a couple of kids, a house in the Village, summer vacations. I wanted my student loans paid and a hefty amount of money in savings. I wanted my wishes to come true, but now? Well, now I was focused on what was in front of me—the flower shop, my father, and my dream of someday publishing my own books about floristry.

I'd squeaked out nearly twenty thousand followers on Instagram and collected a decade of notes, a list of titles and themes just waiting to be explored. And someday, I would.

But first, today. And today was for predictability.

Wild could wait.

Things You Can Count On

LUKE

"**Y**ou're late."

Tess scowled at me from behind the counter, her palms flat on the surface and her apron already streaked with dirt.

"Good morning to you too," I said cheerily as the door closed behind me.

She rolled her eyes before turning to the shelf behind her. "You already have deliveries, so don't bother getting comfortable."

"It's only eight in the morning."

"No, eight was when you were supposed to be here. It's eight-thirty," she said, thunking a vase on the counter.

"Three orders this early? Who says we're not busy?"

"Don't get excited. They're all to Judy."

A laugh shot out of me. "News travels fast."

"You're disgusting, you know that?" *Thunk* went another vase. She pinned me with a glare before turning for the last.

"All I did was come back to town."

"You'd send your mother to an early grave if she knew you were running your gigolo clients through her flower shop." *Thunk.*

"Please. I haven't been a gigolo in years."

Her eyes narrowed to slits, and I got the distinct impression she was trying to explode me with her corneas.

"I'm kidding, Tess."

Another roll of her eyes as she slapped the ticket next to the vases. "The truck is out back. By all means, take your time coming back."

"You wound me," I said, smiling at her like a fiend, fueled by her scorn.

"The indestructible Luke Bennet?" She snorted. "You act as if I don't know you."

I stalked up to the counter, my smile tightening. "Oh, I don't think you know me as well as you think you do."

She took a step back as if to keep the distance between us. "Hey, whatever helps you sleep at night."

At that, my smile fell completely. "You sure are full of venom for this early in the morning."

"Some of us are here before the sun." She turned for the back. "It's not early."

"Hey," I called after her, "I'm sorry again, Tess. For yesterday. I shouldn't have grabbed you like that whether I thought you were Ivy or not."

She shrugged a small shoulder with a flick, the motion anything but blasé. "No, you shouldn't have. But if you leave with those bouquets in the next five minutes, we'll call it even."

The lie rolled off her tongue, but I didn't buy it any more than she meant it. So I let it go, recognizing a brick wall when I saw one.

"Think you'll manage the counter without me?"

She shot a look back at me, her small nose down and her eyes narrowed. "Beyond all the odds, we've somehow managed all this time without you. I'm sure we'll survive." She turned, striding away. "Tell Judy we said hi," she said just before disappearing around the corner.

"Ohhhhkay," I muttered, grabbing a box for the vases.

Tess had always been prickly, but this was a new level of disdain. Never had my very presence seemed to offend someone so deeply. The knowledge rankled me. Really, it was the *lack* of knowledge that got under my skin. I didn't know what I'd done—or not done—and I had the distinct feeling that asking her would only end with me getting snapped at and evaded.

So I'd just have to convince her she was wrong about me. I was charming as fuck, so all I had to do was figure out how. I wondered if donuts would do any good. Everybody liked donuts. I could always try to kiss it out of her, but I had a feeling I'd end up with pruning shears between my ribs.

"Luke Bennet. Aren't you a sight for sore eyes?"

The sound of Ivy's voice put a smile back on my face. I'd expected to find her giggling, as she was, and I'd expected her to launch herself into my arms, like she did. What I didn't expect when I looked down was to find her visibly pregnant.

I caught her with ease, hugging her for a second before setting her down to get a good look at her. The same bright eyes I remembered, the same red hair. Though unlike Tess's, which was lush and russet, Ivy's was copper and curly and wild as she was.

"Well, would ya look at that?" I said, nodding to her belly.

She flushed, laughing as she rolled her eyes. "Six months in, an eternity to go. We all knew I'd end up knocked up, didn't we?"

"Who's the lucky guy?"

"Dean Wilson." She beamed up at me, resting a hand on the

curve of her stomach.

"The delivery guy?"

"He runs the company now. Very established," she said with a wink. "I can't believe you're back! God, it's good to see you."

"At least one of you thinks so," I said, glancing in the direction Tess had gone.

But Ivy waved a hand. "Oh, don't worry about her. She's just grumpy this morning."

"She was grumpy yesterday too."

"Well, you humped her in the cooler."

"In fairness, I thought she was you."

Ivy laughed. "Well, sadly, I am off the market and in the family way. Tess, however, is not."

"Right. She seems super available," I deadpanned.

Some mischief flickered behind her eyes. "Oh, don't let her fool you."

My brows gathered in confusion, but when I opened my mouth to speak, she cut me off.

"So Judy's already after you, huh?" she asked, nodding at the vases.

"She's relentless."

"Well, you did sleep with her all summer after senior year."

"Ah, the good old days. I'm telling you—the older ladies are always the wildest."

"You're disgusting, Luke," she said around a laugh.

I shrugged. "Hey, whatever it takes to save Mom's shop."

"Oh my God. You aren't actually going to sleep with her, are you?"

I picked up my box with a smirk. "Depends on which kimono she's wearing. Always was a sucker for animal print."

A bawdy laugh burst out of her, and she swatted my arm. "It's a comfort that some things never change."

I winked at her. "I aim to please. Congrats on the bun, Ivy."

"Thanks. See you in a bit. I'll show you the new register when you get back, okay?"

"You bet."

I made my way into the shop, past the tables where Tess worked with the laser-focus of a bomb disposal tech. She ignored me completely even though I stared a hole in her. It was impressive, the determination she maintained to pretend like I didn't exist.

Donuts. I was one hundred percent bringing donuts back with me.

I didn't get the animosity, and frankly, that made me feel like a dumbshit. By my estimation, I'd never been anything but nice to her, if not a touch too flirtatious, which was something I really didn't get. Who didn't like getting flirted with? I mean, barring breaching the line of comfort. Maybe Tess's line was just much farther out than most.

I thought back over yesterday and the cooler incident, replaying the encounter and the conversation that had followed. The best I could come up with was that I'd caught her off guard—not only with the groping, but with the news that we'd be working together, which seemed to have thrown her contempt in an amplifier cranked to eleven. I would have been surprised Mom hadn't told Tess I'd be working the counter if she wasn't so scatterbrained. Mom could tell me the name, phone number, and pedigree of every single woman in a ten-block radius who would make good marriage material but couldn't recall the date on any given day.

I'd surprised Tess, and she wasn't the kind of girl who liked surprises. I made a mental note to find out why so I could change her mind about that too.

There was nothing in the world like adventure. There was nothing so sweet as discovery. The unknown, the new, only broadened our lives, made us better. Taught us. Made us more than we were. I sought it at every turn, craved it with every sunrise. California had been a feast, from the people to the jobs, the food to the lifestyle. I'd had jobs ranging from glass blower to stunt man. I worked with a contractor buddy, renovating houses. Was an extra on TV. At one point, I'd even modeled baseball pants for Dick's Sporting Goods, which had left me fielding cracks from my brothers for … well, I was still fielding them years later.

I wanted to learn everything, wanted to experience it all. I couldn't imagine living a life like Tess, in the same job—her only job—for ten years. Monotony sounded like death, a life that would slowly chip away at my soul until there was nothing left but a husk punching a clock every day.

I couldn't understand how anyone would choose that life.

Marcus said I was undisciplined, a flake. Hedonistic and selfish. But then again, Marcus had eaten a peanut butter sandwich with a banana every single day through high school without ever questioning how weird that was. As such, his argument was invalid.

I passed through the double doors that led to the greenhouse, the humid air thick and sticky. It smelled like earth, like damp leaves and living things, and I took an instinctive breath to fill my lungs with its rich perfume.

Dad hefted himself to stand—a motion that seemed to take more effort than I remembered him requiring. He hooked a small spade in his belt and dusted off his hands.

"I see you've been summoned," he said with a smirk and a nod at the box in my hands.

A laugh burst out of Kash, and he leaned on the handle of his hoe. "Judy sure didn't waste any time."

"Don't act like you weren't the one who called her and told her I was back," I said, adjusting my grip on the box.

"Who, me?" he asked innocently. "Never."

I snorted.

"Pretty sure Laney's planning to put out an ad announcing your return," Kash said. "She's got a couple pictures picked out for the spread. There's a good one of you hauling potted palms with no shirt on that's in the running. But I voted for the one of you at four, bare-assed in a planter box."

Dad nodded his appreciation. "I think I've got one of you shoveling the garden with nothing but Laney's pink rain boots on."

I gave them both a look. "You act like I'm not the first to suggest objectifying myself. Feel free to post all the nudes you want, if it'll help sell flowers. I'm still waiting on word about the naked sandwich board. Just let me know a couple of days in advance so I can cut back on my salt intake."

Kash rolled his eyes. "There he is. Good old Luke." As I headed for the back door, he added, "Don't let Judy scratch you up. We need you camera ready!"

If I'd had a free hand, I would have flipped him off. As it was, I opened the door with my elbow and stepped into the alley.

A small driveway led to the greenhouse, and in it sat the delivery van, painted with a bouquet and the words *Longbourne Flower Shop* on the side. I don't think Mom had filled the van up in years for a delivery beyond the occasional wedding.

As I turned the key and left for Judy's, I felt a spark of determination to see that change. Even if I really *did* have to get out on the sidewalk in a sandwich board.

When I was a kid, the shop had been the cornerstone of an empire with a handful of stores spread all over the city. Dozens of employees, several full-time delivery drivers, a constant whirl of action. It was never quiet, nor was it empty. But now … now, it was deserted. Passersby didn't stop at the windows, didn't pop inside to take a look. As classic as the shop was, it wasn't timeless—it was dated and dark and dull. There was nothing fresh about it, nothing new. Nothing to catch the eye of a man on his way to his girlfriend or a woman looking to bring something fresh into her home.

The truth was, since its establishment, the store had largely taken care of itself, providing the business needed to expand without much tending. My grandmother had been the one with the business mind, a trait she had not passed on to her daughter.

And when technology rose, Longbourne was left in the dust. Ecommerce. Social media. Big-box delivery companies. The old way of doing things died, and Longbourne withered from the drastic shift in the weather.

For years, Mom convinced us everything was fine, and we were too busy living our own lives to acknowledge it wasn't. We started losing weddings to Bower Bouquets. The shops began to close one by one as Longbourne retreated in an attempt to stay afloat. Our inquiries and attempts to help were brushed aside.

It wasn't until only the flagship store was left and our trust funds, which the accountant deposited in monthly based on the shop's income, began to dwindle that Marcus finally approached Mom.

What he found was shocking.

The family accountant and shitty, outdated business advisor—who was older than actual dirt, by the way—had done a piss-poor job advising them and sent them not only into deep tax debt, but had inadvertently misled them as to the state of the estate.

So Marcus used his substantial wealth to invest in the shop, buying it from Mom so she could "retire"—which she had done very little of—and then called us all home to help. We had to save the shop, not only for Mom and our legacy, but for Marcus's sacrifice and the future of our inheritance.

We had a long way to go, and each of us had our parts. Though mine was unclear—I'd been tapped to come back and be the shop patsy, the bulk of my responsibility seeming to revolve around menial tasks with little to no stakes. Like deliveries.

But they'd forgotten that I was an idea guy. I just wasn't a get-it-done guy.

By the time I pulled up to Judy's building, my imagination had painted a picture of all the things we could do, all the ways we could update the shop, ideas bubbling like a stream. So much so, before I got out of the van, I fired off a text to my siblings, calling a meeting—kids only. Tonight, after Mom and Dad went to bed, we'd formulate a plan.

My mind wandered as I trotted up the steps, making more important plans to pick up donuts and coffee on my way back. I wondered briefly if I could make Tess smile with my offering, then remembered myself, shooting instead to get her to stop insulting me.

I hitched the box on my hip and knocked on the familiar door, which opened before my hand returned to my side.

Zebra print. Should have made a bet with Kash.

Judy stretched her arm, her face twisted in a seductive smile, silk kimono sliding off one shoulder. "Why, hello, Luke."

"Special delivery," I said, amused. "Where do you want it?"

"Anywhere you'll give it to me," she said, grabbing a handful of my shirtfront to drag me inside.

And with a laugh, I let her.

TESS

"What in the world did that hydrangea ever do to you?"

When I looked up, Ivy was smirking at me from the other side of my table. I'd been too busy fuming to notice her approach.

"Guess it was just too pretty," I said, snipping a branch and depositing it in the water bucket.

"Like somebody else we know," she teased.

"I can't imagine what you mean, Ivy Parker." Snip. Dunk. Fume.

She gave me a look as she picked up a pair of shears. "Tess, it's been ten years. You haven't even seen him in five."

"I know," I huffed.

"Surely you can't still be mad."

I plunked my shears down on the table and gave her a look right back. "I'm not. Honestly, I haven't even thought about it in years."

Ivy gave me a look.

"I mean it. Honestly, it was a relief when he moved away. I'm not mad he forgot about the kiss. Annoyed maybe. Irritated? Sure. But the truth is, Luke acted exactly like I should have expected him to. And him forgetting the kiss busted my rose-colored glasses. I saw every shitty thing he did, and that was all I *could* see."

"*Can* see," she corrected lightly, snipping a branch.

"He's just so…" *Arrogant. Conceited. Vain. Maddening.* "He's so completely Luke. He hasn't changed a bit. In fact, I think the years have made him worse."

"Or made you more grumpy."

I sighed.

"I'm glad to hear you admit you're not mad he forgot he kissed you when you were sixteen. Otherwise, I'd tell you to get yourself some real, adult problems."

"The fact that he kissed me and pretended like I didn't exist afterward doesn't exactly help his case any."

"No, I guess it wouldn't."

I eyed her. "But…"

"Well, Luke's a lot of things, but an asshole isn't one of them. I think if you told him, he'd feel bad. Don't you?"

"Does Luke Bennet actually feel anything?" Snip.

She ignored me. "You didn't even tell *me* until he moved to the other side of the country. Five years, you kept it from me, your best friend. You even let me fool around with him right there under your nose."

I kept my eyes on my hands, which were busy. "Because it obviously didn't mean anything, Ivy. Why make a fuss?"

"Because you were hurt. I wouldn't have ever kissed him again if I'd known—you know I was about as serious about him as he was about me, which is to say not at all. I don't even think I considered him when he wasn't in the room. I didn't even know you had a crush on him, and if I'd known I wouldn't have ever fooled around with him again. Either I'm the most dense woman on the planet, or you're better at keeping secrets than Batman."

I laughed. "Trust me—it was my doing. I didn't want you to know, Ivy. I didn't even want to like him, never mind admit it out loud."

"I could never keep something like that to myself," she continued, disregarding what I'd said beyond a warming of her eyes. "I think I'd combust from the pressure. And especially if I'd just been through what you'd been through."

My mom.

Silence stretched between us as we both went back to that time. I'd always been reserved with things that caused me pain, preferring to shoulder the burden on my own. That way, I was in control. Telling someone else ... well, that was harder. To open up and expose my softest places, my deepest bruises also left me open to getting hurt.

Like that night with Luke. When he'd somehow coaxed the truth out of me—the loss, the depth of my pain, the crushing weight of responsibility. When I lost myself in his arms, cried until the well dried. When I looked up at him and was cursed with the kiss of my lifetime, heavy and deep with emotion.

When he'd told me he was mine and asked me to be his.

And forgotten he'd ever uttered the words.

This was my most guarded secret, the one I'd never spoken to a soul. The humiliation was just too much to bear. And like I'd told Ivy—that night was the blasting of the iron curtain. The boy I had seen post-kiss was not the same one I'd thought I knew pre-kiss.

Ivy broke the silence, snipping off another hydrangea. "Really, I can't believe you didn't tell me."

"I didn't tell anybody. Why would I?"

"I don't know. To get it off your chest?"

"I'd rather everyone not know exactly how I feel all the time."

"And I say exactly what I feel, when I feel it," she said. "It's how I form bonds. I hate being alone."

"I love it."

"Think *Luke* will leave you alone?" Ivy asked with a brow up.

"I'm not that lucky." I looked around the shop, feeling the sharp edges of change in every corner. "It's been you and me for so long. Having anyone in our space, interrupting our routine, will be hard. When that someone is Luke Bennet, we should just prepare for anarchy."

She chuckled. "Oh, he's not so bad."

"Please. His head is so fat, I'm surprised he can fit through standard doorways."

"I think he's gotten just about anything—and anyone—he's ever wanted," she said, and I wasn't sure if it was to argue with me or to agree.

"And yet his ambitions remain firmly in the gutter. Honestly, Luke is the patent opposite of everything I value—he's aimless, unpredictable, unreliable. I can't imagine why you're shocked that I'm not his number one fan."

"I'd take fan two-forty." She shrugged, her eyes on the flowers. "I think he's exciting, always was. Luke could make grocery shopping a good time. If ever I wanted an adventure, Luke was waiting with a hand extended and a wicked smile on his face."

Adventure. The word struck me like flint and set an angry fire in my chest. I might need adventure, but not with him.

"Why do you look like you could spit acid?" she asked, snapping me back to myself.

"I don't know," I shot, annoyed.

"Tess," she started, pausing until I met her eyes and she was sure she had my full attention, "Luke is a good guy, one you have not seen in years. One who has grown up, just like you. He's Mrs. Bennet's son, who came all the way back from California just to help out. Has he ever intentionally done anything to hurt you?"

"No," I grumbled.

"Sixteen-year-old Tess is still butthurt about it."

"It was a good kiss, and he should have remembered," I joked.

"Yes, he should have. But if you really want reconciliation, then tell him."

"I don't want reconciliation, Ivy."

"Why not?"

"It was ten years ago. He'd think it was ridiculous, and it is."

"Then get over it and move on."

"I have! It's not like I have an effigy of him in my closet or anything, Ivy. It's just that…" I sighed, running a hand over my face, then swearing when I remembered it was dusted with dirt. "He caught me by surprise yesterday," I said, swiping at my face. "The knowledge that he'll be working here with us every day is the worst news I've had in ages."

She reached across the table and wiped away the dirt I'd been smearing around. "You were surprised. But he didn't do anything wrong, did he?"

"Besides harass me? It doesn't really absolve him that he thought I was you. If we had an HR department, they'd be having a field day."

"Fair enough, but deep down, you know his intentions were innocent. Luke would never in a million years have come on to you like that. Right?"

My sigh weighed a thousand pounds. "I mean—"

"*Right,*" she answered for me. "And what about all the good things he's done?"

"So far he's groped me, been late, and if I had to guess, he's about to bang Judy. What has he done right again?"

Ivy rolled her eyes so hard, her irises almost disappeared. "Came back to help Mrs. Bennet. Dropped everything to rush back. Came into the shop before noon. What?" she added, watching my expression. "That's a big deal for him, and you know it. You're just so focused on all the bad things, you can't see the good."

I was pouting, and I knew it. I just couldn't seem to erase the expression her bitter truth had inspired. "The product of years of practice, I guess."

"Well, maybe it's time to unlearn it, if for no other reason than to keep the workplace hospitable. You're going to make the flowers sad with all your bad energy."

I chuckled, picking up my shears again to avoid her eyes. "We can't have that."

"No, we can't. Give him a chance—if not for the shop, for Mrs. Bennet. It'd kill her to think you hated him like you seem to."

For a moment, I imagined the sadness and disappointment on her face if she knew I'd rather eat mulch than make nice with Luke, and my guts twisted against the sight. "All right," I conceded, snipping a branch off. "I'll try to be good. But if he pushes it, I swear ..." I pointed my shears at her in warning.

"Hey, if he deserves it, all bets are off."

"If who deserves what? And who's getting stabbed with those shears?"

Luke's voice set my spine straight as an arrow, my gaze snapping up to find him standing at the end of the table.

God, he was handsome, his jaw square and smattered with dark stubble. Those full, wide lips were constantly fixed at an irreverent tilt. His nose was as Roman as his name, with the slightest flat plane on the bridge, just enough to make him look rugged without interrupting the elegant lines of his brow and cheekbones. Crisp and bright were his eyes, sharp with wit and mischief.

He had been designed to entice and did so at his leisure. As easily as he lured you in, so easily would you be consumed.

And I had no desire to be consumed.

I blinked, realizing we had yet to answer. I found myself unable to fashion a response.

Ivy picked up that ball and ran, betraying me with a smile. "If you deserve a dressing-down, you'll get one. And the shears too, if you're not quick on your feet."

"Ah," he said, still smiling. "Well, I don't think Tess minds dressing me down whether I deserve it or not."

That made me both huff and swat away a flash of guilt. But before I could decide how to answer, he placed a pink box on the counter, revealing a paper caddy carrying two cups of coffee.

"Speaking of—" He set down the carrier and bowed ever so slightly in my direction. "I come bearing gifts of peace. Coffee," he said, gesturing to the obvious, "and donuts."

When he opened the box, Ivy and I leaned in.

"Blanche's!" Ivy gasped, full-on clasping her hands to her chest. "Oh, tell me you got the lavender and lemon ones."

"Is there any other kind?"

"No," I said, smiling.

His eyes shifted to mine, catching them, holding them. His smile softened into something more sheepish, the effect making him look like the boy who'd once kissed me in the greenhouse.

Brutus leaped onto the table, striding over with his tail flicking. But before he got close, Luke scooped him up, petting his short, dark fur.

"Those aren't for you, buddy." He scratched the cat's head, which didn't seem to distract Brutus. His golden eyes were locked on that box. "I got raspberry creme, lemon-blueberry, and strawberry icing with sprinkles. But Tess gets dibs," he said, giving Ivy a chastising look.

Ivy in turn gave me a look, one that said, *See? Donuts*!

The realization that she was right—thus making me wrong—sent a twisting cramp of aversion through me. I hated being wrong. I hated that Luke made me feel this way, and I hated that he'd done something nice when all I wanted was to keep on hating *him*.

But you know what I didn't hate?

Donuts.

I licked my lips, peering into the box and deciding on a lavender-lemon donut. When I looked up, his eyes were on my mouth, hungry as I was for the pastry in my hand. And then they met mine with a nearly audible click.

I took a breath, filling my lungs to power my will. "Thank you, Luke," was all I could manage.

And the words set his smile tilting again.

"You're welcome, Tess. I really am sorry about yesterday."

"I know," I admitted. "Me too," was the closest I could get to an apology, considering he was the one to grope me. "For being so…"

"Bitchy," Ivy finished.

We laughed, and I flushed. She wasn't wrong. But Luke did that to me.

"So, truce?" he asked, eyeing me with mock doubt.

"Truce," I echoed.

At that, he grinned, flashing brilliant teeth. "I knew donuts would work. Donuts always work."

I rolled my eyes. "Don't talk. You ruin it for everyone when you talk." I took a bite, and the second it hit my tongue, the donut melted like spun sugar.

"Not the first time I've heard that today."

Just like that, the donut turned to ash on my tongue. I'd forgotten he'd just come from Judy's. Had he slept with her? And why the hell did I care? And why the hell was I scanning him for signs—mussed hair, hickey, anything.

And why, oh why, did I find myself so satisfied to find none?

Ivy shot me another look as she took a rude bite of her own donut. *Be nice*, that look said.

I forced a smile. "Your mouth might be the only predictable thing about you."

Ivy choked on her donut.

But Luke smiled. "Oh, my mouth can definitely be counted on."

For lies and kisses you don't remember.

"Ivy, weren't you going to show Luke the registers?" I offered in my best effort to put some space between me and the devil.

"Mmhmm," she hummed around her food.

"Oh," Luke said with a snap of his fingers. "We're meeting here tonight to talk about plans for the shop if you two want to come. Around eight-thirty, here in the back. You in?"

"Of course," Ivy answered with a smile.

"Wouldn't miss it," I said, meaning it. This shop was all I'd known, and its future was too tied up in mine to miss a single decision they'd have me be a part of.

"Good." His smile was too pretty to be real. "Then it's a date."

He turned before I educated him on the meaning of the word date, and Ivy stayed me with a glare, just in case I had a mind to speak. But I kept it to myself, choosing instead to fill my mouth with his peace offering as I watched his stupid, fine ass walk away.

I'd agreed to a truce, dazzled by pastries and struck by Ivy's insistence. I'd give Luke Bennet a chance.

And I sure did hope he didn't waste it.

Big Ideas

LUKE

"All right, all right—settle down," I said over the din of my siblings.

No one settled down.

We sat around one of the big tables in the back, all hitched on stools. The only lights were the hanging tin farm lamps over the table, making it feel more like a clandestine mob meeting than a chat among siblings about the future of a flower shop.

"I need a gavel or something," I said half to myself.

"Here," Tess said, thrusting a hand spade into my palm.

"Thank you," I said before banging the handle on the wooden tabletop.

Slowly, the noise dimmed, their faces all turning to me.

"All right, Bennets, Tess, Ivy. Tonight marks our first meeting, hopefully of many. We all know the shop is in trouble, and it's up to us to save it. I was thinking about it this morning and have some ideas."

"Before or after you boffed Judy?" Kash called from the back.

"Before. A little during. Mostly after."

Laney groaned, Marcus rolled his eyes, and I didn't miss Tess stilling next to me.

Marcus folded his arms across his chest. "This is going to be like the lemonade stand all over again, isn't it?"

My siblings burst into laughter, but Ivy and Tess looked confused.

Kash leaned on the table, smirking at them. "Luke's notorious for rallying us for some big cause—lemonade, cookie sales, dog-washing for tips. Ask me how many he actually worked at."

Another round of laughter and a superior, though amused, look from Tess.

"Listen—the lemons would have stung my cuts from Mom making me work on the roses, I wouldn't have stopped playing with the dogs long enough to wash them, and I'd have eaten all the cookies before we got our first customer. You guys didn't want me there."

Marcus shrugged. "Guess we'll never know, will we?"

"Oh, give him a break, warden," Kash said. "You lorded over us with a cash lockbox, a calculator, and a legal pad. It's not like we blamed him. And anyway, you have to admit—he always had good ideas."

"And I've got another one," I started, glancing around the table to meet everyone's eyes.

They sobered, waiting silently.

"We all know why we're here, why we've come back. Longbourne needs us. Mom and Dad need us. Their future depends on this shop. And I know we can save it all, but not if things stay the same. We have a legacy, but there's nothing fresh about our presence. We have no social media to speak of. Our website hasn't been current since 1999. The storefront hasn't changed in fifty years. We have no window display, no aesthetic, no vibe. Longbourne's been left untended for so long, it's overgrown and being choked to death by proverbial weeds. How's the money, Marcus?"

His brows drew together, his lips flattening. "Not good. The finances have been mismanaged for a decade. The debts are so substantial, Marty shouldn't have been depositing anything into our trusts. If we doubled the shop's income tomorrow, it would take us somewhere around five years to really get back on track."

A sigh, deep and painful in my ribs. "Do we have any capital to work with?"

"After buying the shop, acquiring the debts, and trying to figure out how much we're actually making, I only have a little capital left to invest. So we'd better have a workable plan."

"Shoestring budget—got it. I can work with that."

"To do what?" he asked dubiously.

"Implement phase one: give this place a complete facelift."

"What do you have in mind?" Laney asked, her excitement visible in the lighting of her eyes and straightening of her spine.

"Storefront first—that place is a cave. I mean, when was the last time the windows were cleaned? The brick is dark, the ceiling dark … I say we paint everything white."

Laney, Tess, and Ivy perked up.

"It would brighten everything up," Tess said, her smile growing as she imagined it. "The lighting could be incredible."

"And," I added, smiling back, "we have piles of ancient pieces to use for displays. Tables and drawers, old desks and benches. Buckets and rope and God even knows what else we'll find in storage. Laney, what are you thinking for social?"

"I've got big ideas too, starting with a new logo. Check it out." She passed her phone down the table and to me.

The logo was hip and current, two arrows crossed with LFS in the left, top, and right spaces and an illustration of a rose below. It was simple and modern and absolutely perfect.

"I've got Facebook, Instagram, and Twitter set up, and Jett and I are working on the website," Laney said.

"We're gonna need pictures though," Jett added, looking a little worried about the fact.

"I can help with that," Tess offered. "I've been playing around for a couple of years with studio lighting, and my Instagram is pretty strong."

Laney chuckled. "You're being modest—your Instagram is enviable. I was going to ask if you'd be interested in heading up ours."

"I'd love to," Tess answered, flushed and smiling.

"Anyone have any objections to the logo?" I asked.

Negatives came from the lot of them.

"Good. I can paint the walls and wash the windows, go through storage and take inventory. Laney, how do you feel about designing us new signage?" I asked.

"Real good."

Marcus looked skeptical. "I think we should wait until we get some more capital in the door."

"Even if I can get us a discount?" I asked. "My buddy Davey's brother makes signs. I just need a design to show him."

"Davey?" Marcus's eyes narrowed.

"Yeah, we used to wait tables together."

"Which time?" Kash asked like the smartass he was.

"Does it matter?" I asked, forging on before he answered. "I can prep to paint tomorrow. Jett, can you help run deliveries?"

"I'm not going to Judy's, if that's what you're asking."

A laugh rolled through them.

"You say that now."

"I can help paint tomorrow," Tess offered. "It's my day off, but I don't have much else going on."

At that, my smile ticked up a notch. "Sounds good. I'll pick up supplies in the morning. I'll get back into storage too, see what I can drum up. We can rearrange the interior, and then comes the fun part.

We're not going to be ready to advertise, not until we have this place cleaned up, the signage done, our social moving. So I was thinking—what's the best way to get people in the front door?" I paused, scanning their faces. "We go old school. Window installations."

"Luke, that's genius," Tess breathed, and it might have been the nicest thing she'd ever said to or about me.

"Thank you." I smiled, feeling like I'd won a major award. "I renovated houses with a contractor for a while in LA, and I worked set design too. I even helped with installations at The Getty and for a while at Anthropologie in Santa Monica. Dad has all the tools I'll need to build you guys whatever you want."

"It's perfect." Laney beamed.

Kash laughed openly. "You worked at Anthropologie."

I shrugged. "I dated a girl who managed one, and I happen to like their candles." I'd earned another chuckle. "Anyway, as far as I'm concerned, you're the brains here, Laney. I'll be the muscle, and Tess, I think, should take the lead on design."

Tess's face swiveled around, her eyes wide and stunned. "Me?"

"We've all seen what you can do," Laney said, backing me up like I knew she would. She'd be crazy not to. "Of all of us, you are the one with the aesthetic and know-how when it comes to floristry. Luke is right. This is your wheelhouse, and I think we should lean on you."

The color rose in her cheeks, her lashes brushing them when she looked down at her hands. "I … I'm not sure what to say."

"Say yes," I urged. "I want to stop every person who passes our window dead in their tracks. I want our windows to lure them in. I want to become a staple in this city again, and this? This is going to set us apart."

She'd looked up during my speech, her eyes soft and rich, stirring something in my chest. A familiarity, like a memory I couldn't grasp, like a dream that had slipped away when I woke. But then it was gone.

"All right, I'll do it."

A chorus of cheering and relieved laughter filled the room.

"Ivy can take over for you in the back while we get plans together for the front and implement them for the weekend—there's a big event in Washington Square, and we should have more foot traffic than usual. It's the perfect time to unveil the new look," I said. "Kash, you keep doing what you're doing in the greenhouse. Jett, you'll float between doubling for me and helping Mom around the house. Marcus, keep working on untangling the finances. Laney, you let us know what you need for marketing. And I'll back up Tess. Tomorrow, we start. Tomorrow, we're going to take the first step to turning this ship around. And if we don't make Mom cry from sheer joy by the time it's done, I'll eat Laney's raincoat."

Another laugh, this one a little bawdier.

Chatter broke out among them, and for a moment, I stood at the head of that table and watched them all, the accomplishment empowering and the excitement intoxicating. I could see it all, see the shop full of customers, that little bell dinging until the clapper wore out. Ideas on ideas on ideas fluttered through my mind—painting the front door a bright, cheery shade of blue, running beams across the ceilings so we could hang planters and racks and installations from them, imagining the walls crisp and white against the dark old counter and the black-and-white-tiled floor. I wondered what kinds of ideas Tess would have, wondered if she'd let me in on them or if she'd just give me orders and expect me to march on them.

Either way, it was going to be a thrill. We were going to make this place everything it was meant to be, everything it had once been. We were going to save it.

I wandered into the front while their attention was off of me, making lists of inventory, considering how we might organize it. Golden streetlight streamed in through the grate outside the window, and I made a mental note of the approximate size and depth of the window space, noting the casings and devising ways to hang things from it without ruining the old wood. There were so many things I could build out of raw wood, and I felt a greedy anticipation at what I'd find in storage. A hundred seventy years of history, I supposed, history we'd bring back into this space with its second life.

My siblings weren't wrong, ribbing me about the lemonade stand. I loved the rush and possibility of new ideas, but follow-through had never been my strong suit. The only thing I'd really tried to stick out was my marriage, which taught me two important things: sticking things out could ruin you, and I was terrible at relationships.

But this time? Right now? This would be different. Quitting wasn't an option, and giving up wasn't on the table. It was do or die. And I was prepared to ride or die.

It was why we'd all come home, and our future was at stake. Our family was at stake. And one thing I would never walk away from was my family.

"Hey," a gentle voice said from behind me.

I started at the sound, so lost in my thoughts, I hadn't heard Tess approach.

She chuckled. "Sorry to scare you. I … I just wanted to say thank you. For suggesting that I take on so much responsibility."

"You act like you haven't been running the shop for years."

I noticed her cheeks flush, even in the dark shop. "Maybe, but I'm not a Bennet. I feel lucky to even be included in these kinds of meetings."

I turned to face her, pinning her with a look I hoped communicated my earnestness. "Tess, you are as much a part of this family as anyone. You have been Mom's hands for years. She taught you everything she knew, and then you did the unthinkable—you surpassed her."

Tess drew a shallow breath.

"Don't you dare tell my mother I said that."

Her surprise left her on a laugh.

"This store is just as much yours as it is ours. More maybe. Other than Kash, you're the only one who didn't leave. So please, don't thank me. It's me who should be thanking you."

She watched me for a moment with a smile on her lips. "Well, how about that? Ivy was right."

I frowned. "Right about what?"

"Maybe you aren't such a dick after all."

Laughter shot out of me, a little too loud and completely unbridled. "Let's not get ahead of ourselves, Tess."

She shrugged a small shoulder, smiling sideways as she turned to walk away. But as she left, she looked back over her shoulder. "Really, Luke, thank you."

I slipped my hands into the pockets of my jeans. "You're welcome," was all I could say.

Surprise had otherwise rendered me speechless.

Princes & Pirates

TESS

It took entirely too long to decide what to wear to paint a flower shop.

Clothes lay in a heaping pile to rival Everest, so many that a glance into my gaping closet showed little more than hangers. In my defense, I had a lot of needs to fill—must be old and-or disposable enough to get paint on them, must be appropriate for climbing ladders, and most importantly, must be adorable.

If my ass was going to be in Luke Bennet's eyeline all day, it'd better look good.

I shifted three-quarters, inspecting my reflection. Auburn hair in a messy bun, bangs thick and shaggy, a blue bandana tied in a band with the knot on top. Mom's old Cure T-shirt, dotted with paint from my bathroom when she'd painted it years ago. I'd knotted the hem to make it look fitted, cuffed the sleeves to put them at a modern length.

And I topped it off with a pair of overall shorts because that seemed too obvious to pass up. My face was fresh and untouched by makeup, but I wasn't so confident that I was willing to ignore mascara.

I was the poster girl for the basic bitch painting uniform and resisted the urge to change again.

"You're just painting the shop, not auditioning for *Top Model*, for God's sake," I muttered at myself, annoyed.

I blew out of my room before I could change my mind again.

It was anxiety, I realized, and took a second to catalog the details I was aware of. I didn't exactly hate Luke anymore. I mean, he was a pig and a flake, but when he'd stood at the head of that table and told us his ideas, the energy in the room had shifted in his direction. He could be a force to be reckoned with—when he applied himself. When he had passion.

That was really the thing that was the most astounding—witnessing his passion. He cared more than I'd realized, worried more than I had known. He believed we would succeed with optimism and hope, and he imagined all the ways we could make it happen.

We. All of us. Even me.

It was the cherry atop the humble pie I'd promised to eat. Now that I was paying attention to the good, the bad had fizzled out like a bunk firecracker—still full of gunpowder, might blow my hand off if I touched it, but probably harmless.

Probably.

Dad was in his recliner in the living room, listening to The Allman Brothers, reading glasses on the tip of his nose and a book about the Civil War split open in his lap.

"Hey, Pigeon," he said, smiling when I walked in. "Don't you look adorable?"

My nose wrinkled as I moved to the kitchen to change the water in my vase.

"What? You don't want to look adorable?"

"No. I mean, yes, I like to look pretty, but I don't know that I should want to look adorable."

"Ah. Luke will be there, then." He didn't ask. He stated.

I huffed, setting the bouquet on the counter and turning for the sink to wash the vase. "It's not easy or simple. Nothing is when it comes to him and me. But he … well, he wants to save the flower shop, and he put his trust in me. Makes it kind of hard to want him to swan dive off the Flatiron Building."

He chuckled.

"I stayed up half the night, sketching out ideas for window installations. I'm not going to let Mrs. Bennet down. Longbourne will survive—thrive—if I have anything to do with it."

"I don't doubt you'll make it so, Tess. You've done everything you've ever set your mind to, and I can't fathom this will be any different."

I stuffed a paper towel in the vase, drying it off before filling it up again. "Text me if you need anything, okay? Leftovers are in the fridge for lunch. I have a feeling we're not going to finish painting today. I researched it last night, and I'm not even sure Luke knows how to paint brick properly. We have to wash all the brick, wait for it to dry, and then caulk the cracks before we can even prime it. Knowing him, he's just gonna slap paint on there, willy-nilly."

"You act like the poor boy couldn't find his way out of a paper sack."

"Sometimes, I wonder," I said, depositing the bouquet back in its vase and fiddling with the arrangement.

"Well, good luck. Try not to kill him. I don't think Mrs. Bennet would ever forgive you."

"No, her precious golden boy can do no wrong, and she would be unamused if I dumped a can of paint on his head or hog-tied him and hung him up as our first window display. I could put some pansies in his mouth and call it a day."

I made my way over to his chair and kissed his forehead.

"Have a good day, Daddy. Don't get into any trouble, all right?"

"I'll try to contain myself," he said with a half-smile.

And when I pulled on my Vans and snagged my bag, I was out the door.

We lived around the corner from the flower shop, which sat proudly on Bleeker Street among the shops and cafés of the Village. The July heat hit me like a wall, that heavy humidity that clung to you like an aquatic second skin, the kind of heat that made you forget winter ever existed or what it was like to be comfortable.

The bad news was that it was only eight in the morning.

But there was little that could dampen my cheer. I felt the winds of change—even if I couldn't feel the actual wind on that still summer day—sensed the beginning of something big, something magnificent. And it was just around the corner.

Presumably behind the old green door of Longbourne.

I pushed open the door to the familiar ting-a-ling of the bell and stopped just inside.

Music floated around the room from a speaker on the register counter. The room, which was usually full of old display tables and buckets of flowers, had been cleaned out but for the massive, square farm table in the center of the room. The black-and-white floor tiles had been covered in plastic sheeting, and two ladders, a pile of supplies, and a bucket with a push broom sat proudly next to one of the long walls.

And beside them was Luke.

He was already glistening with sweat and had shed his shirt, leaving him in nothing but basketball shorts and sneakers. The golden hue of his skin spoke of countless hours of leisure, and the rolling topography of his musculature spoke of countless hours in the gym. I'd always hated basketball shorts, but on Luke Bennet's ass, they looked like they were meant to be there. I found I didn't have a single complaint.

Especially not when he turned around and I caught sight of the anaconda he was packing.

God bless the man who invented those shorts.

"Morning, Tess," he said with that patent smirk of his, hands still on the broom he'd been using to wash the brick.

To my surprise, the surface was filthy—the brick he'd already cleaned was cheery and red and what he hadn't was a grimy shade of brown.

I blinked at it. "That's what the brick looks like?"

He leaned on the top of the broom handle, flicking a glance at the wall. The effect broadened his shoulders and narrowed his waist, fanning his forearms out. Sweat trickled down my neck, and I couldn't be sure it was strictly from the heat. It really was indecent, him running around topless like that.

"I know. I'm thinking we leave the brick in the back of the store, just clean it up, paint the rest white."

"I love that," I said, scanning the space and imagining what it would look like.

"Good." He smiled, not only like he was genuinely pleased, but like he could eat me for breakfast.

Not that I was special. He looked at every female and food product exactly like that.

I moved for the extra push broom, effectively putting my back to him and breaking the moment.

"So," I started, taking a second to inspect the wall, "let's start with you and me cleaning this wall together, then one of us can clean the next wall while the other caulks this one."

I could actually hear him smirking. "Think you can handle the caulk?"

I shot him a look over my shoulder. Stupid, handsome bastard. "Oh, I can handle the caulk."

"You sure? It's got to be squeezed just right—not too hard, not too fast, just the perfect amount of pressure so you can fill all those holes."

"Lucas Bennet, you are disgusting."

He wet his brush in a paint tray full of water. "Contracting is a dirty job, Tess." With a salacious flick of his brows, he turned his attention to the wall. "So much hammering and nailing and wood. Screwing. Laying studs. We've covered the caulk."

I snorted rather than respond, unable to think of anything to say with the dirty-mouthed, half-naked figure scrubbing the wall in front of me.

I didn't look at the muscles of his back bunch and stretch as he scrubbed. I didn't watch the heavy bead of sweat run down the valley of his spine. And I most certainly didn't watch his ass bounce when he jumped a little to reach the very top of the wall.

Not intentionally at least.

With an inward slap, I dipped my brush in the water and moved past him. "I'll go low, you go high," I suggested by way of command.

"Yes, ma'am," he snarked.

I scrubbed for a minute, satisfied on some deep elemental level as the brick came clean and fresh. "Did you get the right kind of caulk?" I asked with no small amount of skepticism. "It's got to be the quick dry, the kind that—"

"Cures under primer. I know. That's what I got," he answered lightly. "It's like you didn't believe I could do this right, Tess."

"Well, you have to admit—you're not the most reliable Bennet."

"No, that title belongs to Marcus."

I chuckled. "Don't get me wrong. I'm impressed, that's all. I didn't realize you knew so much about this kind of thing."

"Well, I've worked somewhere in the neighborhood of a kabillion jobs. I had a buddy in LA who'd call me in when he needed help renovating houses he flipped. I'd met him bartending in Hollywood."

"Ooh, sounds swanky," I teased.

"It was a pain in the ass but good money. I think I met a million people working there—that at least was a good time. Though the *best* time was when I worked at Cirque du Soleil for a summer."

A laugh shot out of me as I rewet my brush. "Tell me you wore spandex. Or feathers. And that they pushed you off of something."

"Nah, I worked the ropes. It's more fun backstage. Less pressure."

"Is there anything you haven't done?"

"Rocket science," he answered without hesitating. "Ride a unicycle, though not for lack of trying. Underwater welding—Mom wouldn't let me. Too dangerous, she said. I even worked on a rig in the Pacific for a few months. That was some *Groundhog Day* action— every day the same thing, same view, same tiny room and clanging machines. I'd never been so happy to get my feet on dry land."

"And nothing led to a career?" I asked, unsuccessfully attempting to school the judgment from my voice.

He shrugged his wide shoulders and kept on scrubbing. "I get bored and move on. Part of it, I think, is that I love to learn. I want to know a little bit about everything."

"Without actually becoming an expert at anything," I added with no small amount of criticism.

But Luke, as always, was unfazed. "If I'd found something I wanted to become an expert on, I wouldn't have moved on."

A brief thought of what kind of thing might convince him to stick around was overridden by, "How do you know if you've never had a long-term job? I mean, have you ever had a job for longer than six months?"

He frowned at me, affronted. "Of course I…" His brows ticked a little closer. "No. I guess I haven't."

I laughed, waving around my rightness. "Exactly."

"Easy for you to say. You've never worked anywhere but here," he said with unmistakable disdain.

"And what's so wrong with here?" I snapped.

"Nothing. It's just not where I want to work. Not forever at least."

I scowled at the wall, scrubbing with more force than was necessary.

"Oh, come on, Tess. This shop is my home. Who wants to stay home forever?"

"Me. I love living at home, and I love living here."

"But don't you miss that … I don't know. Adventure?"

"I'm not interested in adventure. I'm interested in stability. Comfort."

He stopped scrubbing, turning to face me as he leaned on the handle again.

I studiously ignored him.

"You mean to say, you don't do anything that makes you uncomfortable? When was the last time you did something that scared you?"

"This morning, when I came here to help you."

A chuckle. I still wouldn't look at him.

"I don't know, Luke. I'm too busy to run off on adventures. I have my job here to think about, your mom to help. I take care of my dad. I like to take pretty pictures of flowers. And by the time I'm done with all that, there's not a lot of time left to thrill-seek." *Or have a life.*

He stilled. "I forgot you took care of your dad."

"Yeah, well, you forget a lot of things," I snapped at the wall.

But he didn't notice. He'd already started scrubbing again. "It's true. I have the memory of a goldfish—by the time I swim around the bowl, I forget everything I saw, heard, or tasted."

Flake. Unreliable. Undependable. Unaware flake with too many muscles for his own good.

"How long do you think it'll take us to finish painting?" I asked, annoyed at my annoyance and desperate to change the subject. Luke inspired that in me—the irrational urge to fight. I hated that urge.

Worse—I was beginning to realize that it was me who was the problem, not him.

"We should finish tomorrow, if we play it right. Man, I can't wait for Mom to see this. Oh, and? I found a bunch of stuff in storage. I'll show you when we finish for the day. Maybe you can use something for the installation." He paused, and the sound of music and brushes on brick filled the space between us. "Have any ideas?"

"I was thinking something with succulents," I said. "It's so hot and sunny, I thought maybe passersby would find it fitting."

"I like it." The genuine enthusiasm in his voice disarmed me.

"We'll see. Maybe there's something in storage we can use. I've got some sketches, but I want to see what we find back there before committing."

"Tess? With a plan at the ready? Never."

I huffed a laugh.

"I have a good feeling about this," he started. "I've been thinking … you know how Mom always talks about the old magazine feature *Home and Garden* did on my grandma?"

"I've stared at that framed magazine cover in the shop for ten years. It's one of her proudest memories of her mother, I think."

"I know. And I was thinking that maybe once we get things on track with the shop and find a groove with the window installations, we could approach some magazines."

A smile spread as I imagined it. "Oh my God. She'd die. Like, you might actually give her a heart attack."

He laughed. "Laney thinks it's possible to land a feature, depending on how the window displays go."

"No pressure," I joked.

"If anyone can do it, it's you," he said, stripping me of the last of my armor. "Just say the word, and we can do whatever you want. Your wish is my command."

I wish I hated you. I wish you'd be an ass. I wish you remembered kissing me.

I rolled my eyes at myself. I'd had a dozen boyfriends and a thousand kisses in the last ten years, but I couldn't seem to remember a single one, except the one he didn't.

Maybe the torch still burned because my wound had festered for so long, buried in my heart. Maybe it was because it had happened in a moment when I was vulnerable and lost. Or because I'd trusted him with words too raw and real to utter aloud. Or because he'd promised me something he never acknowledged again, leaving me feeling nothing but betrayal and pain in a time when I was already shattered.

I hadn't been lying when I told Ivy I hadn't thought about it in years. But the second I'd seen his face, I'd been transported back to that day when I'd stood almost exactly in that spot, waiting for him. And he'd promptly ignored me, making his way to Ivy for a kiss right there, right in front of me.

Ten years. Really, I needed to let it go. But the wound was the sort that never healed, the kind that flared when the seasons changed or a storm blew in. And the season was changing.

I wondered if it already had.

Luke lived by laws that offended the very foundation of what I believed in. He spoke of adventure like it was nirvana. My nirvana was security. And security was not found in risk, but in consistency.

But we could be different, and just because he was different didn't mean he was wrong, no matter how much it felt like it was. The truth was that Luke was leading the charge in revamping the store, lending his generous muscles to the task. Even today, he'd come prepared, and that earned my respect even if it was tarnished a bit by my terrible attitude.

All you can control is your reaction, I told myself, an adage my mother had imposed on me.

And so I spent the next hours appreciating the view and reminding myself that good manners were made of small sacrifices.

By the time I finished caulking the second wall, Luke was right behind me, touching up my work, which was both annoying and thorough, the feelings negating each other.

I climbed off the ladder and stretched my back out, twisting against the ache. "All right, ready to prime?"

"Can't prime, not until tomorrow. Brick's gotta dry. But we should definitely have the whole space painted tomorrow."

"Oh, good. I can help again, if you want." I shuddered to think what I'd wear after the dramatics this morning and mourned the use of my cutest painting outfit on caulk.

"Hey, I'll take all the help I can get," he said with a sidelong smile, setting his caulk gun on a ladder step. "Come on—let me show you what I found in storage."

Luke looked like a kid on his birthday, full of possibility and excitement, and when he passed, he snagged my hand as if it were the most natural thing, towing me toward the greenhouse.

My hand disappeared in his fist, and his wide back obstructed my view, but I followed him like I had the option not to, nearly two of my steps to his one. He pushed open the swinging double doors to the greenhouse and turned to head down the main aisle.

The greenhouse inhabited the space behind five buildings, an oasis teeming with flowers begging to be cut. Every morning, I walked into this place empty-handed and walked out with my arms full of an almost unimaginable bounty of fresh-cut flowers.

This was my happy place. The smell of soil and leaves and blooming flowers. The blanket of humidity. The sunlight filtering in through the glass roof and walls, bathing everything it touched. Mr. Bennet's head popped up between vertical planters of lavender delphinium, offering a knowing smile and a flick of his eyes to where Luke had a hold of me. Kash jerked his chin at us in greeting as he pushed a wheelbarrow full of dirt down one of the side aisles, a similar smile on his face, though his was less innocent.

Under their scrutiny, I fought the urge to jerk my hand away, not sure I could get it out of the vise if I wanted to. Which I otherwise didn't.

Luke towed me around the corner and down the ramp to the basement, chattering on about vegetable storage containers and old ladders, wire baskets and stands with baskets and more. By the time we reached the foot of the ramp and flicked on the lights, he was practically giddy.

Tin lights sparked to life, and I caught sight of a blur with a tail— Brutus, hot on the trail of a rat, I was sure. And there Luke stood, next to his bounty, with all the pride Brutus would display when he dumped said rat at my feet.

I gasped, smiling as I made my way toward the goods he'd arranged in the center of the long, crowded space, surrounded by the chaos of a hundred seventy years of discarded supplies. And just like he'd said, there was a small organizer made of wooden shelves and angled wired baskets, so you could reach right in and grab whatever suited you. There were several ladders, coils of rope, piles of ancient, salvaged wood. Sideboards, an apothecary cabinet, washboards and washtubs, pails of every shape and size. I imagined them all full of flowers and sitting proudly on the big farmhouse table and thought for a second that my heart might burst.

"Luke … I can't believe all this stuff," I breathed as I stepped into the mix, running a hand over one of the sideboards. "When was the last time your mom came down here?"

"I dunno, but it must have been forever. No one's updated the shop since my grandma in the seventies. To be honest, she was probably the last person to come down here for anything other than fertilizer or hoses."

My eyes widened, my smile wondrous. "I just had an idea." I moved for the haphazardly stacked wooden crates. "We could make planters out of these, hang them vertically. Half of them with succulents, the other half with leafy greens—ivy, spider plants, baby rubber plants, oooh, or some coleus … their leaves have that purple in the middle. Do you know what I mean?"

"I do," he said, still smiling. "They'd go well with Persian shield."

I brightened up another dozen watts. "Genius. I think that should be our first installment. And what if…" My wheels turned, zipping through the catalog of riches Luke had uncovered. "I could make a flower cloud … pampas grass and heather, wheat, maybe…" I said to myself, thoughts clicking together behind every blink.

"Flower cloud?" he asked with skepticism written all over his face.

"It's a thing," I said absently. "An arrangement, usually monochromatic, shaped like a cloud." I wandered toward some shelves, spotting crates of glassware I couldn't make out from the ground. "What about these?" I pulled the ladder over and ascended. "Are these milk bottles?"

"Careful, Tess," Luke warned, approaching as I climbed.

"Oh, I'm fine," I assured him, reaching for one of the crates. The ladder wasn't quite tall enough, and I flexed my feet to get me a little taller. I stretched for the crate with singular focus on grabbing it without breaking my neck.

"Seriously, this ladder is old—"

"I've almost got it," I insisted, reaching.

My fingers brushed the very edge of the crate before gravity shifted, the round-legged ladder slipping out from under me. My weight pulled me sideways, down, and my only thought was that for the safety of the clinking milk bottles.

Luke caught me with an oof and a small bounce, the landing

easy and gentle even though my limbs had flailed, wheeling as I fell. Somehow, he hooked me almost perfectly, though I managed to crack him across the face with my forearm.

He shook his head, blinking and wincing as he tried to clear it, and I didn't think, just grabbed his face, wide-eyed as I inspected it.

"Oh my God, are you okay?" I breathed, tilting his face so I could look at his nose, wondering if it would bleed. I'd felt his teeth through his lips, so I checked those next, moving his face around with my hands so I could examine it.

When he laughed, I noted a slight swelling on the plump part of his upper lip but nothing more. "You almost broke your neck, and you're worried about me?"

A smaller, more nervous laugh left me. "You caught me like a sack of flour. How'd you manage that? I must have looked like a windmill."

He shrugged, his cheeks high under my palms and scruff tickling my skin. "Just lucky, I guess. And you looked more like an octopus than a windmill."

Another laugh, this one easier, lighter. And when it was gone, I took a breath that locked in my lungs.

His face was close to mine, his arms holding me like a crucible. And I melted in them like metal, an amalgamation of emotion. Surprise and desire, need and want. No logic was present, only the creases of his lips and the sweet puff of his breath. Only his jaw, hard in my hands. The heat of his skin, his chest bare and pressed against me. His eyes, blue as a cornflower. His lashes like raven feathers.

There was a kiss waiting on those lips, waiting for time to start again.

There was a kiss on those lips, one I wanted.

The realization was a snowball in the face of my desire, and I jerked my hands away, laughing like a crazy person while my brain chemicals went ballistic.

Those lips of his ticked down, but he took the hint, hinging to set my feet on the ground.

"Thank God you were there to catch me," I rambled, putting a few feet between us. My face was on fire. "That'll teach me not to listen to you."

"I'll remember you said that."

I kept laughing to cover my confusion and discomfort, the sound strange, my cheeks hot. I bumped into the table, catching the tobacco baskets before they toppled over and onto the ground.

"You all right, Tess?" he asked with that smile on his face and his chest on full display.

I set the baskets to rights and straightened up, putting my own smile on. "Yeah. Uh-huh. Just the adrenaline, I think. I mean, I did almost just die."

"That would make me a hero."

I rolled my eyes. "Let's not get crazy."

"And that would make you the damsel."

That earned him a mocking laugh and a flash of annoyance that I'd actually needed saving.

"I mean, I did catch you in a princess hold after you fell dramatically from that ladder."

I ignored my curiosity over how he knew what a princess hold was in favor of, "And what, you're the prince?"

He narrowed his eyes like it was a real pickle. "I'd say more of a knight."

"More like a pirate."

"With a heart of gold," he added.

"Well, thanks," I said. "For catching me."

"Saving you," he corrected.

"Saving me," I amended, rolling my eyes hard enough to almost hurt.

He stepped to the crates, inspecting one. "Is there anything specific you need me to do for the planters, or can I just go nuts?"

"Go nuts—as long as you don't get mad if I make you redo them."

A smirk cast down the line of his shoulder, straight at me. "Impress Tess or else. Got it. Meet me back here tomorrow at eight, if you want to help paint the shop."

"I'll be here," I promised.

"Thanks," he said. "For the help."

The echo of my own thank you brought an unbidden smile to my lips. "You're welcome. I'll see you tomorrow."

"Until then, Tess."

I turned, needing out of the room. Out of the building. Off of this block. And even then, I didn't know if the space between Luke and me would be enough.

The mixture of emotions was like cheap concrete—everything from the smooth sand of almost kissing him to the gravel of the fact that *him* was *Luke Bennet*. I wanted to like him. I really did. But I couldn't shake the feeling that I was, on some level, being manipulated by force of his will and charm. It felt disingenuous somehow.

I had no reason to believe him to be anything but sincere, but I didn't trust him as far as I could throw him, and he weighed as much as a baby elephant.

A thought struck me as I hurried out of the greenhouse: I had been operating under the assumption that he wanted to sleep with me, a presumption that had no merit or foundation. He'd kissed me once, drunk on whiskey and full of teenage hormones. That didn't mean he still wanted to kiss me a decade later. He'd been married since, for God's sake.

Maybe he just wanted to be friends.

The thought gave me both a thrill and an aversion. A thrill because I found that part of me did want to be friends with him, and if I wiped away the notion that he wanted something other than that, my claws retracted. And an aversion because sixteen-year-old Tess wanted him to kiss her again and wanted him to regret forgetting. She wanted vengeance, I figured, and who could blame her?

Certainly not twenty-six-year-old Tess.

Friends. I tested the thought, rolled it around in my brain. And I smiled to myself, stepping out of the shop and into the summer heat.

I could be friends with Luke Bennet, so long as he never wanted to kiss me again.

Rhymes With Yes

LUKE

I wanted to kiss Tess Monroe.

I'd wanted to kiss her the second she walked into the shop yesterday, wearing overalls and a Cure T-shirt. I'd wanted to kiss her as I watched her scrub the wall with her little face wrinkled up in concentration. I'd wanted to kiss her when she fell off the ladder and into my arms. And all day today while we painted the shop, I only thought about one thing.

I wanted to kiss her. And I was accustomed to getting what I wanted.

"Did you hear me?" Kash asked impatiently.

"Hmm?"

He rolled his eyes, his long body stretched out on the bottom bunk in our old room. "Man, what's with you?"

"I've been scrubbing and painting the shop for two days. I'm tired."

"Right." he said. "And the redhead in the overall shorts has nothing to do with it."

I leaned back in the wooden desk chair I'd taken up residence in, the hinge squeaking. "As if Tess Monroe would willingly give me the time of day."

He shrugged. "Seems to me like she's given you the time every hour, on the hour, for two days. What's with her? She was different today."

It was true. This morning, she'd walked into the shop, bright-eyed and bushy-tailed, ready to work with a smile on her face. She'd only insulted me seven times, and one of those was a backhanded compliment. My stats were down: the day before, it'd been twenty-three insults and a jab with a broom handle that I couldn't be sure was accidental.

Not that I was counting.

"I dunno what's gotten into her, but I'm not looking a gift horse in the mouth. I'm just taking the boon and moving on."

"Man, she looked so cute with that bandana in her hair and paint on her nose. And her ass in those overalls..." He whistled up at my old bunk.

I fought the urge to chuck my Batman paperweight at him.

"So are you going after her or what?" Kash asked, smirking.

"I just got her to quit treating me like a dog. Pretty sure anything more is off the table."

"Maybe I'll go after her then. Think I've got a shot?"

I snorted to cover my immediate fury at the thought. "She's a girl with standards, Kash. If I don't have a shot, you've got none in hell."

"Maybe she just needs somebody older. More mature."

"We were born in the same year, asshole."

"I'm just saying. Maybe she's looking for stability. Everybody knows you're about as stable as uranium."

"And you're running your mouth like you want a foot in Uranus."

Kash laughed. "I'd love to see you try."

I eyed him. "You don't actually like her, do you?"

"Nah," he said, smiling. "I just want you to admit you do."

A sigh of concession blew out of me, the pause filled with my thoughts. "We almost kissed yesterday," I admitted.

Kash sat up so fast, he thunked his head on the bottom bunk. "Goddammit—" He rubbed at his forehead "—Warn a guy before you go saying things like, *I almost kissed Tess.*"

I laughed openly at his misfortune, hoping it left a mark. "She fell off a ladder in storage, and I caught her. Topless."

His eyes bulged, hand still pressed to his forehead. "Tess was topless in storage?"

"No, I was."

He rolled his eyes, chucking a pillow at me. I caught it midair and chucked it right back at him.

"I'm surprised she didn't deck you," he said, fluffing the pillow before leaning back again.

"Me too, if I'm being honest. She hates me. Hated me. Maybe still hates me a little."

"What'd you do to her?" he asked. At this point, the question was rhetorical—neither of us knew, no matter how many times we'd asked.

"Who knows? But I think the last couple of days have helped my case. All I had to do was show up and not fuck up."

"Don't worry. There's still time," he reassured me.

"Trust me, I'm aware. I've been working on the installation for her in the back, and I'm both convinced I'm going to disappoint her and that I'll knock her socks off."

"Or her bra. Think you can knock that off?"

"If she were anybody else, I'd guarantee it. But Tess?" I made a resigned noise.

He watched me for a second in that way he had about him, the quiet assessment that ran under his outward charm. It was a mask—that much I knew for a fact—armor to protect his soft spots. Everyone thought he was nothing but a girl-crazy flirt, just like me. But that was just how we liked it. Let them think we were empty.

There was comfort in being underestimated. We were constantly set to impress everyone.

Something in his expression shifted, and I knew what he was going to say before he said it.

"Wendy's back in town."

A long, noisy draw of breath filled the space between us. "Laney told me."

Another pause, his eyes the deepest, darkest blue of all of us. "What do you think she wants?"

"I don't know. Can't be a coincidence that she's on my heels."

He frowned. "Didn't think so either. Think she heard Marcus bought the shop?"

Unease twisted around in my stomach like a nest of snakes. "Maybe. Though I don't know why she'd bother coming all the way back. I've only seen her a handful of times since … well, since it ended. The last time was a few weeks ago. She seemed her usual then."

"Charming? Messy? Manic?"

"All of the above."

His frown deepened. "Was she up or down?"

"Up. She wanted to hike Cahuenga, so we did. It was … nice. Like the old days."

"The thrill isn't worth the fallout."

"You say that like I don't know."

Kash huffed. "You didn't sleep with her, did you?"

I shrugged. "It's Wendy," was all I said. Which, of course, meant yes.

That earned me a roll of his eyes. "You're so predictable."

Rather than argue, I ran a hand over my mouth. "You know how it was with her. I loved her—or who she was when she was lucid. And when she wasn't…"

"You wanted to save her. Help her. I get it. But man, you are a glutton for punishment, getting back in bed with her."

"It was the last time. She told me afterward she had a boyfriend."

"You're fucking kidding me," he said flatly.

"Don't worry. Lesson learned and all that. At least she's consistent."

This time, his eye roll was accompanied by a snort.

A rumbling came from the hallway, the unmistakable thunder of someone running up the stairs.

"Dinner!" Laney called, the word trailing down the hall and up the next flight.

"Who knows?" Kash asked, hauling himself out of the bed. "Maybe Wendy'll actually use whatever lives between her ears and stay away."

"Let's not press our luck," I said on a tight laugh, following him out of our room, thinking of her.

Five years ago when I'd met Wendy, my orbit had shifted, centering around her. She had the energy of the sun, warm and bright. It was intoxicating, the vitality radiating from her, and I siphoned it off to fuel my own.

But that's the thing about a star. Get too close, and you get burned.

Whatever I schemed, she was down for. Whatever I wanted to do, she was in. I thought I'd adventure through a lifetime with her. So when she hit lows, there I was, stable and steady, a lifeline in the storm.

She needed me. So I gave her everything, heart and soul.

I told myself it wasn't her fault when she refused meds, dropped out of therapy. I blamed her parents for their neglect, their irresponsibility, for the lack of love she received. I wanted to save her from them. From herself. I wanted to give her the life she'd never known.

So I used my trust on our house in Santa Monica. Let her shop without constraint. The debts grew, and my trust dwindled. My odd jobs wouldn't pay for Hermès purses anymore, wouldn't fund the house. So we packed up, headed into the Valley where it was more affordable, and found an apartment in Reseda. My thought was that when things turned around, we could settle down there and raise kids, despite the fighting it had taken me to get her off the west side. And that fight seemed to bleed into everything. The good times quit outweighing the bad, her lows longer, harder. I thought we'd never make it when I found the Vicodin, when I uncovered her addiction— that fight was so intense I left the house when she started slinging plates at me like frisbees. When I came home, every ceramic in our kitchen had been reduced to rubble, the room a wreckage of porcelain bursts and nicks slashed in the walls.

I found Wendy in our room, unresponsive. A handful of pills, a couple of drinks. An ambulance. Stomach pump. Her tears, her sorrow when she woke, as desperately real as her rage had been.

Wendy had two triggers—financial security and abandonment. And that knowledge should have been my clue. I should have known then that it was going to fall apart. But like a fool, I had faith.

And then I found her with him.

It was the stuff of nightmares. After all we'd been through, after everything I'd given, I came home to find her fucking him in my living room. Everyone has a line, a boundary that once crossed could never be retreated beyond again. And that was mine.

I believed her when she said she was sorry—not to get me back, but because despite it all, she didn't want to hurt me. She moved back to Santa Monica with him. And when he dumped her like a broken armchair, she came back, begging. I was sick enough to consider taking her back.

But what I'd told her was as true then as it was in this very moment—I couldn't forgive her just because she was sick. Not for what she'd done.

The most I could offer was to help her find jobs—which she would inevitably lose—or help her secure apartments—which she would live in until she either couldn't pay rent anymore or found a new guy to shack up with. She bounced from man to man, always rich, always connected. And when they discarded her, as they always did, she would come to me. It would start as dinner and end up with us in each other's arms. But there was always a surprise—she needed money, had been dumped. Or worse—she came to me for comfort when she had a boyfriend I didn't know about. Which made me the other man.

Beyond the pale. That last time was the last time.

But still I knew deep down that I'd answer the call. Because if I didn't help her, no one would.

When Marcus had summoned us home, I realized I'd only been staying for her. And coming back broke the shackles I hadn't realized I'd been wearing.

Hearing that she'd followed had them hovering over my wrists all over again.

But this time, it was different. This time, I wouldn't sacrifice. It was time I moved on, and for the first time in a long time, moving on felt possible.

I mean, aside from the fact that I was living in my childhood home with my siblings.

Our old room hadn't changed much, though Kash had moved into Laney's old room when she left for college—it was bigger and had a bay window. Of course, he'd relinquished it to Laney when she came home. And since Marcus's room had been turned into a junkyard of homeless boxes and furniture, Kash and I had ended up back in our room together.

He'd called bottom bunk, and when we'd wrestled for it, he'd won, thanks to a well-placed punch to the nuts. Always was a cheater—it was the only way he could beat me. As such, every night, I climbed a tiny ladder and slept close enough to the ceiling that I couldn't raise my arms without putting a fist through sheetrock. Lucky for Kash, I wasn't claustrophobic.

We trotted down the stairs, passing framed pictures of all of us, from naked butts to posed studio pictures. Kash and I took turns insulting each other, Laney chiming in with a flick of my ear that ended up with her over my shoulder, squealing. Marcus remained civilized, only offering an occasional one-liner, and Mom followed behind, fussing over his suit and warning me not to knock anything off the walls.

We burst into the dining room like a herd of wildebeests. Dad sat at the head of the table, sighing as he closed his newspaper, his moment of solitude passed. Jett entered the room with a casserole dish in mitted hands and Mom's apron tied around his neck and waist—the purple one with the little yellow flowers.

The rest of us stopped with a nearly audible screech, paused, and busted out laughing.

His face flattened. "What? I didn't want to mess up my shirt."

Kash bellowed, grabbing Jett around the neck. "You look so pretty, Julie."

Jett rolled his eyes, elbowing Kash hard enough to make him *oof*. "Watch it, Kassie."

"Come on, don't let him get to you," I soothed. "Not when you look so pretty in purple."

"And you look great in black and blue," he shot.

"Now, hush," Mom said, shooing us toward our seats. "Your

brother cooked dinner for you ungrateful Bennets. Shame on you for teasing him. He was the only one who offered, knowing I can't cook anymore." Her voice was high and lilting but tight around the edges with guilt.

We shared a look before mumbling our apologies.

"Smells good," Laney said, pulling up her chair. "Enchilada casserole? Man, I've been craving this for years."

"That's more like it," Mom noted, beaming at her children as we all sat, her discomfort gone—or at least packed away for the moment. "What did everyone do today?"

Laney reached for the spoon and divvied herself out some Spanish rice. "I worked on graphics for the store all day and almost have the website finished."

"Oh, good. I can't wait to see," Mom said as she filled her plate. "Marcus?"

"Oh. Here's the guacamole."

"No, what did you do today?"

He frowned, setting the dish back down. "Considering I have a dozen banker boxes full of handwritten receipts to go through, we can assume I'll be doing that until I die."

She flushed, tittering. "I've never had a head for math."

Marcus smiled in an uncharacteristic display of compassion, the kind he reserved for Mom. "It's all right. Once I get it sorted, I think we might refile with the IRS for a few years back. I have a feeling there's another twenty to thirty thousand in deductions that were missed."

"Well, what a surprise!" Mom said. "We should take a cruise."

Kash's nose wrinkled. "Stuck on a boat with a bunch of strangers and buffets covered in E-coli? Pass."

"And you, Lucas? What did you do today?"

"Tess," Kash said, smiling innocently at Mom.

Her brow quirked in confusion, and Laney snickered.

"What he means is that Tess and I finished painting," I answered, kicking Kash under the table.

His knee hit the tabletop hard enough to disturb the silverware.

"How exciting!" Mom was all smiles, completely unaffected. "I like to see you two getting along," she said pointedly.

"Oh, they're getting along all right," Kash said, sniggering. "Luke just can't seem to keep his mouth shut about it."

I was ready to fling my fork at him like a ninja star, but Mom went on, unaware.

"Good," she said. "That makes me unreasonably happy. Can I finally come see what you've done, or will you keep me out of there another day? You know I don't do well waiting, Lucas."

"Tomorrow," I promised. "We've still got to put everything back where it goes. Plus, I've got a couple surprises for you."

"I love surprises," she said, her face all soft and dreamy. "And I'm glad you and Tess are working together. She is such a treasure." Tears filled her eyes, happy tears. Proud tears. "She's been my hands for so long, I almost don't miss it. Almost."

Every face at that table warmed.

Dad reached for her hand. "Tess would argue it's you who's the treasure."

Mom smiled, sniffling. "Oh, she would, but it'd be a lie. But I appreciate a well-formed fib as much as I appreciate a good surprise."

I picked up the Tess torch and ran with it. "She jumped right in to help, got her hands dirty, has loads of ideas. We're working on a few things to show you, things I think you're gonna flip your lid over."

"I'm sure my lid will flip elegantly and stick the landing." She let loose a happy sigh. "I will never get tired of seeing all my children at the dinner table again. Will you, Mr. Bennet?"

"Surely not, Mrs. Bennet," he said with a smile only for her.

"And all to work in the shop. Here I thought only Kash had

any interest. And just like that, all five of my children are home and pitching in. I must be the luckiest mother in the whole world."

Marcus eyed her with suspicion. "Mom," he started in warning. "What?"

"How many blind dates have you set us up on?"

She glanced up at him, attempting at innocent. "Marcus Bennet, I can't imagine what you might mean."

"There was no nuance, Mother."

The color rose in her cheeks. "Well, who could blame me for wanting to see my children in love and married? How else will I ever hold grandchildren? When will I weep at a wedding? Lucas ran off and married that girl, and I didn't even get any pictures. Laney and Jett are thirty-one. Thirty-one! And I'm only getting older. Soon, I'll be feeble and frail, and how will I hold babies then?" she rambled her consternation, face flushed and attention on dishing herself out casserole without thought until an insurmountable pile sat on her plate.

"Mom," Laney warned. "Did you really?"

Kash smirked. "Hey, I'll take a blind date. Last one she set me up on was with Charity Smith."

He and I shared a knowing look. The only thing Charity was charitable with was in her pants.

"See?" Mom said, digging into her mound of casserole like it wasn't outrageous in portion. "I'm being *helpful*. Thank you, Kassius. At least one of you is trying."

"How many of us did you set up?" I asked, forearms on the table and brows together.

She shrugged, her face too benign. "Oh, I don't know. All of you?"

The table erupted in noise, and Mom took a prim bite like she couldn't hear us.

"Honestly, Mom," Laney huffed, "it's not like we can't get our own dates."

"I know you can," she insisted, dabbing her lips with a napkin. "You have your apps and your matchmaking websites nowadays, but there's something to be said for a good, old-fashioned setup, isn't there? For instance, at garden club yesterday, Vera Archer said her daughter just moved back from San Francisco and needs some friends. Of course, I offered for Jett. Plus—"—she leaned in, smiling wickedly—"she's filthy rich."

Jett groaned.

Laney rolled her eyes. "Mother."

"What?" she blustered. "I only want my children to be happy and healthy and find love. And if the person they fall in love with is rich, that couldn't possibly *hurt*, could it?"

"Of course it couldn't hurt," Dad said, "beyond the bite of the hayfork you use to shovel them off to the marriage market."

Mom swatted his arm. "Oh, I'm not shoveling … just giving them a little nudge. Isn't that our job? Encourage them to fly out of the nest?"

"Fly or swan dive?" Marcus asked.

"Fly," she insisted. "Your date is next Tuesday, by the way. With that sweet little Jenny Arnold. Do you remember her?"

Marcus's face flattened. "I think she gave me a religious tract outside the bathroom in high school."

Kash laughed. "She still does that. I saw her in Blanche's Donuts last week, just hanging around outside the restroom door waiting to proselytize to poor, unsuspecting donut enthusiasts."

"I'm not going," Marcus stated in a tone that brooked no argument.

One Mom was deaf to. "Oh, you'll go. Otherwise, you'll have to tell her yourself, to her face."

And just like that, she had him, check and mate. No way could he bear the look on poor Jenny Arnold's face when he told her he'd rather eat a dirty boot than take her to dinner. Instead, he'd sit through an entire dinner, listening to her talk about her favorite Psalms while he thought of all the ways he could off himself with things within his reach.

I laughed at the thought, but the sound died in my throat.

She'd said she'd set *all* of us up.

"Mom," I warned, "who'd you pair me with?"

She smiled, lips together to guard her secret. "I'm still firming yours up."

I frowned, aversion sliding over me like a slug. There was only one girl I wanted to ask out, and her name rhymed with *yes*.

"I'm too busy with the store," I insisted. "Give Kash my date."

Kash shoveled a bite into his mouth, saying around it, "I'll take it."

But Mom tsked. "No, this one is special for Lucas. You can't have her."

My frown deepened, my attention inward as Laney climbed on her soapbox to rant about societal pressures to get married and how unfair it all was.

I'd find a way out of whatever date my mother devised. That was all there was to it.

I had other plans.

The vision of Tess in my arms arrested my thoughts. The almost imperceptible smattering of freckles on her nose and cheekbones and the unbelievable length of her eyelashes. The little details of her face that I hadn't seen until she was close enough to kiss, like the burst of honey gold around her pupils, the color vivid and full of light against the deep brown of her eyes.

I liked Tess, and it had been a long, long time since I felt like this … like there was *possibility*. She was the kind of girl I could see myself with because who else could truly tame a Bennet but a girl like Tess? She wouldn't give me an inch. And she believed I wasn't the kind of man to be responsible.

Which made me want to prove her wrong.

Despite that, she liked me. In the moment when she'd almost kissed me, I knew. Maybe against her will, but she liked me at least equally as much as she hated me.

And that was something I could work with.

Double Take

TESS

I was all smiles, bouncing into the shop the next morning like a rubber ball.

The difference with the white walls was night and day, and to see it in full daylight was astounding. The space looked twice as big, bright and full of sunshine, the effect lost on me and Luke last night when we'd finished after dark. But this morning, Longbourne was illuminated. The long walls were pristine, the tables and displays back in place, and in the back, the register counter was framed by freshly scrubbed red brick.

He must have hung up the old wooden Longbourne sign above the counter this morning, and my heart twisted with emotion at the sight.

I hummed behind smiling lips, making my way through the shop. Ivy smiled up at me from an arrangement she was working on—succulents, ivy, flowers in water tubes, all planted in a glass apothecary jar. One of our living arrangements I'd come up with last year, which had become an instant success. Dean stood next to her as he sometimes did—especially when he delivered supplies a couple times a week—a human brick wall with a smile as shiny as Las Vegas, his big hand resting in the small of her back.

"Well, aren't you chipper this morning?" Dean said.

"I know!" I answered.

Ivy shook her head, but she smiled broadly. "Gee, I figured all that manual labor would have you moving a little slower than this." She gestured to all of me.

"I can't help it. It's window day!" I cheered. "Can you even imagine what it's going to look like when I'm done with it?"

"I honestly can't," she admitted, "but knowing you, it's going to be brilliant."

"Come here and hop into my pocket so you can remind me of that all day."

Ivy laid a hand on her belly. "I'm not fitting in anybody's pocket anytime soon."

With a cluck of his tongue, Dean pulled her into his side. "Just a couple more months, and I'll have two pocket-sized girls."

"Couple more months," she grumbled. "She'd better be really cute."

"She will be, 'cause she's gonna look like you."

She nudged him but gave him the sweetest glance, just a flick of her eyes that conveyed her utter adoration. "Flatterer."

I chuckled, resisting the urge to grab her around what was left of her waist and waltz her around the room. Things were looking up and looking bright. Everything I needed for the window installation had been delivered, and today, I'd finally see what Luke had been working on in whatever spare time he'd mustered.

I glanced behind Ivy, looking for him.

"He's in storage," she said with a smirk.

"Thanks, Ivy." I beamed, pressing a quick kiss to her cheek as I bounced away again. "Bye, Dean!" I called over my shoulder as I pushed through the doors to the greenhouse.

The sound of an electric saw buzzed through the greenhouse, and as I descended the ramp to the basement, I saw Luke, his back to me and eyes down. That back, that shirtless back in all its muscular glory, was on display, already glistening with sweat at eight in the morning. I wondered how long he'd been here. But then, he'd been here every morning before me.

It was a new side of him—the responsibility, not his massive back—one that I was impressed by. One that inspired him to rise early and stay late, fueled by nothing more than his excitement and vision. His duty and dependability.

Extraordinary how it changed him.

Somehow, he'd gotten more handsome in the last seventy-two hours. Someway, when he spoke, I didn't have to fight the urge to stuff moss in his mouth or shove his face in a pile of topsoil. It was probably because I'd decided to be his friend instead of assuming he was trying to sleep with me.

There was an enormous amount of relief in that. Not because I didn't want to sleep with him. With him running around shirtless and using power tools, any hetero woman in her right mind would want to sleep with him.

No, it was because I didn't know if I'd stop him if he did happen to make a move.

That was what I'd really been afraid of, I realized—my lack of will, given the assumption he wanted to make out with me.

You are such an egomaniac, I told myself with an eye roll.

By assuming he *didn't* want to theoretically make out with me, I absolved myself from theoretically having to make out with him. And so, by taking the threat off the table, I'd cut my anxiety down by eighty-nine percent, thus easing my white-knuckle grip and generally making things more pleasant between us.

I thought that maybe, in time, Luke could make a great friend. And working with him was far easier than I'd imagined. I'd thought he'd fight me the whole way, be contrary as a rule, make it his personal mission to irritate me. But over the last few days, we'd found a rhythm. He came up with the ideas, and I figured out how we'd get it done. He took my direction without complaint and executed it with precision.

It was more creative fun than I'd had in years. And I was high on the feeling.

I stopped behind him, admiring the expanse of his back and shoulders with a giddy smile on my face. I tapped him on the shoulder, trying for cute.

He jumped six inches, the saw coming to a stop just as he wheeled around, the motion fast enough to nearly knock me over.

"Jesus, Tess. Didn't anyone ever tell you never to sneak up on a man using power tools? I could have lost a finger."

I flushed, laughing. "I'm sorry."

He gave me a sideways smile. "No harm done. Just remember—I can't make you things if I have no hands."

I peered around him, looking for the crates. "Speaking of…"

Luke chuckled softly. "They're over here. Come on, let me show you."

He walked me over to the big worktable, and on top was one of the crates and my entire order of flowers, plus some things I hadn't ordered but would match perfectly.

But my eyes were locked on the crate, and as I approached, he smiled, folding his tremendous arms across his chest. I didn't even care how smug he looked.

He'd painted them a buttery, sunshiny yellow, lined them with moss, filled them with soil, topped them with chicken wire to hold the dirt in place. On the tops, he'd installed metal drawer pulls, two on each, to hang them by, I figured.

"The color is perfect, Luke."

"It'll match the other window. I found a whole box of drawer pulls and thought that'd be better than just using screw hooks. And I had another idea," he said tentatively. I'd have called him nervous if I thought Luke was capable of the emotion. "Wait. Let me back up."

He moved down the table, his hands disappearing behind the metal buckets full of waiting florals. And when he stepped back around it, my smile was wide enough to open up in a grin.

In each meaty fist was a rope, and at their ends was a board of wood as old as this establishment. It was worn and grooved, dry and etched with age. He'd made a swing.

"So when you said you'd make a flower cloud, I thought ... what if we made a scene? The succulents, those can be sunshine. And this one can be rain. The cloud, the swing. In each, we could hang filler flowers in an arch like rays or rain—feverfew daisies for the succulents and purple sweet peas for the swing. Oh, and look." He set the swing down to reach under the table, returning to view with an armful of rain boots.

The sizes varied, from men's to women's, big to small. Some had to be from the thirties or forties, the style both foreign and familiar, the shape of the toe, the craftsmanship of the buckles. All of them were worn, loved.

"We could set them up in the windowsill and fill them with flowers. Maybe ranunculus ... have you walked through the greenhouse rows lately? It's legitimately exploding."

I reached for a boot, the feel of cool rubber under my hand as I inspected it with awe and appreciation. This boot had lived a lifetime, as had the components of the swing, of the crates he'd turned into planters for me.

For the shop, I corrected.

Emotion washed over me, my surprise and sentimentality over

all he'd done overwhelming. "It … it's perfect. Just perfect."

He smiled, setting the boots on the table. "Man, I'm relieved. I figured you were going to hate it."

I made a face. "Hate it? How could I possibly hate this?"

Luke scratched at his neck. "I dunno, Tess. I figured I'd screw it up somehow, especially since you didn't weigh in on a lot of this. I changed your plan."

"You *adjusted* my plan. Lucky for you, they're good ideas," I teased.

"I mean, don't overdo it on the flattery or anything."

"Thank you, Luke," I said quietly, my smile small and awed. "I could never hate this or anything you create. You, my friend, are truly talented and in ways I could never be. And I'm sorry I ever made you feel like I wouldn't approve. I haven't been myself lately. You … you tend to do that to me." I snapped straighter, smiled wider. I'd said too much. "So please, go nuts anytime you want with zero concern for what I think."

He watched me with his thoughts clicking behind his eyes, though they were otherwise hidden from me. "That'd be impossible. But thanks all the same." I opened my mouth to respond, but he spoke first, changing the subject. "Now, what do you say we get started? I want to show Mom tomorrow. If we don't, I'm pretty sure she'll bust in here like the Kool-Aid man whether we like it or not. It'd blow our whole surprise."

Our surprise, he'd said. My smile widened.

"All right. Let's hang sheets in the window, just in case she decides she needs to take a walk."

"Smart thinking. She's up there, scheming—I swear I can practically hear her—but Jett's got strict instructions to keep her still. If he has to watch another historical film, I think he's going to go ballistic and start wearing a top hat and cravat and calling everyone madame."

A laugh burst out of me. "How do you know what a cravat is?"

He shrugged. "He's not the only one who's had to keep Mom busy so someone else can make trouble. BBC makes for a great diversion," he said, moving for a flat cart.

"What's your favorite?" I asked, helping to load our haul onto the cart.

"I dunno." He stacked one crate on another, then a third, and picked them all up like they were nothing. "I'll tell you what I didn't like—*Poldark*."

"Really? I figured you'd relate to old Ross Poldark."

He snorted, setting the crates down with a thunk. "Please. That guy's a douchebag. The second he cheated on Demelza with Elizabeth, I was out. I played Candy Crush and half-listened to Mom fume through the rest of the seasons."

One of my brows rose as I picked up one measly crate, which might as well have been a sack of bricks. "Look at that—Luke Bennet, the monogamist."

"Elizabeth married some other dude instead of waiting for him to come back from the war!" he shot.

"She thought he was dead," I argued.

He was mad, actually mad about it. "Fuck her. If she'd really loved him, she would have waited. And instead of writing her off for being the cold bitch she was, he pined after her like a teenager, even after he was married." He made a noise. "Stupid asshole. Demelza gave him everything, that ungrateful shit."

My amusement bubbled out of me by the way of my laughter, which surged when he aimed a solid pout at me.

"I'm not wrong," he said petulantly.

"No," I said around a laugh. "You're not wrong."

"Then what's so funny?"

My mouth opened, looking for words as I moved another crate. "I'm just surprised is all."

His arms folded, this time making him look like Paul Bunyan, with tree-trunk arms and brawny shoulders as he looked down at me. "That I watch historicals?"

"No, that you disapprove of him cheating on her."

Oh, how his frown deepened, forming an expression of betrayal. "What do you mean?"

"Well," I hedged, suddenly unsure of myself, "only that … well, I just didn't think you were one to attach emotions to sex."

"That is mighty presumptuous of you, Tess."

"It's just that you seem to really enjoy women," I clarified, avoiding his eyes by keeping myself in motion.

"Sure, but that doesn't mean I don't respect them." He picked up another stack of crates and loaded them a little harder than necessary. "If I'd nearly died in war and come home to find the girl I loved married to someone else—my dickface cousin named Francis, no less—I'd have been broken. But I would have gone on. Because if she'd loved me, she would have waited. And if I'd found someone who loved me like Demelza, I wouldn't have looked back."

I watched him stack the last crates with that pout still on his face, unable to reconcile the man who watched BBC with his mom and ranted about the love story and the guy I'd thought had zero regard for anyone's feelings other than his own. Not that he did it on purpose. His head really was that far up his own ass.

Or so I'd thought.

"Well," I started, grabbing a couple of buckets of flowers, "I'm with you. And when she punched him in his stupid slack jaw, I jumped off the couch and did a Herkie."

"A what?" he asked on a laugh.

"A Herkie. You know, the cheerleading jump where your legs go like … like one of them sticks out and the other bends?"

He frowned. "I don't get it."

I sighed, setting the flowers down and taking a few steps back to get into a clear space. "Like this."

I wound up and jumped, kicking my right leg out in front of me, toe pointed, and bending my left leg, putting my foot right by my ass. My hands punched out to the sides like Bruce Lee knocking out two drug lords at once.

He clapped when I hit the ground, and I curtsied, lifting invisible skirts.

"Thank you, thank you," I said.

"Where'd you learn to do that? I don't remember you being a cheerleader."

"I wasn't. Ivy taught me," I said, picking up my buckets again as he grabbed the cart handle. "I used to help her, spot her and that sort of thing, and she showed me some stuff. That one was my favorite."

"As far as I'm concerned, you shoulda made the squad." He winked as he passed, and I followed him.

"Oh, I didn't really have time. My mom … well, I'd just started taking care of my dad full-time. There wasn't time for much else."

He slowed, looking down at me as I caught up. "I imagine you didn't have much pep either," he said gently, quietly.

"No, not a lot of pep or cheer. Not to expend on a basketball game anyway. I spent that energy on flowers instead."

He didn't say anything for a second as we walked through the double doors and into our workspace, and neither did I. It wasn't something I wanted to talk about, nor was it something I wanted to dwell on.

"Well, you did good on that, Tess. And look at you now—head of design and production at Longbourne Flower Shop."

I chuckled, thankful he didn't press. "What a fancy title. I'll have to put that on my business cards."

"You have business cards? Do they have your number on them?"

he joked, waggling his brows at me.

I rolled my eyes. "No business cards."

"If you did, would you give me one?"

"Probably not."

"So there's hope?"

I laughed, bumping him with my arm. But I didn't answer.

I was a terrible liar.

The day went by in a blur, that kind of creative time warp that left you shocked when you looked up and it was dark out, the sort that had your stomach grinding on itself because you'd missed a meal. We ordered sandwiches, ate them sitting on tables across from each other in the storefront, feet dangling as we talked.

Luke and I worked around each other in a symphony with no sound. I planted the succulents and leafy plants, and he hung the frames and swing. I built the flower cloud with a wad of chicken wire, using wispy gray pampas grass like feathers, lavender heather, white wheat stalks, baby's breath. It looked like a thundercloud hanging over that swing. Then we strung the filler flowers, hanging them upside down from frames Luke had whipped up like it was nothing. When I backed up, the flower heads made a pattern that looked like it was raining or sunshiny, depending on which installment we were looking at.

It was late as I put the finishing touches on it all. Luke had disappeared an hour before, but I'd barely noticed, my mind focused wholly on what I was doing. I stepped back to admire our work when I heard him approach.

"What do you think?" I asked without looking, still smiling at the installments, hands on my hips.

"Damn," he breathed. "It really is impressive when you step back and look at it all together. I can't wait to see it from the outside. Especially when we hang these."

My brows quirked as I turned. He'd put his shirt back on when the sun went down and the shop cooled off, much to my disappointment. But he was dusted with sawdust, and little flecks of wood stood out like snowflakes against the dense black of his hair.

In his hands were two signs, and he held them up one at a time, as they were too long to display at once. In a gorgeous handwritten script were the words rain and shine, carved out of the wood, which he'd left raw.

My jaw hit the ground. "Luke, did you ... you didn't make these, did you?"

"Yeah," he answered, inspecting *rain*. "Do you like them?"

"Like them?" I took *rain* from him, my eyes combing over it. "They're ... they're gorgeous. How the hell?" I asked myself, turning it over like I'd find proof of magic.

He shrugged like it was no big deal, casual and confident, like this was just an everyday, regular thing. "I drew it out, used the scroll saw. Didn't take long, thirty minutes for each, since they were just fonts, no borders or anything."

I turned to meet his eyes, blinking at him stupidly. "You drew this?"

"I mean, I used a font as a template, but yeah."

"And then you just ... cut it out?"

"That's how it usually works," he said on a laugh. "I would have painted them, but I didn't know what color you wanted to do."

"Turquoise," I said without hesitation. "To match the door."

"Got it. Be right back." And with a smirk and a wink, he was walking away again, leaving me in the quiet shop.

Luke Bennet, my hero.

It wasn't even right.

I swallowed the bitter pill that I'd been wrong about him as I walked to the swing and sat, gripping the rope. But the aftertaste of that wasn't something I could rid myself of so easily.

I liked him. And I liked him enough to do something about it.

This was a dangerous realization, my teenage self screaming *Don't do it!* like I was willingly stepping in front of a goddamn freight train. Because I'd been down this road once before, and though we had just been teenagers at the time, in moments like this, the wound stung like it was fresh.

Luke Bennet had been my friend. He'd been my first crush, the first boy's name I doodled in my notebook, the boy I rushed to work after school to see. Funny, charming, beautiful Luke Bennet, who had convinced me to come to the greenhouse that night, who listened to me cry about my dead mother with that heartbreaking look on his face. Who kissed me in the moonlight and then forgot me completely.

He was unpredictable. What he said, he didn't always mean. He was dangerous.

We were kids, I told myself. *He's grown up since then.*

Teenage me made a face at the thought. Did people really change, or did they only shift, shimmy, slide? And even more troublesome—had he changed, or had I pegged him wrong all along?

His hands on my back nearly shocked me off the swing. With a quiet laugh, he gave me a little push.

"Look at that. It holds," I said over the thumping of my heart in my ears.

"You doubted me?"

"Considering I didn't know you knew how to make anything but trouble a couple days ago, I'd say a healthy amount of concern isn't out of line."

"Fair enough."

He pushed me again, as firmly as he could in the space we had, and for a moment, neither of us spoke. The window stretched almost to the floor and all the way to the ceiling, the installment several feet inside of it. I glanced up at the cloud, which was built to look like it was suspended over the swing, the pampas grass swaying with the motion.

"You did good, Luke," I admitted, not sure how to fill the silence between us.

"You did too. Difference is, I never doubted you." It wasn't an accusation. The words were touched with levity, like he was smiling.

"Well, I've never given you a reason to doubt me, have I?"

He considered for a beat. "No, I guess not. You've always been capable, reliable. Dependable, even when we were kids. But what have I done to convince you I'm not?"

There was something in his voice, the edge of a wound, a tendril of hurt.

"Well," I started, not wanting to hurt his feelings, but compelled to be honest, "aside from you never holding down a job? Or being in a serious relationship?"

"I was married, Tess," he said quietly. "How much more serious could I get?"

But I laughed it off, hoping to defuse the tension. "I mean, was Wendy *really* serious?"

He pulled the swing to a stop. "You think I'd get married if I wasn't serious?"

I gripped the ropes, shifting so I could look back at him. The hurt on his face was unmistakable.

"I … that's not what I meant."

"Well, what *did* you mean?" He waited for my response like he'd wait until hell froze over if he had to.

My lips gaped just a little, my mind scrambling with how to explain, and when the words came, they were honest and blunt, wielded with the unwavering certainty that nothing could faze him. Nothing could hurt him. "It's just that you've always been a player. You fooled around with Ivy for years. Never had a girlfriend in high school, just a string of hookups. And then, out of nowhere, you disappeared with Wendy, who was a notorious flake and player equal to you. You were always so … I don't know. Unattainable. No one could lock you down. You toyed with every girl's emotions in a twenty-block radius, so when Wendy did, I assumed it was just a game. Temporary."

His gaze hardened, his jaw stiff and square. "How do you always do that?"

"Do what?" I asked, genuinely confused.

"Find ways to insult me, even when you're being earnest?"

I opened my mouth to defend myself.

But he cut me off. "What did I ever do to you, Tess? We used to be friends, and somewhere along the way, you turned into *this*. You have berated me, insulted me. Treated me like I was second-class. You act like I was put on earth solely to annoy you, and I can't understand why. So enlighten me, Tess—what did I do to deserve this?"

I hopped off the swing, my face drawn as I turned to him. The secret I'd kept from him, the truth of that night, all of it waited on my lips. But I couldn't speak the words. I couldn't admit it, not after all this time.

"Nothing. You did nothing, Luke. Like always."

All of hell fueled my fire as I blew past, wanting nothing more than to get out of that shop and far, far away. But he hooked my arm, stopping me.

"What the hell does that mean?"

"It doesn't matter."

"*What* doesn't matter?" His brows were knit so tight, they nearly touched. "What happened, Tess? What do you think I did?"

"I don't *think* you did anything." I jerked my arm from his grip, fists like hammers at my sides and jaw like a vise. "If you can't remember kissing me, I have no interest in reminding you."

His face clicked open like pins and hammers of a lock.

But I didn't wait for a response. I didn't want one. Not when I was sure he'd say exactly what I feared: *you meant nothing to me.*

There was only one thing to do, one thing I needed—a city block between Luke and me. And with furious tears in my eyes, I brushed past him to put it there.

You Can Try

LUKE

I blinked as she passed like a thunderbolt.

She hadn't said what I thought she'd said. There was no way I'd heard her right. None in the history of the world.

Never in a trillion years would I have forgotten kissing Tess Monroe.

My hand shot out like a grappling hook, snagging the crook of her elbow. I turned her around, my fingers clamping her arms to hold her still.

"Tess," I started, my voice calm, still, like she was a wild animal set to bolt, "I have never kissed you."

She shook her head, her eyes shining. "You did. I'll remember it until I die whether you do or not."

I swallowed hard, my mind scrambling backward in time, searching for the memory. "I don't know who kissed you, but it wasn't me."

Fury and hurt lit her eyes like a brazier. "The greenhouse. Laney bought you a bottle of Wild Turkey."

I frowned. "That I remember. I drank a third of it waiting on you to sneak out. Your mom had just ... I'd wanted to cheer you up. But I didn't kiss you."

"Are you sure about that?" she shot.

"We talked and drank and ... that's it." *Wasn't it?* "We were friends, Tess."

"I thought so too. And then you kissed me. You told me you wanted to date, kissed me all night, and forgot me by the morning."

I found that night in my memory and flicked through it. But the end was a blank space. I didn't remember anything until the next morning when I woken up, half-hanging from the bunk with a thumping headache and a stiff neck.

"I ... I don't remember."

"I know you don't. You didn't remember when you came to work the next day either. When you patted me on the head and made out with Ivy in storage."

I shook my head, half to argue, half to shake the cobwebs out. "No." I pulled her closer, closer still, my eyes bouncing between hers. "I'd never forget you."

"Except that you did. Because that's what you do. I didn't mean anything to you—nothing seemed to—so excuse me for assuming things hadn't changed."

"Tess," I said, the word bouncing off her lips and into mine.

"What?"

"I owe you a real kiss."

"No, you don't." The words trembled, her tone belying their meaning.

I let her arm go, my hand sliding up the line of her jaw, the shape fitting in my palm neatly. "Yes, I do. All I need is five minutes."

"F-for what?" she breathed.

"To change your mind."

A shift of permission—the simultaneous intake of breath, fluttering of lashes, tilting of her face, parting of lips. For a protracted heartbeat, I gazed into the face of submission, held it in my palm.

And then I took it for mine.

Lips, a hot crush of lips, soft and eager, willing and earnest. A noisy breath, the scent of earth and life and loam filling my lungs, filling my mind.

I was slammed back in time with a jolt.

The moonlight in the greenhouse, the sigh from her lips, the sweetness of her, the fire in me. Tess. Whiskey on her breath. Her mouth, her tongue had been timid, inexperienced. She'd had to go home—I didn't want her to. I'd wanted her to stay. I'd wanted her to stay forever, and I'd asked her to, first with my kiss, then with my words.

My grip on her tightened, and I pulled her closer—this Tess, my Tess—as if the taste of her, the feel of her against me could prolong the memory. There was nothing timid about her roaming hands now, nothing inexperienced in the way she wound around me. We went up like a torch in a twist, a tangle of arms, our bodies locked and seeking the other. There was no space—the flame had devoured the distance, the air, her and me.

Consumed.

Her arms tightened around my neck, my hand hitching her thigh, my tongue sweeping the depth of her mouth and hers dancing against it.

I didn't know who slowed, who came to their senses, who remembered the earth existed and tethered us. But the kiss broke. And I looked into the lust-drunk, blinking face of Tess.

"You had to go," I said, my voice gravelly and raw. "I didn't want you to go home that night, and I told you so."

"You did," she whispered.

"I remember," I breathed. "I kissed you. I wanted you, thought I had you."

"But then you forgot."

"Then I forgot. And you hated me … I thought it was your mom, everything you were going through. I thought you needed space, so I never tried, not knowing I'd pushed you away myself."

She swallowed, looking up at me with uncertainty.

"I owe you more than a kiss, Tess. Let me make it up to you," I begged, her face in my palm, my fingertips in her hair.

A flicker of a smile. "You can try."

And with a smile of my own, I kissed her again with the intention of doing just that.

TESS

Beyond all logic and with all the rightness in the world, Luke Bennet kissed me.

Slower, deeper was this kiss, without the frantic frenzy of the first. He breathed in my fire, stoking it until it raged. But his lips moved with intention, a savoring, sampling game of catch and release. He tasted me like it was the first time so many years ago, like he wanted to memorize the details he'd once forgotten.

Disarmed. He disarmed me, stole my grenades, took down the wall brick by brick, left me defenseless. I was helpless to fight, and my desire to was gone, replaced by another desire entirely.

This was a moment I'd thought about too many times over too many years, one that had found its way into my dreams, unbidden, unwanted. I'd written him off, but then he had come back and did everything right, said everything I wanted to hear without knowing I wanted to hear it.

It was a rewriting of history, that kiss. And I chose to lose myself in the moment.

I should have stopped. I should have refused. I should have stepped back and run out of that shop like it was on fire. Part of my brain screamed for me to, but I pushed her into the cellar and locked the door. This time, I wouldn't stop. This time, he wouldn't forget. Tonight, I would be selfish and make a new memory to replace the old one.

I couldn't ask him for more than that.

Because in the end, I was still me, and he was still him. He would move on again, and I would stay here. I'd be brushed aside the minute Judy called in an order or Wendy blew back in town. He wouldn't want me for more than this, so I should never let myself want him. Not for more than tonight. Right now.

Letting him in for more than that would be naive. A cavalier risk, not a calculated one. Because the data told me one thing: Luke Bennet would hurt me if I let him.

So I wouldn't.

A shocked hiss left him when my hand slipped up his shirt, breaking the kiss.

"I've wanted to touch you for days," I whispered my truth, my lips closing over the soft skin beneath his chin. "You've been so … shirtless."

A quiet laugh, his hand still holding my face with tender care as I kissed his neck, his fingertips in my hair. The other hand cupped my ass, squeezing it as if to test the weight.

"So you've forgiven me for the grope?" he asked, his hand shifting to the seam of my jeans.

My body clenched when his finger stroked the line. "You made me a swing," I muttered, lids heavy. "So, yes."

"And you've forgiven me for forgetting?" The question was softer, less sure, more repentant.

"Depends," I said, tugging at the hem of his shirt.

"On what?" He let me go to reach behind him, pulling it off and tossing it away.

My teeth pinned my bottom lip, my thirsty eyes on his chest, hungry hands on his abs. "On how well you plan on making it up to me."

He bent to kiss me, grabbing me by the thighs to hoist me up and wrap me around him. His narrow waist in the circle of my legs. My fingers in the silky depth of his hair. My lips pressing his, demanding and submitting all in the same motion.

He walked us to one of the tables, setting my ass on the edge, spreading my thighs to nestle his hips between them. The length of him fitted against me—his basketball shorts masked nothing, and I praised their creator once more—and with the arch of my back, I stroked him, stroked myself.

A deep rumble in his chest, past his lips, across my tongue.

A flash of lightning in my heart.

It was fear, white-hot and electric. Because I'd never had a fling, never had a one-night stand. I'd never separated sex and feelings—I'd never had to. And with Luke, that separation was imperative.

Let her be wild. Tonight. Only tonight.

And so I let go.

Luke didn't break the kiss, but his hands had their own agenda. The line of my jaw, the column of my neck. Collarbone, the tender flesh in the dip, the hard bone of the ridge. My T-shirt bunched in his hands, rising up my torso—this was what paused the kiss. Over my head, behind him somewhere into the void.

The room was warm, but a riot of goosebumps broke out across my skin, my nipples tight and straining against the thin fabric of my bra.

The second my lips were free of my shirt, they were his again.

A mewl into his mouth when his thumb brushed the aching peak of my nipple, my fingers twisting in his hair, my hips wild, angling for his.

I wished we were somewhere else. Somewhere soft where I

could feel the weight of his body on mine. But this would have to do.

I flexed my legs, squeezing until his hips pressed into mine, hard enough that it was almost painful, if it didn't feel so good.

Oh, this will do, I thought, my tongue brushing his, his hand on my neck, thumb tilting my chin, pinning it so he could delve deeper into my mouth. *This will do just fine.*

My arms circled his neck as I wrapped my legs around his waist, angling my body so he could do what he would with my breast. Fingers hooked my bra and pulled, freeing my breast. God, I wanted his mouth on me, wanted the heat of it, the slick satin of his tongue on my skin. But I settled for the lock of our lips and his hand on my breast. My ribs. My stomach.

His fingers found my button and opened it with a snap. The vibration of my zipper as he lowered it thrummed down the seam of my pants, against the delicate, aching flesh between my thighs.

Fingertips grazed the hem of my panties, the satiny front, cupped my sex. Tested the valley, circled the peak, his hips grinding into the back of his hand, the pressure spurring a grind of my own.

The kiss broke, leaving me stupefied and slack-jawed, my lids too heavy to keep open. His arm, hot and strong, wound around my waist, and he picked me up. The steaming skin of his solid chest against my exposed nipple sent a shock of pleasure down to the place that needed him so. My legs locked tight enough that he let go, slipping his hands into the back of my jeans until his hands were full.

Before I realized what was happening, his hands shifted, working my shorts and panties half off in the same motion as he set me back on the table. A yelp of surprise into his mouth, and my jeans were moving down my thighs. One sneaker in his palm, then on the ground. The other followed. And in little more than a handful of breaths, I was naked but for my bra.

Too stunned to parse, too hot to care. His lips moved down my body, closing over my nipple just like I'd imagined. But imagination was nothing compared to the real thing— the slick heat of his mouth, his fingertip tracing the slick heat of my body.

Though not for long, not nearly long enough before he moved on, leaning me back, lips on the curves of my stomach, the swell of my hip. His hand on my thigh, a stroke, a pull to open it, to hitch it on his shoulder.

I willed my lids opened, the white of my fingers in the black of his hair. The bridge of his nose, the crescents of his lashes. His lips, swollen and dusky. The flash of his tongue, the feel against my thigh. My other thigh slung over his shoulder. The tan of his fingers against the pale of my skin. A tug of my hips, a flick of his eyes to catch mine and hold them. To make sure I was watching when he ran the flat of his tongue up my center and closed his lips over my hood, sucking gently.

I drew a ragged breath, my lids fluttering closed, head lolling and thighs trembling. His tongue shifted, soft and hard, flat and firm, slow and fast.

Seconds. Seconds of his mouth on me, and my awareness sharpened, zinging across my skin. My heart thumped, every nerve in my body zeroing in on the place he was latched to me.

A hiss through my teeth. Fist in his hair. Thighs locked, hips flexed, core tight, tighter, squeezing nothing.

Seconds, that was all it took.

I came with a gasp and a cry, my body flexing for a long, suspended moment, and when it let go, it was with a burst of pleasure, a fluttering pulse of my core, my heart, my breath.

But he didn't stop. He slowed, eased, but didn't stop. The rhythm of his tongue and the pressure of his mouth tuned to the rhythm of my body, spurring the orgasm on when it would have fallen. Instead, it floated on, galloping through me, holding me captive.

It didn't end until he willed it, his lips in the crease of my thigh, the bend of my hip. Up he moved, and I was too tired to hold myself up. But there was no room to lay—a hutch was at my back, potted plants everywhere but the space where my ass rested and elbows planted. Fern fronds tickled my shoulder blades. I hadn't noticed it until just then.

His arm hooked around me, hauling me to sit with the sole intention of kissing me. I was boneless in his arms, at his mercy like a sacrificial lamb. And when he'd kissed me thoroughly, he broke away, smiling down at me.

"Jesus, Tess," he breathed.

My cheeks flamed with embarrassment that I'd come like a rocket after a solid four seconds of contact with his devil mouth. Because surely those lips were a sin, and damn me to hell for wanting them like I did.

"I ... it's been a little while," I admitted too hastily.

But he laughed. "Don't bruise my ego, Tess—I just unlocked a life achievement."

I frowned. "Making me come so fast?"

"Making you come at all."

He kissed me before I could laugh. And before either of us decided on it, we were twisted together again, breaths noisy and bodies hard.

His especially. His impressive length found its way between my thighs again, this time with nothing but those goddamn basketball shorts between us. He wasn't wearing underwear—I could feel the ridge of his head, thick and hard against the slick center of me.

He'd made good on his promise. And I had a feeling he'd do it again with the aid of the steel pipe in his pants.

Seemed I maybe owed him too, and I planned on making good on that.

Into his shorts my hands dove like a champion swimmer, sliding down the satiny skin of his shaft, the impossibly soft hardness of him in my palm heavy, thick. I'd known he was packing, but seeing was believing. Part of me didn't know where he was going to put all that. The rest of me didn't care.

I freed him, pushing his shorts off his ass.

He stayed himself with a long, steady exhale that broke our kiss.

"Tell me you have a condom," I breathed, stroking him.

He hummed, catching my lips once, his hands patting his pockets before delving inside and emptying their contents onto the table. Keys. ID. A credit card.

And a condom.

I gave him a look and burst out laughing. "You are such a whore."

But he smirked, smug and sure of himself and unruffled, as always. "Didn't you just beg me for one of these?" He held up the packet in display before ripping it open.

"You don't even have a wallet, but you have a condom?"

A shrug, his hand covering mine, gripping his base as he rolled the condom on. "I'm a minimalist, Tess. What can I say?"

A chuckle puffed out of me, our hands working his shaft together, our lips coming together, open, then closed. And then the laughter was gone, burned away by anticipation, by the shift of his hips that nestled his crown in the rippling flesh of my body. My hand clamped his neck, holding me steady as I leaned back, ass hanging off the table, lips parted, inches apart, eyes locked. Breath heavy.

His body rolled, slow and deliberate, and with the motion, he inched into me. Every wave brought him closer, closer, deeper, until he filled me completely and left us both breathless. And neither of us moved, his forehead pressing mine for a long moment. The pulse of his cock in me sent an echo back.

And then he kissed me.

Hungry was the kiss, his restraint pulled tight enough to snap, a devouring kiss.

A retreat and a thrust.

A gasp of pleasure-pain, thighs wide. He forced my knee higher, glancing down the line of my body as he pulled out slow, rolled his body to fill me up. Again but harder, the table jostling, the clanging of pottery. Again, he pumped his hips, brought his lips to mine. Tucked my knee into his ribs, leaned over me, pressed himself into my body, and I held on. That was all I could do—there was no pleasure I could give him he wouldn't take for himself. But there was pleasure he could give me, and he did with single-minded focus. Every thrust, he rolled his hips, stroking me outside and in.

Seconds, and another orgasm slipped over me in a whisper, then a sigh, then a moan. Then a cry as it pulled me under, as my body pulled him in, swallowed him up, flex by flex, pulse by pulse.

I sagged, edging consciousness. He sped, fingertips dragging ruts in my thigh. A gasp. A strangled grunt, a lock of his hips for a second—one long, protracted second of weightlessness—and he came like thunder, hard and hot, wild and untamed. His body was locked, every muscle stone as he pumped, released, let go of the reins and rode away.

He kissed me as he slowed, the kind of kiss heavy with relief and gratitude and something deeper, that unnamable sense of connection, as real as a tether, binding us together.

Even if only for a moment.

For that moment, there was nothing required but that kiss. No words, no demands. No desire—that we had slaked for the time. It was just the simplicity of that kiss. Of him and of me. Of the years between us and the days that had passed.

He held my face with one hand, holding me upright with the other. Broke away to look down at me, to search my eyes. His lips tilted, the smile so desperately *Luke*, the one it seemed I had known for what felt like forever.

"Did I make good on my promise?" he asked, his thumb stroking my cheek.

A twist of my heart as I looked up at him, knowing this was my only taste, my only chance. But I'd keep him here all night, and I'd take everything he was willing to give me, giving him everything I had. For tonight.

"It's a start," I said, smiling.

And he kissed me, just like I knew he would.

Ever the Gentleman

LUKE

"**N**o peeking," I warned my mother as I helped her down the stoop.

"Lucas Bennet, are you accusing me of cheating?" Her gnarled hands rested over her eyes, which were open and actively trying to see out from between her fingers.

"I've played Monopoly with you, so yes."

Tess, who had her other arm, smiled at me. "You're the picture of virtue, Mrs. Bennet."

"I've always liked you best, Tess," she said.

"Why, because she always agrees with you?" I asked.

"Maybe," Mom answered lightly.

My siblings waited in front of the shop in a chattering pack, my father standing silently on the edge, smiling faintly. It was his resting face—eyes soft and smile only at the corners, his expression in a constant state of both amusement and amiability. It was rare that he put up a fight. But when he did—boy, look out.

They quieted as we approached, and I moved Mom front and center on the sidewalk across from the door.

"All right," I said once I got her positioned. "Are you ready?"

"I've been ready for two days, Lucas. Say when before I die of old age and infirmity!"

A chuckled rolled through us.

"Open your eyes, Mom."

For a moment, she didn't move her hands, as if now that the time was upon her, she was afraid. A breath, shaky and deep, sawed in and out of her. And then she found her courage and looked.

The shift of her face stole my breath. A softening, a flush. A widening of her eyes, the shine of tears against the crisp cerulean of her irises. Her trembling fingers pressed to her lips. Tears slid down her cheeks in plump droplets.

She didn't speak. This was a miracle of its own—my mother had never been at a loss for words in her life.

Her brows drew together with a shake of her head as she took it all in. The windows, teeming with flowers. The taste of the interior, bright and white and crisp and clean. The shop—her shop—transformed, made new.

The joy and shock on her face was the most satisfying thing I had ever seen.

Second to which was the joy on Tess's.

Her cheeks and nose were pink and splotched, the sweetness of her lips—lips I'd familiarized myself with last night—caught in that gentle half-smile, half-frown only achieved when crying. Those tearful, dark eyes were absorbed with my mother, who choked on a laugh doubling as a sob.

"I … what have you done, my impossible, sweet children?"

"It was Tess," I said, pulling Mom into my side. "She came up with the idea."

Tess shook her head. "No—all of this was Luke. Without him, we wouldn't have ever had the impetus. He made all this happen."

Mom laughed. "You two. You even argue when you're complimenting each other."

"Come on," I said with a smirk at Tess, who chuckled, swiping at her cheeks. "Wait until you see inside."

Mom's arm wound around me, her other trembling hand resting on my chest as she looked up at me. "I can't believe this," she said. "I can't believe you did this."

"Am I so unreliable that my own mother didn't believe in me?" I joked, smirking and squeezing her shoulder.

She swatted at me. "Oh, you know that's not what I meant. I'm just so …" Her gaze drifted back to the windows. "I just never imagined it could be like this. Generations of women have passed this store down to their daughters, and the last person to update it was my mother. I … I wish she could have seen it. I wish she could have seen what you did."

Mom reached for Tess's hand, squeezed it as they smiled at each other.

"They were wise to have you do this, Tess. Never in my life have I seen such a beautiful display, and never could I have believed we would have something like this in our shop. You are a treasure," she said with a sob.

She'd said it before, and I agreed more now than ever. Tess was a chest of doubloons, waiting for an eternity under a waterfall, just waiting for someone to find her. To open her up and admire her riches. And I was the greedy pirate she'd accused me of being. I'd found her, and as far as I was concerned, that made her mine.

"Come inside," Tess coaxed, taking her arm. "Luke made magic."

We headed in, past the turquoise door, across the threshold of the shop, over the black-and-white checkered tile. Tess had set up a display of foxtails on the front table, the stems dyed neon pink and tops blonde and grainy. And all around the display were potted succulents for sale. Mom took in every detail, gasping over our old finds, wandering into the window installations, crying again when she saw the rain boots.

She knelt, running her hands over them. "This was my mother's. And this little one, that was mine. My grandfather's. Your f-father's." The words dissolved, and for a moment, she collected herself. When she stood, it was with pride on her face and tears still in her eyes. "I am beyond words."

"Then that means it's time to drink," Kash declared just as he popped the cork of a bottle of champagne.

The lot of us jumped and laughed. Laney provided plastic cups, and Jett popped a second. And around the bottle went until we all had a bubbling glass raised, ignoring the early hour in the spirit of celebration.

"To all that's old and new," I said, smiling down at my mother. "May we be immortalized by the deeds we do and the love we give."

Hear, hear, we cheered before joining in silence as we drank deep from the well of beginnings and the familiarity of home.

Chatter rose as everyone began to talk among themselves, wandering around the shop to point and nudge and smile at every corner of the space. Dad scooped Mom into a hug, whispering something in her ear that made her smile-cry again. And I took the opportunity to put myself in Tess's space.

She smiled at me over her champagne, taking a deliberately delicate sip as I approached.

We'd left the shop the night before in a trail of kisses, neither of us wanting to go. I couldn't speak to her reasons, but as for me … I wasn't sure if that was it. If she wanted me for anything more than last night.

A flash of fear shot through me, as it had a dozen times since last night, at the thought that it might have been the only time. That all she wanted from me was the use of my body, the blanket of my charm, the comfort of companionship for a moment, nothing more.

But Tess was different. The things she wanted. The way her body sang to mine. Tess didn't fling. And I didn't want to.

I wanted to build things for her and watch her face light up. I wanted to surprise her, wanted to give her the unexpected. I wanted to discover her, and I wanted to live in every little joy that discovery would bring. But I wanted more than just that.

I wanted to be the man she didn't believe me to be.

Tess's eyes were deep and dark, touched at the corners with mischief.

"Well, cheers to making her cry," I said, extending my glass for a tap.

She obliged. "It's all thanks to you."

I made an argumentative noise and took a sip. "You're the brains. I'm just the brawn."

Tess made a derisive face, though it was soft with affection. "Please. You did more than me, and your ideas were even better than mine."

I chuckled. "Mom's right. We even argue when we're getting along."

Her face lit up when she laughed. "If we're not insulting each other, we're trying to out-compliment each other. It's sick, really."

"Disturbing," I agreed, stepping closer without meaning to. "Also, for the record, I never insulted you."

"That's true," she admitted, her eyes flashing down to the golden bubbles in her cup. "I'm sorry for that, Luke. I've been cruel."

"Well, I did forget I'd kissed you for ten years."

A chuckle, but she didn't meet my eyes. "It was just a kiss, and it was forever ago."

"It wasn't just a kiss, and I shouldn't have forgotten."

"I just … I'm sorry for judging you unduly. I shouldn't have assumed so much."

"Don't be so hard on yourself. It's the general consensus that I'm a shameless flirt and an irresponsible slacker. You aren't the first one to be wrong, and you certainly won't be the last."

The joke, the one I always told, the one with the kernel of truth I usually ignored. Easier to own it than to fight it, I figured.

But something made her look up at me with earnest intentions lining her face. "I *was* wrong. I was wrong about a lot of things."

I smirked against the squeeze of my ribcage . "So does this mean it's your turn to make it up to *me*?"

She rolled her eyes as she laughed. "You're impossible, do you know that?"

"I do, and is that a yes?"

An arch look colored her face, followed by a flash of indecision. "Luke, I don't think we should—"

But before she finished, I leaned in, not wanting to hear the rest of that sentence. I brought my lips to her ear, my breath moving her hair in puffs when I whispered, "Because if you really want to make it up to me, I'll be in the back of storage in ten minutes. The spot where I saved your life."

Her breath was shallow, her pulse fluttering in the soft dip behind her jaw. I wanted to kiss that spot, to feel the heat of her skin under my lips. But not in front of my mother. God knew what sort of proposal she'd make if she knew.

No, for now, Tess was all mine, if she'd have me.

I leaned back, taking a moment to soak in the surprise and desire on her face before I turned and walked away, leaving her stunned behind me.

My heart *tha-dumped* as I ambled through the store, wondering if she'd meet me. Wondering what she'd say. Wondering if I would kiss her again or get rejected.

I brushed the thought away and hugged Mom again, kissed her cheek, modestly batted away her praise. Because the truth was, without Tess, none of this would be what it was. I had ideas, sure. But what I didn't always have was the motivation to follow it through.

Tess, I found, was the greatest motivator of all.

My siblings congratulated me even though they'd all seen the shop at various stages of production. I had to admit, the full effect was staggering. As I stood, admiring the shine installment, I noted the faces on the other side of the window as people stopped, smiling into the shop.

It was going to work. I knew it would.

It had to.

I glanced at the clock on the wall behind the register, noting the time. Everyone had begun to disperse. Mom and Laney headed back to the worktables where Ivy had been hard at it for hours. Dad and Kash wound their way toward the greenhouse. Jett and Marcus chatted behind the register, talking about *point of sale* and *conversion rates* and a bunch of other nonsense that sounded like noise. And I caught Tess's eye as she moved pots around on the display table without purpose.

"Tick-tock," I said, smiling sideways at her to cover my uncertainty as I passed.

I somehow avoided being stopped, everyone engaged in their own conversations. Mom, Laney, and Ivy bent over a vase of zinnias. Dad and Kash talking about the pH levels of the yarrow beds. And silently, casually, inconspicuously, I walked back to storage.

The building was dark, and I was greeted by the smell of earth and old wood, the sharp scent of fertilizer and mulch, the sweetness of a hundred years of memories and age and familiarity. And I leaned back against the shelves next to the ladder where I'd caught Tess.

Had it only been a few days ago? It seemed like years. Too much had changed for it to have only been days. Days ago, I'd been convinced she hated me. Hours ago, I'd had her body at my disposal. And if I'd learned anything from last night, it was that a taste wouldn't be enough.

Not when it came to Tess.

I couldn't understand why. Because it was true—she had been shitty to me and for no other reason than she thought I was impervious to pain. Which was fair enough … that was armor I wore quite often and with great purpose. Maybe it was that I'd won her over, and that battle had been hard-fought.

But on inspection, I knew the real reason was this: Tess Monroe was a mystery to me, and I wanted to unearth the answers to all my questions. Like why she was so averse to adventure. Or why she wanted to do the same thing, day in and day out. I wanted to know what it had been like for her all these years, taking care of her dad, living without her mom.

I couldn't imagine life without my mother. She was the brightest, boldest fixture in my life, a constant support and constant love. And I knew one day, she would be gone. I knew that someday, she would leave this world. I knew that my youth was a gift, that as I grew older, so the stakes would rise. Now was the time when tragedy rarely struck. My family was healthy, whole, happy, but the years would wear that away. It was only a matter of time.

And Tess had already done the unimaginable—survived loss at an age when her biggest problem should have been which lip gloss to wear. She'd taken on the responsibility of her household when she should have been sneaking out to go to parties.

It was no wonder she was cautious. If I'd lost in the ways she had, I wouldn't be so free.

I heard her before I saw her, talking to Kash at the top of the ramp, and a rush tore through me.

She came.

"There's some stuff I need. I mean, Mrs. Bennet wanted me to get the ... uh ... the old ... um, Luke said there were more rain boots! Yes. Rain boots," she rambled. "And I, um, I was just going to see if I could find them."

Kash laughed. "Right. Boots."

"Yup! So if you'll excuse me, I'd better get those for her before she starts to worry. You know how she is."

Another chuckle. "Sure. Don't get lost in there. And tell Luke to be a gentleman, or I've got a shovel that wants to give him a little smooch."

The loudest, most awkward cackle burst out of her. "Oh my God, whatever, Kash."

I caught sight of her, the slanting light at her back and her face cast in shadow. And then the darkness swallowed her up.

My eyes had adjusted, and I could see her silhouette as she walked tentatively through the room and toward me, hands slightly out.

"Luke?" she whispered.

My relief was palpable. Because she'd come to me when I asked. She wanted to see me again, and I wanted to see her. Well, eventually—I wasn't seeing much in the dark.

I snagged her hand and pulled, my smile widening at the little yelp of surprise that left her before she was in my arms.

And then our lips were too busy to make a sound.

She was stiff for a moment of hesitation, long enough to convince me she was going to push me away. But with a sigh, she melted into me like hot butter. Her arms wound around my neck, her lips parting to grant me all the access I wanted. She tasted like champagne, sweet and lush, her lips soft and pliant. But after a second, she broke away.

I smiled down at her, regardless of the fact that she couldn't see me. "I've been thinking about that since you walked out the door last night."

"Me too." I could hear something else under the words. "But ..."

"No buts. I want to see you again. I'd like to see *all* of you again. Do you want to see me?" I asked, my tone light and my chest aching.

"Might be kind of hard to see much of anything in here," she hedged.

"Simple question, Tess. Do you want to see me again?"

A pause, heavy with her thoughts. "Yes, but—"

"I said no buts. Tonight. Meet me in the dahlias at ten."

Another pause, this one laced with hope.

"Come on," I coaxed, my desperation expertly masked. "For old times' sake."

A little laugh. The weight of her hand on my chest sparked a flash of desire that didn't want anything but a yes from her lips.

"All right," she said. "For old times' sake."

And before she could change her mind, I kissed her to occupy those wayward lips of hers.

I was so preoccupied with those lips that I didn't hear my dad until my tongue was deep enough in Tess's throat to taste her toothpaste. We popped apart when he entered and flew apart like shrapnel when he flicked on the light.

On his face was a mild smile, and in his eye was a roguish gleam.

"Oh, hello," he said genially, as if he hadn't known we were back there.

I made a face. Tess looked like someone had a rifle pointed at her.

"The, ah, rake broke. Just needed to grab a new one."

Tess swallowed hard and put the most ridiculous smile on her face I'd ever seen. "Thanks, Mr. B!" she said with an awkward wave before bolting past him and into the greenhouse.

He and I shared a look.

"I don't think she's ever called me that before. Any idea what she thanked me for?"

"Not a clue," I answered with a triumphant smirk. "But a word of advice: when it comes to Tess, take what you can get."

Curiosity Kills

TESS

The bell over the door did not stop ringing all day.

Ivy and I were slammed in the back. We had run out of our prepared bouquets within an hour. Twelve orders for bouquet deliveries had hit us before lunch. Jett had been called in to run the counter. Kash had been tasked with cutting flowers and carting them up to us. And Luke had been in and out with deliveries nonstop.

Seeing him sent a simultaneous thrill and worry through me. Today had not gone as planned—not only had I not clarified last night's intentions, but I'd kissed him and agreed to see him tonight.

His lips were apparently the antidote to my willpower. And they were as convincing as a politician on the campaign trail. He'd asked me point-blank if I wanted to see him again, and the honest answer was yes, even though I shouldn't want to.

I'd tell him tonight. I'd meet him and tell him that was it. Simple, so long as I could avoid kissing him again.

Kash set two massive buckets—one of cosmos in shades of purple, pink, burgundy, white. The other was full of roses—delicate peach eglantines, buttery crown princess, vibrant colettes.

"Can you grab us some more snapdragons?" I asked, not looking up from my hands as I tied another bouquet bundle.

"Madame butterfly or chantilly?"

"Chantilly. Oh, and some celosia. Yellow, red, and pink, please."

"You got it," he said amiably before heading back to the greenhouse.

The brown paper crinkled as I wrapped the bouquet and gathered up the dozen I'd made, three sets of monochromatic bouquets in four colors—peach, yellow, white, and cotton-candy pink. I giggled over the top of them at Ivy.

"Ridiculous!" she said on a laugh, her hands flying over the arrangement she was working on for delivery.

I hurried to the front. The storefront was busier than I'd ever seen it, even in its heyday. Mrs. Bennet saw me coming and excused herself from the customer she was talking to.

"Here, let me help you, Tess. My, these are just beautiful," she said, her voice sweet and touched with awe. "You are an artist, my dear."

"I learned everything I know from you."

She blushed, tittering. "The bunny tails in these bouquets! I never would have thought."

"Don't give me too much credit," I deflected. "They just happened to be what was in reach. We might clean out the greenhouse today."

She laughed openly at that. "That would be a sight I've never seen before."

"I can't believe how many people are here," I said with a shake of my head. "We've sold twenty market bouquets today, and I've got twelve more here that I suspect will be gone before dinner."

"It's all thanks to you. I … I don't know how I'll ever thank you, Tess." Her voice quivered, then broke.

And when my hands were free, I pulled her into a hug. "Mrs. Bennet, we would do anything for you and for this shop. All we did was spruce it up so people would notice it again."

"You kids are too smart for this old lady. I never would have imagined to do all this."

I leaned back to look at her. "Oh, you would have. You're the most creative florist I've ever known, and I know a few. In fact, I was wondering … would you help me with the next installation?"

Her flush deepened. "I can't do much anymore, Tess."

"Why? Don't tell me you've got dementia. I'm not ready for you to lose your marbles."

A laugh, touched with sadness. "No, not yet. Though when I do, I can only imagine the conversations you'll have to endure. I doubt losing my wits will stop me from talking, and if you ask Mr. Bennet, he'll tell you that's my superpower."

A woman said from behind us, "Oh, these are beautiful. Are those zinnias?"

I moved out of the way so she could reach the bouquets we'd just loaded. "They are."

"What a beautiful monochromatic bouquet. I've never seen anything quite like it. Are you the florist?"

"She is," Mrs. Bennet said proudly. "She designed the installations too. Did you see them?"

"That's why I came in," she admitted. "I swear I've walked by this shop a thousand times and never knew it was here. Looks like I'll be getting all my flowers here."

"Well then," Mrs. Bennet said, "we'll see you again soon."

The second she turned to head to Jett at the counter, Mrs. Bennet grabbed my hand. "You! You, my sweet Tess, are a godsend."

"Takes one to know one." I kissed her cheek.

"You and Lucas are a good team, Tess. You ground him, and I think he loosens you up a little." Her smile was coy, and she shifted, bumping me with her hip.

My cheeks caught fire as I laughed her off.

"He's a good boy, Tess. I promise. Now, go! Shoo! Go make more witchcraft back there with our flowers."

"And you keep hustling, Mrs. Bennet."

She beamed, turning for a customer as I bounced to the back again.

Could she be right? Could it be me who'd inspired Luke's newfound purpose?

But I brushed the thought away, laughing at my self-importance. He was here for the shop, for his family. I had nothing to do with it. Of that I was certain.

Ivy sighed, running the back of one hand across her forehead. The other hand reached for the small of her back and pushed. "This is madness. Jett just gave me three more orders!"

"Well, we'd better get started then," I said with an unstoppable grin on my face as I reached for the orders. "You should sit," I suggested. "Or if you need a break, I can handle it for a bit. Rest your feet, Ivy."

Another sigh, and she pulled up a stool. "Oh, that feels nice," she said once she was sitting.

I chuckled, making a recipe in my head for the orders. The table was covered in buckets of flowers, harvested in droves by poor Kash. Hibiscus and begonias, dahlias and ranunculus, orchids and snowberries.

"So are you going to tell me what the hell happened with Luke last night? Because we have been too busy to talk, and I'm busting at the seams to know."

"You're busting at the seams anyway," I teased, choosing a vase from the shelves under the table.

"Ha-ha, Tess. Don't you dare deny it again either. He's been looking at you all day like he eyes a ham sandwich."

I filled it with cold water from the farmhouse sink, scooped some preservative in. "You'll be happy to know I told him about the kiss."

Her mouth popped open. "You're kidding. I didn't think you actually had the stones to do it. I was going to have your headstone engraved with, *Here lies Tess—He should have remembered.*"

I shook my head, laughing.

"So what did he do? God, just spill it already."

"He kissed me and promised me he'd make it up to me." My eyes were on my hands as I chose a variety of dahlias and a couple of the big ranunculus.

"And did he?"

"He did. Twice, right over there." I jerked my chin in the direction of the shop. "And once over there. Oh, and another time there."

This time, her jaw came unhinged and hit the table. "Don't toy with me, Tess. You don't want to be responsible for putting me into preterm labor, do you?"

I shot a smirk at her.

"Oh my God. *Oh my God,*" she hissed. "You did not!"

I still didn't answer, just kept on smirking as I snipped stems and filled the vase.

"You slept with *Luke Bennet.*" She whispered his name, glancing around like someone might be listening. "I think this is the most spontaneous thing you've ever done in your whole life."

"Other than kissing him the first time."

"Yes, other than that. What does that mean? Are you guys, like … dating?"

A laugh burst out of me. "God, no. I might be crazy, but I'm not stupid, Ivy. It was a one-time thing, a fling. For fun. To rewrite what happened before. I'm being adventurous like everyone loves to accuse me of *not* being."

She eyed me with no small amount of skepticism. "You. A fling. With Luke."

"Yeah. What's the big problem? Literally everyone has had a fling with Luke. Why not me too?"

"Because you don't know how to have sex without feelings."

"Please. Luke and I are exactly wrong for each other. But man, that boy knows how to kiss." I sighed, smiling at the flowers. "If there's one person in the world to fling with, it's a guy like him."

Her suspicion deepened. "And what does Luke think of it being a one-time thing? Because I saw the way he was looking at you, just like I saw you follow him back to storage."

I kept my eyes down, saying matter-of-factly, "I'm telling him tonight."

A bawdy *ha* shot out of her. "Oh, Tess."

"What?"

"You're going to meet him tonight, alone, to tell him you don't want to climb him like a jungle gym ever again? Right. Sure. Whatever you say," she said lightly.

"It can't ever be anything more than that. You said yourself, I can't have sex without feelings."

"Which is exactly why going to see him tonight is a mistake. Unless you really do want to fling again."

I frowned. "Of course I want to fling again—I'm not dead inside. But I shouldn't. Honestly, I shouldn't have last night, but I don't regret it one bit."

For a second, she watched me, her eyes assessing and sparkling with an idea. "Then do it again."

My eyes narrowed. "Just like that?"

She shrugged innocently. "Sure, just like that. Maybe it's time you learned to fling. Maybe you should exercise your wildness on

Luke. I mean, he's the perfect candidate."

"What's your angle, Ivy?"

"No angle," she lied. "Look, you don't have to decide now. Wait until tonight."

Not gonna lie—the thought of flinging another dozen times sounded like exactly the right thing to do even though I knew it couldn't be more wrong. And as suspicious as I was of Ivy's intentions, I was happier that she'd told me what I hadn't realized I wanted to hear.

She didn't think I could fling. Which sparked a hot desire to prove her wrong.

"Tonight then. I'm a hundred percent sure the wild lifestyle is not for me, but a girl can dream, right?"

Ivy laughed. "I don't even know who you are right now, but I love it."

Holding my hands up in display, I said, "It's the new and improved Tess."

An undeniably masculine and outrageously cavalier voice said from behind me, "What if some of us like the old Tess?"

I turned, smiling up at Luke. His dark hair was windblown, his smile bright against the tan of his skin. His T-shirt stretched tight over the expanse of his chest, around the curves of his biceps.

It was ridiculous really. Nobody should be allowed to be that hot.

And I had to somehow figure out how to walk away from all that hotness. Suddenly, I understood everything Ivy had just laid on me.

"Man, the store is crazy," he said, beaming. "Mom's out there hustling flowers like it's her full-time job."

"Well, it kinda is," I noted.

"So much for retirement," he said on a laugh.

"I think we all knew she was never gonna retire."

I didn't realize we had stepped toward each other until I could smell the sunshine on him. He must have been driving with the windows down. I wondered if he was going to get a sunburn on his left arm, and I fought the impulse to go get the sunscreen out of my bag for him.

Ivy cleared her throat. "We've got some more orders ready for you. They're in the cooler."

He blinked at me and stepped back, looking to Ivy. "I'm on it. Haven't seen this much action in forever."

Ivy snorted, and I shot her a look, taking up my station at the table again as Luke loaded a box with orders. When he stood, the weight of the box in his hands engaged all those muscles he possessed, the veins on his forearms visible from across the room.

"All right, girls—don't get into any trouble." He flashed a hotshot wink at me as he passed, and somehow, even that was sexy. A wink.

I wondered absently if I should get my head checked. Surely, something had to have gotten into me.

Besides Luke.

I laughed at my hands, and Ivy gave me a look.

"Seriously, you are giddy. *Giddy*," she said. "Don't get me wrong—I don't hate it. But you don't like … smell burned toast or anything, do you? Because if we need to get you a CAT scan or something, I think that can be arranged."

"I'm fine, Ivy," I said on a laugh. "God, a girl can't even get any around here without the third degree."

"Considering you make most guys wait three dates before hooking up, I don't think I'm being unreasonable by asking."

"Three dates is not that many. And I've known Luke most of my life. You act like I got some strange in a gas station bathroom."

"In Tess-land, it's basically equivalent."

I rolled my eyes at her, but I was laughing again. I couldn't help it. The whole thing was too crazy for words.

"Well, never fear," she said. "I'm here to help shepherd you through it."

"The queen of flings."

"I don't know if you know this, but I'm a little out of practice."

"I heard getting knocked up will do that to a girl."

"It's true," she said with a sigh and a rub of her belly.

"Well, if I decide to go for it, you'd better teach me all there is to know about casual sex. You can officially pass the torch."

"Let's just hope you don't get burned," she joked.

But a flash of worry shot through me at the thought.

She wasn't wrong. Luke Bennet wasn't any less dangerous than he'd been yesterday. In fact, he was probably more dangerous than ever.

But with every kiss, I found it harder and harder to care. And deep down, I knew that I wouldn't be able to put up a fight even if I wanted to.

LUKE

I shifted on the blanket again, wondering if I looked casual.

If you have to ask yourself that, you do not look casual.

It was late, the greenhouse bathed in moonlight, music floating out of my little speaker as I waited on Tess to meet me. I'd brought a couple of lanterns and laid out some camping mats under the big woolen plaid. In the cooler was ice, and on top of it was a bottle of whiskey. And all around was the abundance of flowers reaching up to the skylight.

The bounty of this place was astounding. My father's green thumb had been learned from his father-in-law, who had tended the greenhouse before him, just as my mother's knack for flowers had been learned from my grandmother, passed down to Laney, Ivy, and Tess.

But Laney had never loved it, not the way Mom had and not in the way Tess did. Dad understood. I don't know that Mom ever would. And as such, Tess had become the vessel to pour her passion into.

And really, it was a boon because Tess needed Mom. Needed a mom.

I scanned the greenery, dotted with zinnias. Even after the heavy harvest today, there was more to be had. And over the next days and weeks, more would bloom.

It was one of the many majesties of flowers—the more you took, the more they gave.

One common misconception of gardening was that pruning would hurt the plants. But so long as you did it with conscientious awareness, the bounty would multiply. When control was exerted, when boundaries were put in place, the subject thrived. When left wild, they would overgrow, choke other plants. The bounty would thin. The plant might even die.

Glancing at the greenery, one might think it was chaos. But that chaos was controlled, contemplated, cared for with consideration.

It was like Tess, I realized. Her desire to prune, to control her life, to insulate herself from change and that inevitable chaos of life. Maybe there was something to that. Where I was wild, my bounty was anemic. Where hers was pruned, her bounty was plentiful.

Maybe it was something I could learn from her. Maybe she'd show me where to trim, where to cut.

And maybe I could show her how to run a little wild.

I shifted again, lying on my side, propped up by my forearm. Brutus popped his head out from a peony plant, judgmentally eyeing me.

"I look like fucking Burt Reynolds, don't I?" I muttered to him, sitting up.

"You kinda do," Tess said with a laugh.

I shot to my feet, smiling like I hadn't just had the shit scared out of me. "Hey. You came."

"Sorry I'm late."

"Did you have to sneak out again?"

She chuckled, moving to sit on the blanket I'd laid out. "Not exactly, but I did have to lie about where I was going."

I frowned as I sat next to her. "I thought your dad liked me."

"Oh, I'm sure he does. But I'm not quite ready to explain to him that I do too. Not after years of insisting that I can't stand the sight of you."

I ignored the latter in favor of the former. "You like me."

Tess laughed, her little chin tipping up. "Well, you've been a good friend."

"And a great kisser."

A flush smudged her cheeks. "Yes, and that. Among other things."

A flash of hope smudged my heart. "I've been working on changing your mind about me."

"You don't say?" she deadpanned.

"I know. I'm slick undercover like that." That earned me a laugh, and I reached for the Maker's, holding it up in display. "Care for a drink?"

With a nod, she smiled, lips together and corners curled. "It's that first night all over again."

"Except this time, I'm not drunk and I brought better whiskey. I want a do-over, Tess. You deserve one," I added as I scooped ice and poured us drinks. "I told you I'd make it up to you. What better way than the closest thing to a time machine I could come up with?"

I handed her a drink, which she took with that small, sweet smile on her face. "To time machines."

She held her glass out, and I tapped it with a clink.

"And second chances."

Something flashed behind her eyes—a touch of worry, a hint of indecision. Appreciation, understanding.

We drank without clarifying what it meant.

I knew what I meant.

This—whatever *this* was—was different. I liked her. And not in that I was interested in a distant way like I normally was, with that detached admiration I typically felt for women.

I liked Tess. I liked *her*, not the idea of her, not as one admires art or a bouquet. But in how I craved her company. How I wanted to impress her. How I wanted to prove her wrong about me. It wouldn't be easy. But I had a feeling it'd be the most satisfying thing I'd ever done, if I could pull it off.

The last time I'd felt this way, I'd ended up married. A shot of fear rushed through my chest at the thought. Because that had been a trainwreck.

But it was the closest thing I could compare it to. Tess had gotten my attention. And now, I couldn't look away.

"You did good today, Tess," I started, stretching my legs. "How many bouquets did you make?"

"Feels like a trillion," she said on a laugh. "Pretty sure I'm going to have anxiety dreams about marigolds tonight."

"Mom cried through half of dinner. I swear, I think she's going to erect a statue of you in the middle of the shop as tribute."

Tess blushed prettily. "I can't believe that many people were lured in by window installations."

"People shop with their eyes, right? And you gave them a visual feast. That window display is perfect. It helped that it was gorgeous out."

"And that there was an event in Washington Square."

"I was thinking we should always do the new displays on Sunday mornings, get the weekend crowd. Maybe we could even join forces with a couple of local places, like Blanche's. Have a little coffee bar and pastries for the unveiling."

She brightened. "I love that. Think we can get Blanche's to partner up?"

"Oh, old Blanche can't say no to me," I said with a sidelong smile.

"She'd sneak me donuts when I was little, made me swear I wouldn't tell Mom. Officially, she's known at my house by the name Meal Ruiner."

A chuckle, this time coupled with a sardonic look. "Is anyone immune to your charms?"

"Only you."

Her eyes flicked to the ceiling, but she was smiling. "Please. Me least of all. It's why you make me so mad."

"Make? Or made?"

"Both."

It was my turn to chuckle. "You know, they say there's a fine line between love and hate."

"*They* also say not to shit where you eat."

"Sure, but a bird in the hand is worth two in the bush."

"And curiosity killed the cat." She took a sip of her drink, her eyes smiling at me over the rim.

"Well, drastic times call for drastic measures." I set my drink on the cooler, taking hers once it was free of her lips. Because I had other plans for those lips, plans I didn't care to wait to implement.

"I'll take that with a grain of salt," she said breathlessly, watching me as I moved closer.

And I slipped my arm around her waist and shifted, laying her down. Her hands gripped my arms from the motion, fingers tightening when I slipped my thigh between hers, opening them up.

"Then I'll let my actions speak louder than words," I whispered against her lips before I took them for my own.

This. This was what I'd missed last night. Her body beneath me, soft and sighing, mine for the taking. I'd wanted to lay her down so I could love her down, unobstructed by distractions like physics and furniture.

But she broke the kiss with a pop, her breath noisy and lids heavy as she looked up at me. "Wait," she whispered. "Are you sure we should—"

"Yes," I said and kissed her again. I kissed her until she was wound around me, until there was no space, no air.

But she stopped the kiss again, staying me with her hand. "When you do that, I can't think."

"Then don't."

When I kissed her once more, I felt her give herself over completely, felt her yield, felt the fight in her heart abandon her. And I took the chance to fill that space in her with me. I'd convince her I could be what she wanted, what she didn't think I was. I could be that man.

I would be that man.

As the kiss deepened, I noted the depth of my desire. It reached beyond the surface, into the hidden spaces in me, places undiscovered, untapped. I didn't care what it meant, didn't question the difference. All I knew was this: I wanted to give Tess what she wanted. My body was hers, but that was the easy part.

Because if I knew Tess at all, I knew she didn't do casual. And for the first time in a long time, I didn't want to.

And the strangest part of all was that it wasn't strange. Not even a little.

Not even at all.

Ace

TESS

"I've got it," I lied over my shoulder at Luke, who watched me wrangle the armful of flowers with dubious concern.

"If you'll just let me—"

"I've got it," I repeated with a laugh as I headed for the door to the shop, not entirely sure how I was going to open it. "I just need to—*oof*."

I hit the worktable with a thump and a burst of pain in my hip.

With a chuckle, he took the load off my hands. In his massive arms, they looked inconsequential. In mine, I could barely see over the top.

"Sure you don't want anything else?"

My face flushed. "Well, since I've got more room, I'll just grab some of these." I reached for the bucket of pods. "And maybe some of these. Oh! You know what would look great …"

And seconds later, my arms were almost full again.

He shook his head at me, his smile sidelong and sweet.

"Okay, that's it."

"You sure?"

I cast a forlorn look at the flowers before promising, "I'm sure. Thank you, Luke."

He started walking, and I followed the expanse of his back. Which he'd been on half an hour ago. With me in his lap. Naked.

I realized I was smiling and pursed my lips, taking a breath to try to cool the warmth on my cheeks.

So I'd caved that night in the greenhouse. And then I'd caved again the next day. And the day after that.

And then I'd given up fighting, which was when it had become *fun*.

Luke Bennet singlehandedly made every minute of my days light and carefree, bright and brilliant. His unworried, unhurried attitude kept me more still and calm than I'd been in years, since before my mom died.

We'd closed the shop together every night for a week.

Every morning when I came in, he was already here. I would make arrangements with Ivy all day while Luke ran deliveries between repairing furniture he'd found in the storage shed. Or building things for me. Or discovering new props for the shop in the depths of the forgotten wealth of storage.

Mrs. Bennet had advised me on plans for window installations, her ideas fresh and clever and sparking my own. Laney and I had coordinated our social media for the next few weeks with the store's displays, and Luke had helped build a photo spot for a corner of the store. This week, it was a flower wall with ivy and zinnias in hot summer colors. Next week, it would be a wall painted a pale pink, topped with garlands of roses. The week after would be daisies hung vertically in strands. We'd only had it up a week, but our Instagram had exploded with several thousand followers in just a handful of days. Laney had set up newsletter promos for coupons, bouquet giveaways for our followers, and a dozen other promotions that I would never have even considered.

Luke built whatever she needed alongside putting in beams in the ceiling where we hung planters and some old tobacco racks for displays. We built and created every day, and Luke showed up with the sun with nothing but a smile on his face and the motivation to get shit done.

And I matched him smile for smile.

He brought donuts from Blanche's every morning. I brought us leftovers to share for lunch. We ordered dinner every night and ate sitting on top of the worktables with dangling feet and endless conversation. And then everyone would leave, and it would just be me and Luke.

I looked forward to that part of the day from the second my eyes opened in the morning. The sound of the bolt on the front door sliding home was like Pavlov's bell, indicating that dinner was served in the form of a Luke Bennet buffet.

Somehow, he had become a fixture in every meaningful part of my day. And I didn't hate it. I didn't hate it so much, it scared me.

He is not your boyfriend. He is your fling. He is your friend. Don't you dare expect anything beyond that.

This, I told myself, was why it was fine that Luke was about to come to my house for the first time in a decade. Friends went to friends' houses. They chatted with friends' dads. It was all normal, totally normal and exactly why I shouldn't be super fucking nervous.

Silently, I followed my friend, who I saw naked every day, out the door to the shop—which, by the way, he opened without incident despite the haul in his arms. Once I was past him, he locked up, pulling the grate down and locking it too, one-handed.

Showoff.

I smiled mischievously at him.

When he stood and caught the expression, he answered it with a matching smile before stealing a kiss.

"Lead the way," he said.

So I did.

"Can you believe the crowd today?" he asked, his voice touched with wonder and that smile. "We should rename Sundays the Garden Annihilator."

I laughed. "Thank God we have a week to replenish before we do it again. I thought maybe we should move the new installations to Saturdays, get the whole weekend crowd, but I don't know if the greenhouse would survive."

"Never in the history of Longbourne have we had such a wonderful problem. Thanks to you."

"Psh, you're the one who built me twelve ladders last week."

He shrugged one massive shoulder. "Half of them I scavenged."

"Oh, sorry. You made six ladders with your bare hands. Totally normal, everyday stuff any old joe would know how to do."

"YouTube is a powerful tool, Tess. Anyway, it was your idea to set them up and display flowers all over them. It looks like something out of a magazine. It's no wonder we had to close early."

"It was either that or have nothing to offer but potted succulents."

"Hey, we had some ivy too. Honestly, you could have made bouquets out of dying roses, and I bet people would have bought them. Marcus said we should raise prices. Supply and demand or something."

I frowned. "I don't know if I like that."

"Oh, don't worry—Mom almost cranked open his mouth and climbed into his throat. I'd say there's very little danger of prices changing anytime soon."

I laughed, imagining Mrs. Bennet going after Marcus, finger wagging and face bent up and red. "I was thinking next week, we can use two of the ladders to suspend from the ceiling for me to hang arrangements off of."

"Oh, you know—I know a guy who laser-cuts acrylics and welds. I know you like geometrics, right?"

I glanced at him, surprised. "I do. How'd you know?"

He shot me a little smile. "You just ordered all those planters with the gold wire frames. Kyle could totally make you something like that. Or acrylic planters, big ones. We could do a big display, plant succulents, make it look like a minimalist jungle."

I smiled. "I like it. How fast can he get something to us?"

"Draw something up, and I'll ask."

We walked for a second in silence. The cool of the summer evening was welcome after the sweltering heat of the day. Marcus had just spent a small fortune installing air-conditioning in the front, promising we'd sell more if we kept it under eighty degrees, and he'd tasked Mrs. Bennet with keeping a water dispenser on the display table just inside the door to lure people in.

Honestly, it worked. I swear, some people just came in under the promise that frosted, sweating cooler full of sliced fruit water made. But they always left with a bouquet.

At the last kid meeting, Marcus told us we had a long way to go, years to catch up to the debt, but this was an excellent start. We'd put our best foot forward. I only hoped we could keep up the pace.

"How do you know so many people?" I asked, unable to catalog the array of encounters he'd had.

Seriously, he had a guy for just about everything.

"As you so kindly noted, I've had a lot of jobs. I collect friends like some people collect matryoksa dolls."

My brows gathered. "What dolls?"

"Russian nesting dolls. Wendy and I used to live next door to this little old Russian lady who had about a thousand of them. No lie—I really do think she had a thousand. They covered every wall in her living room. She said her grandfather owned a shop in St. Petersburg about the same time my ancestors were opening Longbourne."

My heart slid into my stomach at the mention of Wendy. "I bet she had stories to tell."

"That she did. She would call me *synochik*, make me tea in a pot older than God, and tell me about her village. Her husband and kids. Her parents and grandparents. Surviving the winter by sleeping on a massive stove made of clay. Foraging and storing food in spring and summer. The war. It's crazy, what she's been through. I used to go down every Saturday morning and eat biscuits with her and just listen."

"Wendy didn't go with you?" I asked tentatively.

He huffed a laugh. "Wendy couldn't be bothered to listen to an old woman talk. She was too deep in her own head for anyone but herself."

I didn't know what to say because I had nothing nice to say. So I asked a vague question in the hopes I'd avoid saying the wrong thing. "Do you miss it?"

"LA? Nah. I loved living there, but I don't think I'd go back."

"All that sunshine's a bummer, huh?"

A chuckle. "You have to drive everywhere. There's no decent public transportation. The highways are a parking lot. And the people are just … I dunno. Different."

"Different how?"

"I can't say without sounding snobbish."

I laughed. "Now you have to tell me."

His nose wrinkled. "It's just like New York in that status is a thing. What neighborhood you live in defines you or what kind of car you drive in LA—that sort of thing. But the difference is, in New York, nobody even sees you. There, everyone's watching you, measuring you up, and putting you on a shelf. From the old lady in the rainbow-striped thigh-highs digging through the sushi at Whole Foods to the model in stilettos and fur coat in Target in the heat of July."

"Do you miss your old Russian neighbor?"

"Yeah, but I send Zhenya postcards every few days. I've even gotten a few back," he said proudly, reaching into my pocket too quickly for me to be shocked. When his hand came into view again, my keys were in it.

"Postcards, huh?" I smiled at his back as he glanced at my keys and unlocked the door to my building.

"She really liked the one of the Statue of Liberty. I told her to wait until she saw the one of the skyline. I'm making her wait," he said with a smirk, pulling open the door.

"Cruel," I said on a laugh.

We climbed the stairs without speaking as I imagined him sitting in a dusty apartment with a little old lady, listening to her talk about her life.

Every day, Luke surprised me. It seemed to be a knack of his.

I didn't think I'd ever enjoyed being so wrong.

My keys were still in his hand, so he unlocked the door to my apartment with the first key he tried.

"How'd you do that?" I asked as he opened yet another door for me like the gentleman I'd never thought him to be.

"What?"

"Figure out which key it was?"

"Well," he started, following me in, "this one and this one are keys to the shop." He displayed it. "And this one is less worn, so I figured it was for outside. Those tend to get replaced more often. And I figured this one was for your house. The teeth are nearly worn smooth."

I gaped at him.

He smirked. "I had a job as a locksmith for a minute after high school."

With a roll of my eyes, I laughed. "Of course you did."

"Tess?" Dad called from back in the apartment. "That you?"

"Hey, Daddy. In here," I called back, setting down my haul on the kitchen island.

Luke set his beside mine, but he was taking in the apartment. "Man, this place hasn't changed at all. That same old wallpaper. But the plants … holy shit, Tess. It's a jungle in here."

I chuckled. "They were Mom's."

"Can't get her to even prune them," Dad said, wheeling into the room with a smile on his face. "Hello, son. How are you?"

When he got close enough, he stopped, extending a callused hand. Luke took it, the knot of their square hands pumping.

"I'm good, sir. And you?"

"Little hungry. No chance there's a hamburger somewhere in that bundle of flowers, is there?"

I gave him a look. "Did you forget to eat again?"

He shrugged, looking cowed. "I was in the middle of the commissioned officers, and I couldn't quit until I finished. Couldn't very well leave the beach on Normandy without its leaders, could I?"

I kissed him on the forehead and made for the oven to set the temp. "I left dinner in the fridge. All you had to do was put it in the oven."

"You always take care of me, Pigeon."

Once I had the fridge open and my hands were full of casserole, I kicked the door closed with a thump.

Luke leaned in as I pulled off the foil, wetting his lips. "What is it?"

"You can't be hungry. You just ate almost an entire pizza."

"What?" he asked innocently. "My mother says I'm a growing boy, Tess."

I laughed. "This, Luke Bennet, is Betsy's Super Tuna Noodle Saproodle."

Dad groaned hungrily. "If I'd known that, I wouldn't have made a meal off pistachios."

"Well, you have twenty minutes to work up your appetite."

"You're welcome to join me, Luke. We'll be eating off that casserole for two days, easy," Dad said.

"I'd love to," Luke answered with a smile that made my heart do a loop-dee-loop. "I was just telling Tess I can't believe this place hasn't changed at all. That's the same couch we used to play Mario Kart on."

"Still have it," I said. "Play you after dinner."

"You mean, you'll lose to me after dinner," Luke corrected.

A laugh burst out of me. "You never could beat me, and I know you've got to be rusty. Dad and I play at least three times a week."

"And she can't beat me," Dad added. "So I'll beat you both after dinner."

Luke and I locked eyes, spitting out, "Dibs on Donkey Kong," at the same time.

Then we were all laughing.

Luke looked around the room, scanning everything with the gears in his head whirring. "You know, it wouldn't take much to get this place out of the nineties. Eighties?"

"It was Betsy's mom's before we lived here. A lot of this was nostalgic. I think that wallpaper and the curtains are from the seventies. All recent decades are represented." Dad smiled fondly, looking around the room. "I've thought about remodeling forever, but I wouldn't even know where to start."

This time, my heart had a very different reaction—a painful squeeze. He'd never admitted that to me, never even mentioned it. And the thought of changing this place soured my stomach.

Luke smiled, completely unaware. "Honestly, it wouldn't take much. The floors are in great shape. But we could paint all the cabinets, maybe splurge on countertops and appliances. There's a warehouse discount place in Hell's Kitchen—we can get stuff cheap. And I know a girl whose dad does stonework. Countertops, flooring, that sort of thing. I could install crown molding real easy, just for the cost of materials. I've got all the tools," he said, almost to himself, too deep in his imagination to even seem to remember we were there. "We could pull the wallpaper, paint … it'd be like a brand-new place."

The pizza we'd eaten for dinner climbed up my throat. "We couldn't ask you to do that," I said, hoping he'd agree.

It was like I didn't know him at all.

"Are you kidding? Man, that would be fun to do. It'd be no trouble. Might take a little bit, just because I'd need to do it between the stuff for the shop, but we've got it in great shape down there. I've got time."

Dad smiled at Luke. No, it wasn't a smile. He was beaming. "I can almost see it. But the only way I'll agree is if you let me pay you."

"For materials," Luke insisted. "That's all. I'm not a contractor. I'm not licensed. Some things will need to be done by the pros, like counter installation. Let me get some numbers together for you and for now, we'll just agree to talk about it. What do you say?"

I didn't hear my father respond, just watched him grinning and shaking Luke's hand and looking thrilled while I panicked.

Luke wasn't wrong—this place was a time machine, and that was exactly the way I wanted it. I'd thought Dad did too, but he'd been thinking about this, wanting to do it, and he'd never told me. Probably because he was worried that I'd feel exactly like I did. Like I'd been betrayed. Like he was ready to move on. Like he wanted to forget.

But I didn't want to. I didn't want to forget anything. I didn't want to change anything. Because it would start here with the wallpaper and the kitchen where Mom had taught me to cook, and it would end with her closet cleaned out and her things gone, donated, lost forever. Where would I go when I needed her if her closet was empty? Because even now, I had a little spot under her dresses where I'd sit when I needed her. Where I'd imagine I could still smell her perfume.

Where her favorite polka-dot dress hung, where the sweater with the big cable knit waited for me to slip into when I needed a hug.

I took a breath, pressed my thoughts down until they were flat. Folded them until they were small. Tucked them away in a drawer in my mind. And carried on.

I scooped up some flowers, and when Luke saw me, he followed suit, as I'd hoped. The conversation shifted, as I'd also hoped.

"Be back, Daddy," I said with levity I didn't feel. "Twenty minutes, and your belly will be happy."

He chuckled, navigating into the living room. "All right. Meanwhile, I'm gonna get warmed up so I can properly whip you two on the track."

Luke followed me to my room, setting his flowers down next to mine on the bed while I busied myself prepping. I turned on my ring light and moved things around in front of my backdrop to stage a shot.

"Wow," he said from behind me. "This is where you take all your pictures?"

"Mmhmm." Avoiding his eyes, I sorted through the flowers, making an arrangement almost without thought.

"We should set up a bigger space at the shop. Somewhere you can shoot installations or … I don't know. Somewhere with room for you to really spread out."

"I don't need more room," I said a little more firmly than I'd meant.

As usual, Luke didn't pick up on it. He stepped between the ring light and the backdrop, turning around with a smile on his face. That smile melted my worries like chocolate in the sun—sticky and messy and impossible to clean up, just like Luke Bennet.

But I was smiling back, simply because there was no choice to be made—whenever he smiled, I smiled.

An idea struck. I handed him the bouquet and picked up my camera.

He gave me a look that was somehow both suspicious and

amused. "What do you want me to do with these?"

"Look hot," I answered, looking through the lens.

He laughed, looking down at the bouquet, blushing bashfully. I pressed the button, the shutter clicking to the same mad beat as my heart. He was so earnest, the compliment affording a rare view of modesty so often hidden by his unwavering confidence.

I glanced at the screen. It was perhaps the hottest photograph I'd ever seen, featuring two of the most beautiful things in my world— flowers and Luke Bennet.

The only thing that would have made it better was if he'd been shirtless.

I sighed dreamily. "Really, you must be an alien or something. Normal people aren't this good at everything. I should start calling you Ace."

He made a flippant sound, stepping toward me so he could look himself. "Trust me, there's plenty I'm bad at."

"Name one thing."

"Relationships," he said without hesitating, but kept talking to cover the admission. "Advanced math. Cooking. Ice skating."

"Ice skating?" I echoed around a laugh.

He shrugged. "Weak ankles."

When I laughed louder, he smiled, set his flowers on the bed, and stepped into me. His big hand circled my wrist, his thumb shifting against my palm.

"Are you okay?" he asked simply, but those three little words held a quiet knowledge that threatened to break me open.

Luke Bennet saw through me more often than I liked.

I opened my mouth to say yes. To lie, to hide how I felt because it was irrational. Because admitting the truth would hurt.

I wanted to say yes, reassure him that I was fine. But with Luke searching my eyes for the truth, I couldn't tell him anything but the truth he sought. "I don't want to change the house, Luke. I don't want the wallpaper gone, and I don't want the kitchen to be different. I don't want *any* of it to be different. Because if it's different, I won't remember. I'll forget everything. I'll forget her." Tears pricked the corners of my eyes, the words gone, cut off by the squeeze of my throat.

The lines of his face softened, his brows drawing together. His hands, so warm and strong, framed my face, tilting it up so our eyes were locked.

"I'm sorry," he said gently. "I'm so sorry, Tess. When your dad said ... well, I just thought ..." He took a breath and let it out slow. "It sounded like he wanted a fresh start, and I didn't even take a minute to consider you might not want the same. If I had, I'd have known better. I'd have asked what you wanted before telling you all the ways I'd rip your home apart."

"It's not your fault," I assured him, leaning into his palm. "I think Dad does want a fresh start, and I'd never stand in the way of that. This is his home. She was just as important to him as she was to me. So if this is what he wants, I'll do it. I just don't want to." Tears fell—stupid, heavy, fat tears that I didn't want any more than crown molding in my living room. I tried to look down.

But he held my face where it was. "Tess, let me make you a promise." He waited to make sure I was listening, his face somber and sincere. "I promise you, if I end up helping do this, I will not erase your mother from your home. There are ways to keep things and change them. You're not going to lose her. I'll promise you that over everything."

I nodded, my face twisted up and a sob lodged in my throat, one I couldn't swallow, no matter how hard I tried. And Luke pressed a kiss to my forehead before wrapping me up in the safety of his arms, shifting his weight to rock me.

He let me cry as his promise sank in. I knew without a doubt that he'd uphold it with all his power.

And for the first time, I wished with all my heart that I could keep Luke Bennet for my own.

Just the Truth

TESS

Two weeks flew by in a blur of flowers.

Bouquets and arrangements. Window installments. The greenhouse. Buckets and buckets of flowers in every color. I dreamed of the feel of stems in my hand, the scent so overwhelming, I could still smell it when I woke.

I wondered if it clung to me, just a part of who I was now. Never had I made so many arrangements, and as our crop thinned, I had to get creative, mixing flowers I wouldn't normally consider together. We'd begun to supplement with deliveries from Long Island and Chelsea while our plants replenished. Mr. Bennet began looking for more vertical growing solutions with Marcus, and Kash had already started planting more bulbs.

Because if it was going to keep up like this, we'd need more plants, and maybe a few more florists.

After years of decline, it was maybe the best problem we'd ever had.

Just like another problem I had.

It wasn't Luke's good humor—his ability to make me stop, slow down, and laugh, even when I was beyond capacity, was nothing short of magic. And there was no problem with his attentiveness. He gave that in abundance along with a healthy helping of fun, excitement, and spontaneity.

The problem was that, for the last few weeks, I'd had a real hard time reminding myself of what Luke and I were and what we weren't.

Spending every night with him didn't help. Not all night—we were bound to the flower shop, since we both lived with our parents. Never before had it felt like an inconvenience. But now, I'd have killed for an actual bed, a shower, or I'd even settle for a door to lock. Of course, I told myself that was good. It kept some boundaries in place.

Because I was not allowed to fall for Luke Bennet. Not beyond his body and his company.

We were not a thing.

Luke didn't do *things*.

It's temporary, I reminded myself over and again.

It was a now thing, and I never looked beyond today. Not aloud anyway. I tried not to think about how I'd feel if he came in and ignored me, if it all of a sudden ended without warning. As much as I told myself it was fine, that what happened tomorrow wasn't important, that I was living in the moment, there was no small amount of expectation that I *would* see him. He would be charming and gorgeous and would kiss me like I was the only woman on the planet. And then he would leave, I would go home, and we'd wake up to do it all over again.

But I wasn't Luke's girlfriend even if it did feel like we were dating. Not that we'd actually gone on a date. Or really been anywhere but our parents' houses or here. In this shop. All day and every night. I'd come in on my days off. Luke had built me a small studio in the back for our Instagram, which he helped me shoot, citing his brief experience as a photographer's assistant in LA as credentials. I'd posted the photo I'd taken of him in my room, and our account had blown up, so I'd taken to photographing him some, hauling things, making pieces for the installments, and more than a few times with flowers.

No lie—posting pictures of a hot guy with pretty flowers made for a whole lotta Instagram love.

When girls started coming into the shop looking for him, I tried to tell myself I didn't want to drown them all in the farmhouse sink. Judy had placed an order a day for weeks, and Luke would send Jett every time. But that had nothing to do with me other than the fact that we were busy with work. Luke wasn't my boyfriend. He wasn't my anything.

Oh, the lies I told myself.

That night, we'd just locked up the shop, waving at passersby who had stopped to stare in the window with a gesture to the sign— *New installment, 8a. Blanche's donuts and coffee!* And then we drew the elegant curtains we'd hung last week and started hauling supplies from the back.

Luke moved the last frames off the flat cart and stretched his back, arms over his head. His shirt crept up, showing a sliver of his abs. I knew every ridge of those abs so well, I could draw a map of them in the dark. My bottom lip made its way into my mouth as I watched him openly and without a stitch of shame. And why should I feel ashamed when Luke took every opportunity to grope, squeeze, caress, or put his lips on me?

Seriously, I had no idea how we hadn't been found out yet. Not officially at least. I had a feeling all the Bennets knew—with the exception of the matriarch—though no one had uttered a word. Well, except Ivy, who waddled out with her hand on the small of her back.

She had plenty to say on the subject of my fling that was feeling less and less like a fling by the day.

"I'll go grab the last load, if you want to get started breaking the installment down," he said, watching me watch him with a sideways smile on his handsome face.

"All right," I answered with a flush of my cheeks.

Ivy watched us a little too closely. "See ya tomorrow, Luke."

"Don't pop yet, Ivy. We've got too much work to do to lose you."

She snorted a laugh. "It'll be like the old days—I'll just have the baby out in the greenhouse and finish picking flowers for the day."

His face wrinkled up. "Please don't do that either."

Ivy laughed, shaking her head. "Bye, Luke," she said pointedly.

"Yeah, yeah, I'm going." He put his hands up and headed back into the shop.

The second he was out of earshot, she made a wicked face at me. "Have fun with your boyfriend tonight."

I scoffed. "God, you are the worst, you know that? He's not made out of boyfriend material, Ivy. He's made out of charm and impulsivity."

She shrugged. "He's had girls coming in here for weeks to throw themselves at him, and he hasn't taken a single one out."

"How do you know?" I deflected against the ache in my chest that he might have done just that without my knowledge. "Maybe he goes out after he leaves here."

"And that would be just fine with you?"

I groaned. "You're a broken record. Why can't we talk about your uterus or something? Braxton Hicks contractions? Mucus plugs? I'd take mucus plugs over this."

"I mean, if you really want to talk about my body fluids, I'm here for it. Just not as an avoidance tactic. You know," she said, stepping closer and lowering her voice, "I heard him talking to Kash in the greenhouse yesterday about you, and it was all hearts and flowers."

"Well, we do work in a flower shop."

"He likes you, Tess," she insisted.

"For now. For *right now*. I can't expect anything else but that."

She eyed me. "Tess, let me tell you something. Something straight from the mouth of your fling queen." She paused. "Are you listening?"

I folded my arms, frowning at her. Because I was a hundred percent sure I didn't want to hear what she was going to say.

"I'm listening," I assured her.

"Flings don't happen every day for three weeks. Flings don't spend every waking minute with each other. They don't eat breakfast, lunch, and dinner together. Whatever this is, it is not a fling. Luke and I? We had a fling—it was never going anywhere, and neither of us wanted it to. He and I fooled around for ages, but never, not once, did he ever look at me like he looks at you. So I'd encourage you to think about that for a hot second and figure out what your next move is. Because if you aren't interested in dating him, you'd better quit this. Now."

Cold dread shot through me, followed by a hot burst of possession and defiance at the thought of quitting Luke. I didn't want this to end, and I didn't want to walk away. Where would I even go? Wherever I was, so was he. And his presence was the bright spot in every single day.

I didn't even have to speak.

Ivy lit up with smug certainty. "Aha! That. Right there." She pointed at my face. "That feeling you have right now? That raging no that just screamed through you? That's why he's your boyfriend. And he wants to be. So quit fighting it and just say so already, for God's sake. It's not like everyone doesn't know anyway."

I sucked a noisy breath through my nose since my jaw was locked shut.

Ivy looked mighty proud of herself. The sight made me want to both cry and throttle her.

Because she was right, and the realization that Luke and I were in a relationship was an ice bucket on my thin delusion. And here I'd been, so happy pretending, and along came Ivy, who had to ruin everything with her damnable truth, the one I'd been avoiding. But now, it had been said. And once a thing was said, the only thing you could do was own up to it.

Ivy rolled her eyes. "I don't understand what the problem is, Tess."

"The problem is, I don't know how to do this. Not with him. He's too … *resplendent*."

She laughed. "What?"

"He's larger than life, somewhere above us all. He's got the gravity of the sun, Ivy. No one can match him. No one can be equal to a man like that."

She made a face. "How are you turning something good into something bad? This is not a bad thing. I'd like to state for the record that I've never seen you so happy and carefree as you have been the last few days. When was the last time you organized the supply drawers?"

I opened my mouth to answer but paused, realizing it had been weeks. "There hasn't been time."

"When was the last time you made a list? Stressed over your pictures for Instagram? Worried over your dad? Mrs. Bennet?"

My brows drew together when I frowned. "I … I don't know."

"And when was the last time you slept in? Did something spontaneous? Laughed until you cried?"

I blinked. "Today. I did all that today."

"And that's because of Luke. Just like you haven't seen him forget something, show up late, give up on a project. He's been the picture of dependability. And that's because of you."

I stared at her, stunned.

"I mean, he's still immature, but that's just a male Bennet

genetic trait."

A laugh burst out of me. "You ... you're right."

"I know I'm right. The question is, what are you going to do about it?"

Before I could answer, I heard the cart squeaking toward us. Ivy nodded at me, her face softening. She pulled me into a hug.

"I love you, Tess. Stop fighting."

I held her close, breathed deep the scent of roses and peonies. Then I let her out, locking the door behind her.

And I turned to face my fate, which lay in the hands of the last man I'd ever thought I'd give such power.

LUKE

My smile died when I saw the look on Tess's face.

It was somewhere between facing a firing squad and getting caught naked in public. Wide, dark eyes. Lush lips flat. Neck long as a swan, on full display, her auburn hair piled high on her head.

"You okay, Tess?" I asked, my brow furrowed and dread gripping my heart. It raced against the feeling.

For two weeks, I'd been waiting for this, whatever it was. A hammer to fall. A shoe to drop. A dozen times, I'd tried to talk to her, to define what we were, to have the dreaded relationship talk. But I never did. Partly because I didn't know what to say. Partly because I had the undeniable feeling she would reject me the second I put her on the spot.

But the unspoken words underscored every moment, every word, swam in the undercurrents of a joke, an offhanded observation. She didn't think I was serious, didn't believe me to be capable. I was a fling, but I was a friend. We'd spent every minute together that we could for weeks, and not strictly because of proximity.

I could hear the truth of her feelings in the way she laughed, feel it in the way she touched me. See it in the way she lit up when she caught sight of me. It was the same fire that lit in me. But if I acknowledged it, if I said the words, I could lose her.

Never before had I been so unsure of where I stood with a woman. And never had I been so certain of where I wanted to stand.

Beside Tess.

Her throat worked down a lump. "I … I'm okay. I think."

"Is Ivy all right? Did she … did she say something to upset you?"

She shook her head. "Just the truth."

I felt my weight sink into my shoes. "Was it a good truth or a bad one?"

"I … both, I think." She paused.

I didn't speak. It was always me, making light. Changing the subject. Ignoring what was left unsaid to spare us both from having to answer to it. But not this time. It had to be her.

And she seemed to know it.

Her chin lifted, though her eyes were afraid. "What are we, Luke?"

The band on my lungs squeezed tighter. "What do you want us to be, Tess?"

"I'm afraid to say."

"Because you think I'll say no?"

"Because you might say yes."

Hope zipped through me like a bottle rocket. I closed the space between us quietly, slowly. "What do you want, Tess?" I asked. "Tell me so I can give it to you."

Her jaw fit in my palm, her eyes searching mine. "What if you can't?"

"There's nothing you could ask for that I couldn't give."

Her brows edged closer, though not in anger. In sadness.

"Do you trust me?" The question was gentle, still, pleading.

"I … I do."

"Tell me what you want." Loud was my pulse in my ears, and in the roar were the words I wanted to hear from her lips, seconds before she spoke them.

"You. But not just this, not just what we've had."

A smile flickered on my lips as I did some quick math. "What we've had? Five hundred hours since the first night. Two hundred and fifty of those, I've spent with you. Know how many of those you've been in my arms? Twenty-one. Give or take."

Her cheek rose against my thumb as she smiled.

"Tess, I know you don't think much of me. I know you don't think I can be what you need. And I plan on showing you every single way you're wrong. All you have to do is let me."

Another hard swallow as she looked up at me with pride and fear. "Why am I scared?"

"I don't know. Because if you don't think I'm serious about you, you haven't been paying attention."

A small, conceding laugh through her nose.

"Let me prove it," I commanded. "I'm not asking you to promise anything. I don't want anything to change. All I know is when I walk through that door, it's your face I look for. Every night when we say goodbye, I don't want to go. And I don't know what that means besides this: I don't want to be your fling, Tess."

"Say it again," she said softly.

With a smile, I looked deeper into her eyes. "I don't want to be your fling. I want to be your everything."

A pause, a breath, a smile. "Never in a million years did I ever think I would hear you utter those words, least of all to me."

"Should I say it again? Louder maybe?"

She laughed, the sound sweet and tender. "No—if your mom hears, she'll come down here, and then you can't kiss me. And I really want you to kiss me."

"Anything you want, Tess," I said, my heart singing as I brought my lips to hers.

I'd kissed her a hundred times. In the dark and in the sunshine. Gently and with demand. I'd kissed her greedily, and I'd kissed her with adoring care.

But this was the first time I kissed her with possession—not only of her, but her of me. The warmth of her body, the light in her heart, the matching of two flames in the meeting of our lips. When the kiss broke, I saw ownership written all over her face. And I knew it was written all over mine.

Her eyes opened slowly, meeting mine as her lazy smile spread. "What are you gonna do with me now?"

"Oh, I have an idea or two," I said, bringing my lips to hers to steal a kiss and seal a promise.

I was about to boyfriend the fuck out of Tess Monroe.

I scooped her up, the kiss breaking when she squealed her surprise. Her arms hooked around my neck, her cheeks high and smiling, flushed and pretty.

"We have work to do," she halfheartedly argued around her laughter as I hauled her to the back.

"We will. As soon as I'm sure you know I'm serious about you."

She giggled. "Even if I already believe you?"

"I don't think there's any way you could possibly know just how serious I am, Tess."

Her face opened up, her smile falling.

I kissed her to cover the depth of the admission, though I feared my lips gave it away.

Into the greenhouse, down to storage I carried her, not setting her down until we were all the way in the back, in the section we'd claimed for our own.

Supplies filled the space, dumped unceremoniously in the back corner near the leftover hay from winter mulching. There were frames for hanging installations. Tables and baskets. Things I'd built, things we'd salvaged. Dried flowers hung in bundles from some racks, and across the space, we'd haphazardly strung white twinkle lights we'd used in the last installation. So we could work comfortably in the dark, I'd explained to my mother.

I'd omitted what exactly I was working on and why I needed to be comfortable.

I moved to plug the lights into the extension cord, snagging the flannel blanket from an ancient rocking chair to spread out into the hay pile.

Tess sighed, smiling sweetly as she looked around. "You know, if I'd organized this, everything would be in neat little rows and tidy piles. And I'd never have known that I preferred it this way. It's organized chaos. Kinda like you."

I stepped into her, sliding my hands around her waist. "And here I thought you hated my chaos."

"Only because it scared me. I don't know if you know this, but I'm a creature of habit."

A laugh rumbled through me. "Who, you?"

She laughed in echo. "The biggest shocker is that I'm admitting it, I'm sure. But … you make it less scary."

"And you make routine anything but boring. I woke up at nine the other day and it felt like half my day was gone."

She wound her arms around my neck, threading her fingers. "Look at you, acting like a grown-up."

"And look at you. A little bit wild."

"Oh, I don't know that I'd go that far, but I'm afraid the taste I've had might have ruined me forever. I don't think I can go back."

"Then don't," I said against her lips. And I took them to remind her why she should stay.

I wrapped her up in my arms, pulled her as close as I could get her, felt every inch of connection from thigh to breast. She was as familiar to me as she was a discovery, the girl I'd known, the woman I'd come to need. This body had been mine for weeks.

Now I wanted the heart inside.

Never had I known a woman who held the power to change me. But Tess did. And as scared as I should have been about that, I wasn't. Because I wasn't just discovering her.

I was discovering myself.

She brought out the best in me, settled me in a way that didn't feel like chains. It felt like roots, alive and sinking into the earth, thirsty and seeking. The depth those roots had twisted had been misjudged until tonight. Until I thought I would lose her but kept her instead.

No, I wasn't scared. I was determined. Hopeful. Zinging with possibility.

Because Tess was my new adventure.

Slowly, I kissed her. Tasted the sweetness of her. Felt the warmth of her. Deliberate hands slid down her waist, under her shirt, up her ribs. A flick of my fingers, and her bra unhooked. I broke the kiss, separated our bodies. She reached for me, but I took her hand, pressed a kiss to her palm, returned it to her side.

She stood still other than the rise and fall of her chest and the flash of her lashes, her face upturned and lips parted, waiting.

My fingertips spoke for me, brushing her cheek, skimming her neck with possession. The stroke of her breast became a squeeze, the weight in my palm exactly right. I wanted her skin. Wanted to see the pale of her nipple as it tightened and rose.

Her shirt was gone before I decided to take it off. Those thirsty fingertips skated over her shoulders, taking the straps with them. Down her arms they went and to the floor. But I didn't register the motion. Not once that flesh I'd wanted was exactly where I wanted it.

I wanted so much.

I wanted her russet hair wild, loose. I wanted it fanned out, wanted it against the pale of her skin. So I freed it, shook it out, slipped my fingers in until they were deep enough to cup her nape. Tendrils of red against snowy white. Dark eyes searching mine. Lips, lush and waiting.

The breath I drew pulled her closer, my fingers tightening in her hair, exposing her neck, offering her mouth.

And I took it for what it was.

Mine.

Our lips were a hard seam, tongues searching. Searching. My whole life, I'd been searching, restless and restive. But in that moment, I wanted for nothing, sought nothing but her. I sought the heat of her with my fingertips as they slid into her jeans. I sought the depths of her mouth with my tongue. Sought the control of her by way of her hair in my fist, my desire to transmit my ownership of her, to translate the weight of proof.

Because even now, she didn't believe. She didn't think I could be what she needed, not yet.

But she would.

I broke the kiss once again, leaving her reeling, hair spilling over her shoulders, eyelids too heavy to open, breasts jostling as I slipped my hand free in order to rid her of her jeans. I pushed them over the swell of her ass, down her hips, to her knees. I captured her nipple with my lips, hands busy with her panties. With a shimmy and a kick, she stepped out of them both. And all I wanted was to drop to my knees right there, to pay homage to her breasts. To kiss my way down her body. To hook her thigh on my shoulder and taste her until she couldn't stand.

But more than that, I wanted her stretched out and comfortable, prone and exposed. I wanted her vulnerable, to strip her bare as she'd stripped me. So I kissed up her body instead, finding every dip—the valley of her breasts, the hollow of her throat, the soft space behind her jaw—as I backed her toward the blanket. I hooked her waist, reached out to brace us as I laid her down. Spread her legs with my thighs. Rose to my knees.

Her eyes smoldered, snagging mine. Her hands reached for the hem of my shorts.

I caught her wrists in one hand. "No."

A sweet pout settled on her face. "But I want you," she said, her voice rough.

"What? What do you want, Tess?"

Her eyes flicked to my cock. It throbbed its answer.

"Tell me," I said, squeezing her wrists.

Her tongue darted out to wet her lips, pink and slick. "I want your dick in my face, Luke."

A smile tugged my lips, just one side. "Next time. This time is mine. I've got something to prove, Tess, and I'm not stopping until I prove it."

She mewled, her hips shifting, calling my attention. I thumbed the rippling flesh between her thighs.

"Don't worry. You'll get what you want."

I reached across my hips to hook her knee, and with a solid tug, I flipped her hips, corkscrewing her body. God, she was beautiful. The shine of her hair, spread out like a siren. The curve of her breast, the line of her waist, the twist of her body, the swell of her ass.

"Roll over," I commanded, grabbing her hips.

She did, her breath noisy. I leaned over her, my eyes trailing up her back, hand brushing her hair from her face, stroking her cheek, thumbing her neck before clamping it with my fist. My free hand skated the length of her body, gripped the bend of her waist, pulled her into my hips, cock nestling in the valley of her ass with nothing but the jersey of my shorts separating us. Those hips rolled, stroking me.

My lips on her jaw, breath stirring her hair, whispering against her shoulder blade. I rose, let her neck go, leaned back. Filled my hands with her ass, nudged her thighs farther apart, and was met with the gentle arch of her back, an offering. A request.

I shifted, eyes locked on the split of her legs. Arms threading under her thighs. Lips tingling with anticipation. Mouth meeting her heat. Tongue tasting the salt of her body. My single-minded focus, aware only on the fringes of the tremble of her thighs, the gasp of my name. I stayed right where I was, taking my time. I knew every peak and valley of her body, knew how to bring her to the edge, knew how to slow her down without losing her.

It wasn't until she shifted that I released her and not by choice, but loss of contact. She sat and twisted, reaching for me as I reached for her, the synchronicity of body and mind instinctual. I knew what she wanted, where I would meet her lips, how I would lay her down again before it happened. Her lips crushed to mine, my body crushed to hers, pressing her into the blanket, the dip of the hay from her body cradling her. Her hands, frantic and frenzied, scrambled for my pants.

I broke the kiss, looking down into her face, smoothing her hair, soothing her breath. But her hips were wild beneath me. I pinned them with mine. Nipped her lips. Only when she stilled did I back away to stand.

She lay stretched out on the flannel, her skin bright against the dark. She was shades of red—the shine of her hair, the flush of her cheeks, the pink of her lips, of her nipples, of the neat thatch of hair in the V of her body. I couldn't look away, and she couldn't seem to either, not as I reached behind me to grab a handful of T-shirt and pull it over my head. Not as I retrieved the condom from my pocket and dropped my shorts. Not as I rolled it on, pumping my cock as I approached.

Our eyes locked—they'd been otherwise occupied. Her thighs spread to make room for my hips. Her arms spread to make room for the rest of me. Chest to chest. Hip to hip. My hand on my base, thumb on my shaft, crown to her heat. And with a flex, I slid into her until there was no space between us.

I swallowed her sigh with a kiss, held her body down with mine. My arms bracketed her face, my hands in her hair. And I spent a long moment right there, through the thundering of my heart, through the pulse of my body in hers, the echo of hers around mine.

My hips were all that moved.

The slow wave, the shift when I hit the end, the pressure she needed, the depth I craved. The kiss broke when she lost her body to the feeling, her head lolling, eyes pinned shut. She couldn't move, couldn't exact pleasure. It was mine to give.

And I wanted to give her everything.

Deeper I drove, kissing what skin I could, breathing into the shell of her ear, tracing the lobe with my tongue. The wave of my body, achingly slow. Deliberate and steady. A deep thrust. Another deeper still. Once more, and she was there, her body tight, her breath shallow.

I lifted my head, pumped my hips, watched her face stretch and brows come together, heard the rasp of my name riding her breath. Felt the flex of her body around mine, so hard and tight. I didn't pull out, just stayed until the pulse burst through her, drawing me deeper.

The pull was too strong, too deep, my awareness shrinking with every thrust of my hips, my senses retreating. Sight gone with a slam of my lids. Sound nothing beyond the thunder of my heart and the sawing of my breath. Touch slipping from every extremity, rushing to the place where my body met hers.

And with a burst of lightning behind closed lids, I came, hanging onto her like I'd fly away if I let her go.

Her arms were the first thing I registered, twined around my ribs. Then, her fingers, the delicate graze of her fingernails up and down my back. The scent of her hair where my face was buried, lilacs mingling with sweet hay. The fluttering of her pulse under my lips as I kissed the column of her neck.

I rose in search of her lips, kissed her with the slow appreciation I'd given her body. And when I broke away, it was to gaze into her face, reveling in the sight of its smiling form in my hands.

"What have you done to me, Tess?" I asked, searching her eyes. "How did you do it?"

Her smile ticked up on one side. "Well, I have this voodoo doll."

I laughed.

"No, really. And there's a shrine in my closet with the standard stuff. You know, some of your hair, red candles, your headshot, some chicken bones."

"What, no sage?"

With a roll of her eyes, she made a noise of dissension. "Please, everybody knows you don't use sage in love potions."

A shot of emotion burst through me at the word love from her lips, and I kissed them to cover it. Fear, surprise, desire. Warning. Welcome.

Love. It meant so many things in so many contexts, a single word to span a hundred emotions. I loved my family. I loved my friends. I loved Wendy, though I never wanted to see her again. I loved Zhenya, my old neighbor, even though I wanted to see her again and probably never would.

The way I felt about Tess was a form of that word. I didn't know what form, not yet. But I knew without knowing that this feeling wouldn't leave. It wouldn't go away. It would only grow.

I only hoped we grew together and not apart.

I packed the thought away, shifting to roll us over and apart. Tess broke the kiss, propping her little chin on her hand to look down at me, hair wild and loose. I smoothed it, tucking a mass of it behind her ear so I could see her face better.

"I always wondered what it was like to be Luke Bennet's girlfriend," she said with that lazy smile of hers.

"Is it as glamorous as you imagined?" I teased, flicking a glance at the hay around us.

"Trust me, it's better," she said, leaning in to press a fleeting kiss to my lips.

My hands bracketed her hips. "So how do you want to play this? Should we put up a sign in the window? Maybe take out a newspaper ad?"

"I was thinking a billboard, or at least a sandwich board."

I chuckled. "Seriously though—we'll have to tell my mom at some point, and she's going to insert herself directly into everything we do. She's going to ask you questions you don't want to answer, like what kind of birth control you're on and if there's any history of heart disease in your family. Maybe your ring size and which cut diamond you prefer."

When she laughed, the flush on her cheeks was almost as deep as her hair. "God, I didn't even think about your mom. I didn't think you'd ever want anyone to know about us."

My smile faded. "Tess, if taking out a billboard wasn't outrageous and inappropriate, I'd fucking do it. This has never been temporary for me."

Her face softened. "I thought all you wanted was temporary."

"And I thought you weren't interested in temporary. I walked into it with the intent to date the hell out of you, Tess Monroe."

She shook her head in wonder. "How do you do that?"

"What?"

"Make me feel like I'm the only woman in the world."

My hand cupped her jaw, my eyes holding hers still. "Because you are."

And I kissed her to prove it.

Things the Cat Drags In

TESS

"**I** told you he was your boyfriend," Ivy said with smug certainty. I laughed, the sound unburdened, just like me. Light as a feather and floating through the breeze, free as could be, despite my exhaustion. It had taken us all night to get the installation done, no thanks to Luke's lips and hands and that *body*.

"You were right, and I was wrong," I said pointedly.

She pressed her hand to her chest, smiling. "It's more common than I get credit for. Are you going to tell Mrs. Bennet?"

My nose wrinkled. "We're gonna wait a bit. Just … get settled, make sure we're stable before she jumps in with wedding invitation samples or something."

"I'd say she'd scare Luke off, but somehow, I don't think it's him who'd get cold feet."

I gave her a look. "Can you blame me? I don't do anything fast."

"No, you don't. And when Mrs. Bennet gets word that her favorite person on the planet who's not related to her is dating her son, she's absolutely going to start planning your wedding. I give it two hours."

"God," I said on a laugh. "Maybe we should keep it from her until we're engaged."

Ivy gave me a look.

"What?"

"You said until. *Until* you're engaged."

My cheeks flamed. "I was kidding, Ivy."

"I'm just saying, Tess. I think somewhere in your rational little mind lies a gooey romantic who knows you two are well-matched."

"We are well-matched. That doesn't mean we're getting married, you weirdo."

She gave me another look, this one telling me she knew better. "You remind me of me and Dean. You just…click, you know? And everyone around you can see it." A wistful smile slipped out of her, her hand absently moving to her belly. "It's your own kind of magic, and I'm so happy you found it. I swear, the electricity flickers when you're in the same room. How Mrs. Bennet hasn't already guessed is beyond me."

"She's too busy fussing over having her kids home to be paying attention. Anyway, when she's down here, Luke and I aren't usually in the room at the same time."

"By design?"

"A little, but also because we're just too busy."

Ivy snorted a laugh. "You act like I didn't catch him feeling you up in storage yesterday."

I shrugged. "You know what they say—a grope a day keeps the single away."

"No one says that," she said around a giggle just as the bell on the counter rang for a second time in thirty seconds.

I frowned, glancing behind me. "Where the hell is Jett?"

"I don't know. He went back to the greenhouse a minute ago. Luke's on a delivery."

I wiped my hands on my apron. "I know where Luke is."

"Oh, I'm sure. It'll become your sixth sense, knowing how far away he is at any given moment. Because you're gonna get *maaaaarried*," she sang, giving me a display of jazz hands for effect.

I rolled my eyes, smiling as I walked toward the front.

The shop was so busy, I found myself surprised Jett had gotten away for so long without the bell ringing.

In the wee hours of the morning—after a too-short nap in the hay—we'd unveiled the new installation to a small crowd, coffees in hand as they waited on the sidewalk. Every week was a little bigger, a little grander, and today was no exception.

It was a surprise to us all. But nowhere near as surprising as who I found on the other side of the counter.

Wendy Westham had always been beautiful, and time had not changed that. In fact, I thought time had made her more beautiful. The roundness of youth had been erased from her face, leaving high cheekbones and a perfectly shaped jaw. Her eyes were more confident than I remembered, more grounded, though still bright with that spark of mischief I so often saw in Luke's. Those eyes were nearly the same color as his, a deep, shocking blue.

If their marriage had yielded a baby, that baby would have had those eyes, clever and ocean deep.

Pain split my ribs as a smile split my face. "Wendy!" I cheered, the sound too light to be genuine. "What … what are you doing here?"

She smiled a smile that belonged on a magazine cover, a smile as perfect and practiced as it was charming and true. "Tess, right? God, it's good to see you. The shop looks incredible. I heard you did the windows, is that true? Because you could get a job in LA like that." She snapped her fingers.

I laughed, wooden and stiff. "I did, thank you. So … can I help you?"

"Oh!" she said on a laugh, adjusting her handbag, which was hooked in the crook of her arm and cost more than a month's rent on Fifth. "I was looking for Luke. Is he here?"

I swallowed the stone in my throat. "You just missed him. He's on a delivery."

Her face fell. "Oh. Do you mind if I wait for him? I've been back in New York for a minute, but I haven't had a chance to see him yet."

With a nod—seriously, what else could I do?—I said, "Yes, of course, though I don't know when he'll be back."

She waved a hand, stepping around the counter to head to the back before I could object. She wore a dress, simple and bohemian in design but colored with little details—a tie here, a ruffle there, clever design that made it feel almost couture. Her beauty was as blinding as it was understated. She didn't have to try. She just *was*.

I didn't know Wendy well—she and Luke had met well after we graduated, and they'd only dated for forty-two seconds before running off to get married. But they'd been a singular unit, inseparable from the second they met. Whenever Luke had come by the shop, Wendy had been at his side. She'd never been unkind to me, though everyone painted her to be a succubus. Everyone just loved Luke too much to accept anything but five-star treatment of him. Anything less was blasphemy.

She wound her way into the workspace. "Thanks, Tess. You work back here, right?"

"Try to." *On days we aren't interrupted.*

As we stepped up to the tables, Ivy looked up, her jaw popping open for a nanosecond before recovering.

"Ivy? How are you?" Wendy beamed, stepping around the table.

175

When she caught a glimpse at Ivy's belly, her face softened, her eyes sparkling with what seemed to be ... *tears*? "Look at you. You're beautiful." Wendy gave her a hug, prompting a terrified look from Ivy over Wendy's shoulder. "Who's the lucky guy?"

"Oh, I don't think you know him. Dean, one of our suppliers."

Wendy's eyes narrowed in thought. "Wait, the big guy? The one who always brings all the pots?" One of her brows rose.

Ivy laughed. "Yes. Pots—and a little pot, if the mood was right."

"Congratulations, seriously," she said, the words tight with emotion she covered by glancing around. "It hasn't changed back here at all. God, I can't count the times Luke and I used to sneak back here." She laughed. "I think we hooked up on every surface in the building."

The wind flew out of my lungs in a nearly audible whoosh.

Ivy tittered nervously, hopping off her stool as fast as any woman in her state and size could. "So what are you doing back in town, Wendy?"

"Oh, you know, just needing home for a minute. Ever get that feeling? When you need a friendly face? Not so many of those in LA these days." She chuckled softly.

God, why did she have to be so charming? And a little sad? And really fucking pretty? And goddamn married to Luke? Once upon a time at least ... though it was all I could think of, along with Wendy's beautiful naked ass all over the shop I loved with the man I thought I could.

The thought tarnished the memories he and I had made here, made them feel tired and used, a repeat rather than a revelation.

In that moment, I could no longer understand what Luke was doing with me. Wendy was his equal in a way I could never be— larger than life, stunningly charming, beautiful in that mythical way that defied your senses. And all that in a summer dress and sandals, and without a stitch of makeup on her face.

And then there was me. Short and freckle-faced, eyes like mud and hair the shade of wet clay. Jeans smudged with dirt and with little holes worn where my thighs met. My pilled T-shirt and sneakers scuffed, the rubber cracked and peeling. Where Wendy was charming and worldly, I was awkward and a little suspicious, and I hadn't left this side of Manhattan in close to a year. My world existed inside the blocks around this flower shop and included the people inside and my father.

Her world—Luke's world—was too big and brilliant for the likes of me.

Wendy wandered over to the arrangement I'd been working on, bringing her pretty nose to the head of a peony. "This is so pretty, Tess. Luke always said you were the most talented florist he'd ever known. I have to say, I think he was right." She smiled so gently at me that the ache in my heart squeezed tighter.

I smiled back and told her the truth. "There's no way I'm better than Mrs. Bennet."

"You're at least equal in my book. Would you teach me something?" she asked earnestly.

Though I wanted to run, there was nowhere to go. So I said, "I'll show you what I know."

And with my stomach sick and twisted, I showed the one woman Luke had ever loved my secrets, all except one.

LUKE

I couldn't stop smiling.

It was like my teeth were greased, my cheeks aching as I pulled up in the delivery truck.

Tess was inside—that was reason one. Reason two was that she was not only inside, but had agreed to be mine. Reason three was that

I had something to tell her.

Something big.

After my last delivery, I'd run to a meeting after getting a text from a buddy I used to bartend with. His sister worked for Floral magazine, and I'd hit him up, asking for a meeting, which he'd delivered in the form of an ambush at a coffee shop. An elevator pitch and our Instagram feed—that was all it had taken to get her to agree to another meeting, a real meeting, one that could end in a feature. A cover feature, if I could manage it.

Tess might have been right. Mom might actually have a heart attack.

Now that I'd convinced Tess to date me, my new life mission was to manage that cover feature.

I killed the engine and popped open the door, waving at my Dad and Kash as I bounded toward the shop.

Toward Tess.

I wanted to see the look on her face when I told her, wanted the kisses she'd grant me after, wanted to spin her around and hear her laugh and to share this feeling with her. Her, before my mom or my siblings, before anybody in the world, I wanted to tell *her*.

I threw open the swinging doors to the workroom like the goddamn King of Siam.

"Tess," I called, scanning the workroom. "You're never gonna believe—"

The words died in my throat, my smile gone for the first time in twenty-four hours.

There was Tess, looking at me like a sheep that just realized she stood in the slaughterhouse, her eyes big and brown and too deep to fathom. And Ivy, who cut a scowl in my direction.

And Wendy. Standing next to Tess. Smiling at me like she hadn't seen me in a decade and had missed every minute.

I stared at them like I was looking at a crime scene, the details sharp and screaming—Tess's shock and worry, the stillness of the room, the hope in Wendy's eyes. And then I found myself, slapping a smile back on my face.

New-new mission: defuse whatever the fuck was happening here and get Wendy the hell out of the shop. Immediately.

"Well," I started, schooling my voice for maximum amiability, "you are about the last person I expected to see today."

"Luke," she breathed, her smile relieved and eyes shining as she stepped around the table.

My eyes flicked to Tess, but she was looking down, her lips pursed and brows together. I had a suspicious, sick feeling that she was trying not to cry.

Wendy floated across the room like the fucking angel of death, and before I knew what was happening, we were hugging. Her arms were around my waist, her face buried in my chest like it had been a thousand times before. The familiarity struck me, but there was no comfort, only a rush of aversion.

But I hugged her around the shoulders with the briefest of squeezes before using my retreat to grasp her shoulders and peel her off of me.

Tess had turned away, the back of her hand swiping at her face.

"What are you doing, Wendy?" I asked quietly, my jaw tight.

Wendy beamed up at me. "I … I wanted to see you. Did Laney tell you I was back?"

"She did." My gaze drifted back to Tess, who was whisper-arguing with Ivy. "Hey, why don't we take a walk?"

"I'd like that," she answered.

I offered a curt smile and started for the front of the shop, my eyes on Tess. "I'll be right back," I said, hoping she heard the apology and reassurance in my voice.

Tess tried to smile but looked away. She looked like she felt ashamed, foolish. And I mentally cursed a roaring tornado of obscenities.

Jett and I had a full conversation as I passed that consisted of a lot of *What the fucks* and *I have no fucking clues* and a solid, *Don't tell Mom.*

I pushed the door to the shop open to the sound of the little bell, and Wendy exited the building.

Thank fucking God.

She smiled up at me. "Where do you want to go?"

I didn't answer, just started walking in the direction of the park. "What do you need, Wendy?" It wasn't cold, nor was it rude. But there was no invitation in the words.

"I ... I just ... when we last spoke, it was ... tense."

"How is your boyfriend, by the way?"

"We broke up." She stopped, snagging my elbow. "I'm sorry to just stop by. I just really needed to see you."

I sighed, running a hand over my face. "It's not good for me to see you, and there's nothing left to say."

"LA's not the same without you, Luke. We ... we moved there together, were married there together."

"Got divorced there."

A frown, slight though it was. "I didn't want to be there without you, so I came home. I missed you."

My eyes narrowed. "What do you want?"

She huffed. "Nothing, okay? Everything ... everything feels fucked up. And when things feel fucked up, it's always your face I want to see."

Another sigh, this one controlled, my jaw tight, the muscle bouncing. "Are you all right? Do you need anything?"

She shook her head, looking down. "No. It's not like that. I just needed a familiar face."

"You can't just show up like this. Not after everything."

She was still looking at her feet. "I'm sorry. It's just that … I feel like I've lost everything." The words broke with a sob as her hand moved to her face.

And with a third sigh, this one resigned, the doubt I'd had about her sincerity was gone. I stepped into her, pulled her in for a hug, let her cry for a minute.

Because I understood. She didn't have anyone—she'd selectively pushed and pulled everyone in her life toward and away like a never-ending yoyo. Her father was largely absent, and her mother existed between cycles of benders and hangovers. Not everyone could handle Wendy, certainly not her parents, and everyone else had left, unwilling to love her enough to shoulder the burden of times like these.

I was Wendy's constant. And whatever had happened triggered her, which meant she was either teetering on the edge of a downswing or about to manipulate me.

I'd keep my eyes open for the latter because I couldn't ignore the former.

She backed away, swiping at her face. "God, I'm sorry."

"What happened?"

Wendy laughed through a sob. "I should have quit dating Hollywood executives. Among other things I should have quit doing." She took a breath and straightened up, smiling a little brighter. "You know, you've always been able to make me feel better."

"I didn't do anything."

She smiled, a small, sad expression. And with her hand on my arm, she stretched to kiss me on the cheek. "You were here," she said quietly, backing away. "Can I text you?"

My lips flattened. "If you need to."

She nodded. "Thank you," she said and turned to walk away.

I stood on the sidewalk and watched her go, wondering why the hell she couldn't have stayed on the other side of the country where she belonged. The sight of her was a shock I hadn't expected.

One I hadn't prepared Tess for.

Tess.

I picked up my feet, hurrying for the shop with my mind on her. By the time I reached the door, I was buzzing, humming with anticipation, an apology rolling through my head on a loop.

I didn't even know what I needed to apologize for. I couldn't control Wendy any better than I could control the weather. But my guilt ran deep—for her presence, for whatever she'd said to Tess. For marrying her. For not walking away. For my sense of duty.

More than anyone, I wished to be able to turn my back on that.

I wound through the store, hurrying into the back, but she was gone. Ivy's eyes were sad, her face drawn.

My heart hit my shoes.

"She's in storage," was all she said.

And I took off before she was even finished speaking. I didn't register my dad and brother, though their disappointment weighed heavy on me as I passed. Not in me. For me.

For Tess.

And that was all that mattered—Tess.

I found her down in storage, in our corner. She faced the wall, her hand over her mouth and shoulders small.

"Tess." I begged the word, and she turned, startled.

Her face shone with tears that she wiped away, straightening her spine, meeting my eyes.

I stepped into her, wanting nothing more than to pull her into my arms. But I didn't for fear she'd push me away.

She swallowed hard, her brows knit together. "What does she want?"

"I don't know for sure. She … she's a little lost, I think, and I'm always the one she comes to when she's trying to find her way." I took another step. "Please, don't cry, Tess."

Her face bent, casting her gaze to her shoes. "I'm sorry. I don't know what's the matter with me."

That was all the permission I needed. I scooped her into my chest, cupped the back of her head to hold her close. "I'm sorry. I'm so sorry," I whispered into her hair.

"You didn't do anything wrong." She sniffled and said against my chest, "God, I'm so ridiculous. You haven't even been my boyfriend for a day, and here I am, blubbering."

"Well, Wendy always did have a knack for making people cry," I teased and was met with a wan laugh. "And I think I've been your boyfriend for a couple weeks now even if you didn't."

She chanced a look up at me. "It was easy to forget about her, thinking she was so far away. She was just a story in your past, not a person in your present. But you were married. *Married*. And she's so pretty and charming and *just like you*."

I sobered, my voice low. "I'm nothing like her. Tess, you've got to understand that she and I are complicated at best. But I don't want her. I want you. And part of the reason I want you is because you're nothing like her. You would never cheat on me, lie to me. Use me. Those lines, once crossed, cannot be uncrossed."

She nodded, but her eyes were still unsure.

I captured her chin in my thumb and forefinger. "You, Tess Monroe, are the most beautiful girl I've ever known. Every little freckle, every little smile. Every hair on your head and curve of your body—especially this one." I gave her ass a squeeze with my free hand, eliciting a chuckle. "You are perfect. And I'm irresponsible and unreliable."

"And hedonistic," she added.

"Yes, which I recall you enjoying." Another laugh. "I don't want somebody like me. I want somebody like you."

Her sigh of concession and relief was coupled with a smile. "Kiss me," she commanded.

And so I did, well and thoroughly.

The kiss broke when the news I'd been hanging on to wouldn't stay put anymore.

"I had a very interesting meeting today," I said, my hands clasped in the small of her back, keeping her flush against me.

"Oh, yeah?"

"With a junior editor at *Floral* magazine."

Her eyes widened. "You're kidding."

"She's interested in featuring us."

Her face shot open like a sunbeam. "Luke …" she breathed.

"I know. She took one look at the pictures you took and was sold. It's all because of you." My heart doubled in size as I gazed into her face. "You've found a way to show the whole world what this shop is, what it means to us. I can make Mom's dream come true."

Her hand untwined from my neck and cupped my jaw, her face soft and open.

"So get ready," I said with a sideways smile. "Because I'm about to get us on the cover of the biggest floral magazine in America."

She laughed, leaping to grab me around the neck, and I lifted her up and spun her around, just like I'd imagined. When her feet were on the ground, I snagged her hand to take her to my mother.

And we ran away with our hopes high and our dreams in tow.

Gold Digger

LUKE

The store was empty and quiet as Tess and I walked to the front that night, the day done and shop closed.

"You sure you don't want to come to dinner?" I asked. "Mom won't mind, especially after today. I'm sure she has a million things to talk to you about."

"Another time. I've barely seen Dad, and I'd love to cook him a fresh meal instead of one he has to reheat."

I pulled her to a stop, tugged her to bring her into the circle of my arms. "You're a good daughter, you know that?"

She flushed, smiling. "Every once in a while, I figure I do something right."

"Tell your dad I've got supplies being delivered tomorrow. Maybe tomorrow night we can have dinner at your place with your dad, and I can make sure everything's in place to get started?"

A nod and a small smile were my only answer.

"You sure you're okay with the renovation?"

An identical nod and smile told me the truth was no.

I frowned. "I really think you should tell your dad. He wouldn't change the house if he knew it upset you."

"I know he wouldn't, which is why I can't say anything." She wrapped her arms around my waist and squeezed. "I trust you, Luke. And I want what Dad wants. Don't worry … I'll be fine."

"You always are. But you don't have to be. You know that, right?"

"I've heard it once or twice," she said with a sidelong smile.

I chuckled and kissed her nose. "Meet you back here after dinner. Let's get the installation brainstormed out so I can start building."

"Deal. And bring your appetite."

One of my brows rose. "You bringing dessert?"

"Yes, in the form of black lace."

I kissed her smirking lips for a long moment before letting her go with regret. "Let's go. Sooner we get this over, the sooner I get my treat."

Out we went, locking up the shop behind us. With a fleeting kiss, we parted in front of my parents' stoop. Well, she parted. I leaned against the rail and watched her, waving when she looked back.

I didn't go inside until she was gone.

The din of my family met me as I closed the city noise out behind me. Marcus and Dad sat silently at the table—Dad with his paper, Marcus with his phone—and when I entered the room on my way to the noisy kitchen, they gave me identical nods. The kitchen was a bustle of motion and sound. Kanye rapped "Gold Digger" from the portable speaker next to Edie's thigh on the counter as she shimmied her shoulders. Jett laughed from the stove, pushing dinner around in a pan as Kash and my mother engaged in a rap battle in the breakfast nook.

Mom was winning. And when she got to the prenup part and shouted, *Eighteen years!* Kash broke down laughing so hard, he lost on the spot.

"Thank you, thank you," Mom said, curtsying before expectantly holding her knotted hand out to Kash.

He flipped through his wallet, retrieved a five, and laid it in her palm. "You earned that," he said, kissing her on the cheek.

Mom flushed, giggling. "Beating you at rap battles since 2002."

Kash shook his head. "You're the reason we can't play Sorry, you know."

She shrugged, tucking the fiver in her back pocket. "I don't know what you're talking about, Kassius Bennet."

Laney laughed. "She gives a whole new meaning to the word."

Jett snorted. "Her *sorry* comes when she flips the board."

"You're the reason we're all so competitive," I said with a smirk. "Except Dad. He's thrown every game he ever played."

"That's because your father knows something very important," Mom stated matter-of-factly, pausing for dramatic effect. "If Mama ain't happy, ain't nobody happy."

Laughter filled the room. Mom stepped into me to give me a hug.

"My boy, how are you?" she asked sweetly. "I can't believe you managed a meeting with Floral! You make magic without even trying, don't you?"

I wrapped an arm around her shoulders. "Anything for you." I kissed the top of her head.

Jett transferred a pot of rice to a serving bowl and handed it to Laney. "You've pulled some stunts, but a prospect for a magazine article? I'm impressed."

"They want to come by next week and scope the shop out. Tess and I are working on an installation tonight."

"I bet you are." Kash made a lewd gesture at me from behind Mom.

I gave him a look.

"You two are working so hard," Mom fussed, letting me go to look up at me. "You're at the shop every morning before it opens and every night after it's closed. You really deserve some time off your feet."

Laney snickered, heading to the dining room. "Oh, I'm sure they're getting plenty of time on their backs."

"I don't see how," Mom said, completely unaware. "I'm going to make you stay home to rest one of these days—you watch me."

"Oh, don't do that, Mom." Jett handed another bowl, this one full of steaming broccoli, to Kash. "I think it might be more punishment than reward."

Mom laughed, completely oblivious. I razed Jett to the ground solely with the power of my mind.

"I never imagined Luke would become a workaholic," she said, laughing softly and reaching for my face. "And here I thought you didn't even particularly *like* the flower shop. Now I can't keep you out of it."

A dish of meat was thrust in my direction, and Jett laid a smirking look on me. "He's in it all right."

I snatched the dish from his hand with an amiable smile. "What can I say? I love some good hammer-and-nail action."

"Oh, we know," he said on a laugh.

"Really," Mom kept on, following us into the dining room, "I never knew you were such a carpenter."

"Always was good with wood," Kash said, tossing a broccoli floret into the air and catching it in his mouth.

I rolled my eyes, setting down the dish and taking my seat. But before I could change the subject, Mom did.

She opened her napkin, laying it in her lap. "I heard Wendy came to the shop today. I didn't know she was in town." The statement was pointed.

I glared at Jett, who shrugged, wide-eyed.

"Oh, please," Mom said. "There are no secrets in this house. The Bennets are known for many things, but tight lips is not one of them."

My siblings at least had the good sense to look cowed. One scan informed me that Jett told Laney, and she told Kash, who would have told anybody who'd listen, even Marcus.

"What did she want?" Mom asked, dishing out rice, catching my eye for a heartbeat.

"Just to say hello," I answered, which was truth enough.

Mom snorted a laugh. "I can't imagine that was all she wanted."

"She moved back," I admitted. "She and her boyfriend broke up."

That earned me a look from the entire table.

"Don't gimme that," I said, ignoring them in favor of the meat. "I sent her on her way."

They were still looking at me.

I set the fork on the dish and gave them all a look right back. "I'm not interested in anything Wendy has to offer or ask for. All right?"

Mom took the fork and dished herself a cut of chicken. "Well, you can't blame us for being suspicious. She's done everything she can to hurt you, Lucas, and I'd rather not see that happen again."

I sighed. "She doesn't mean to."

"That doesn't change the fact that she did—and will again, if you give her the chance. She's not your responsibility. Not anymore. Not after what she did." Mom's face was hard, but her eyes were on her task.

She was right, of course. Wendy wasn't my responsibility. But it felt like she was.

I wondered if I'd ever be free of that feeling.

"I'm just a friendly face," I assured her.

Which earned me an acerbic glance from my mother. "Just don't let anything else be friendly with her."

Kash snickered. The rest of the table seemed to relax. They knew I'd never be friendly with Wendy, not when I had Tess.

"Is she staying with her parents?" Mom asked, her voice tinged with worry.

Because here was the saddest of all truths: despite all that had happened, even my mother wanted Wendy to be happy and safe. We all wanted to save her because there were so few people left who would.

But we couldn't save someone who didn't want to be saved, no matter how badly we wanted to.

"Her mom. Her dad's gone again."

Mom made a scornful noise. "Blowing his paycheck in Atlantic City, no doubt. Is her mom all right?"

"I don't know," I admitted. "Really, I just wanted her out of the shop and gone."

Marcus was frowning mightily. "She knows we're revamping the shop then."

I nodded, exchanging a meaningful look with him.

Wendy had been dumped. The flower shop—and thus my inheritance—was back in play. It was a matter of survival. Where else could she go? It was true that I hadn't held down a job for more than six months, but that was by choice. Wendy had been fired from every job she'd ever had. She couldn't take care of herself. So she used her charm to make connections with people who could take care of her.

It was all of that, true. But it was more than that too. Because I was her safe place. Had I been able to provide for her the way she thought she needed, she wouldn't have cheated. And if she hadn't cheated, I'd probably still be married to her.

I stifled a shudder that crawled up my spine. Now that I had Tess, now that I saw what could be, the comparison was stark and terrifying. What Wendy and I'd had wasn't true love. Dependency, guilt, fear, desire. But looking at my parents, looking at what I had with Tess, I realized love was more than that.

It was equality. Respect. Trust. And I had none of those things with Wendy.

"Well," Mom said, carving her chicken daintily, "I hope she's all right. And I hope she leaves you alone, for all our sakes."

Dad caught my eyes as he chewed a mouthful, swallowed with deliberation, and said, "We're planting a raised row of marigolds."

That was all it took to divert them all, just as he'd planned. Mom lit up and asked what colors and breeds. Kash started on about the new planting system they were in the process of installing, which would double our grow space vertically. Laney brought us up to speed on the website and social, and Marcus got us through the rest of the meal, informing us of the new computer system, which would be in place this week.

I sat among my family, and for once, I said nothing.

Instead, I thought about Wendy. About what she could want and how she could wreck things with Tess. And then I considered all the ways to stop that from happening.

An hour later, dinner had been cleared, the dishes cleaned, dried, and put away. And the family dispersed, my mother last with the declaration of a bath and a book—two of life's great pleasures, she'd noted matter-of-factly.

And with her exit, Dad and I were alone in the kitchen, eating cookies out of the jar between us in silence.

"You talked to Tess?" he finally asked between bites, watching me with clever, knowing eyes.

I nodded, swallowing. "I did. She was shocked."

"Well, that makes all of us."

We chuckled and slipped into silence for a moment again.

"What do you think Wendy wants?" he asked.

"I don't know. I honestly don't. Could be a play to get me back, might be about money. Or it could be as simple as getting dumped and coming home. But I meant what I said. I'm through with her."

He bobbed his head. "Yes and no. You're never really through with her, are you?"

"I can't just … I don't know. Push her away. I don't know where she'll go or what she'll do if I cut her off completely. I've just got to be honest with Tess, and I've got to keep as much distance between me and Wendy as possible."

"Wendy loves you as best she can. And you love her. You went through too much together not to. But Wendy is a loose cannon—we don't know what she'll do or when she'll do it. She's dangerous in that way, and I know you know that. I just thought it served to say it aloud. I don't want you to get hurt, son. And I don't want you to lose what you've found with Tess because of Wendy."

Exhaustion slipped over me, bone deep and heavy. "I know. But if she calls me, I don't know how to ignore her—I've seen what happens to her when I do. I don't know how to survive the guilt any more than I know how to handle her when she needs me. All I can do is be there if she's in trouble and make sure it's clear what she and I are and what we aren't. And Tess—I've got to tell her about Tess. But Dad, it has to be me to answer the call. Wendy doesn't have anybody else."

He watched me for a moment, lowering his hand to the counter. "Your mother's right, you know. You aren't responsible for her."

I shook my head. "I know. But if anyone can help her, it's me."

Dad nodded, shifting to grasp my shoulder. "You're a good man, Lucas. And I'm proud of you. Of the man you've become. Just know what you're worth and give your love to the people who will give theirs back to you."

He turned, taking a bite of his cookie as he walked away. And I hoped against hope that I knew what I was doing.

Fudge Ripple

TESS

I'd barely slept in days, and I'd never been happier.

We'd been in full beast mode, prepping the store for the magazine editor—a new photo corner, some new hanging displays using fresh flowers to replace the dried ones, a rearranging of the furniture to include more tin buckets for our market bouquets. Luke had even refinished a beautiful hutch that we'd stuffed with curios and potted plants.

None of us had stopped moving, and today would be no different. But despite my exhaustion, I bounced out of bed, ready to tackle my insurmountable list with the determination to surmount it.

The house was a wreck of supplies and half-finished projects, though the renovation was finally coming together. I could see the light, the finish close enough to envision. And Luke had done exactly what he'd said—he'd kept Mom present. An accent wall of her ugly, old wallpaper, bracketed by simple, modern curtains that stretched floor to ceiling, the effect making the wallpaper look vintage rather than dated.

The cabinets still held the familiarity of what they'd once been, spruced up with a coat of fresh white paint and new hardware. A new couch and TV stand—an antique sideboard from the shop's storage—had updated the whole feel of the place, but we'd kept the old rug, tying her back in with a thread that ran throughout the whole house.

I found Dad eating a bowl of Cheerios in the early morning light.

"Mornin'" he said around a full mouth. "Get any rest?"

"A little. We've got a big day today, but I'm not tired. Isn't it strange?"

He chuckled. "Passion will do that to you."

I smiled, thinking about Luke. "Funny how things change," I mused. "I never thought I'd enjoy it so much."

"It's easier to see, the older you get, the more seasons you endure. Everything is temporary, no matter how we try to fight it. But when we embrace the change, lean into it, the easier it is to endure. And the more fun it can be."

"Wise words."

"Another perk of surviving those seasons." He took another bite of his cereal. "How's it going with Luke?"

The question was thick with meaning. I hadn't told Dad about Luke and me yet, and with a deep breath, I decided now was as good a time as any. "Good, Daddy. Real good." I took a seat next to him. "I'm afraid I was wrong about him after all."

The corner of his lips flicked up in a half-smile. "You don't say?"

"I know," I said on a laugh. "He's been … well, he's been everything the shop needed. Everything I needed."

"It's about time you bit the bullet and told me. I've been waiting for that for weeks, ever since you came home, all googly about him tapping you to do the windows."

"Hey, I never said we were seeing each other," I teased.

He gave me a look. "Please, Pigeon. You think I don't know when you're seeing somebody?" A derisive laugh. "I've watched that boy puppy-dog after you for weeks, and I've been talking to Matilda about the promise you made to be wild." He nodded to Mom's monstrous ivy plant. "I'm glad you took a chance on him, Tess. And seeing you happy is the most I could have asked for. It's all I want for you."

I covered his hand with mine. "I've been happy," I argued softly.

"There's content, and there's happy. They are not one in the same. And Luke? Well, he makes you happy in ways I've never seen. It practically shoots out of your eyeballs."

I chuckled. "He does. He really does." But my smile faded. "Wendy just moved back. She showed up at the shop the other day, and … I don't know, Daddy. It was hard to witness. They have all this history that he and I don't have."

"Not just history, Tess. Baggage, and a moving truck full of it. I get the feeling Luke's not interested in her in any context. Am I wrong?"

"No, you're not wrong," I conceded even though the worry still scratched at my heart. "But she's unpredictable. And Luke doesn't know why she came back. I just … what if he goes back to her? What if she tells me something I don't want to know? Or tries to come between us? What if—"

"You can't live your life on what-ifs. You just can't. If I'd known I'd lose my legs, I don't know how I would have been brave. If your mother had known what would happen to her, she would have lived her entire life in fear, trying to figure out how to fight it. She wouldn't have lived, Tess. And neither can you, not if you devote yourself to your fear." He paused, turning his hand under mine to thread our fingers together. "Let me give you a little fatherly advice. Have faith. In yourself and your ability to adapt, to shift if something comes your way. In Luke, to be honest and to care for your heart. Has he ever given you a reason for anything less?"

"No."

"Then that's that, Pigeon. I know telling you not to worry is like telling a giraffe to stop having spots, but just remind yourself to *have faith*. You're already equipped to handle whatever life throws at you. Don't waste your time planning for a disaster that might not ever come."

I sighed, venting the pressure in my chest. "All right, Daddy."

He smiled, squeezing my hand before letting it go. "Now, go get to your list. I know you're already checking things off in your head."

"You know me well," I said, kissing his head. "Text me if you need me," I called over my shoulder as I headed for the door, knowing full well he wouldn't.

"You got it," he called back.

And then I was bounding down the stairs, full as I'd ever been on faith.

LUKE

We hadn't stopped moving for six hours.

Not as we moved from project to project, Ivy working her ass off in the back to keep up with orders while Tess and I made our way around the store. We'd hung up a few of the vertical succulent crates, built out frames for our next installation. Ate cold pizza in rounds— Tess ate as she directed me, and I ate as she fiddled with the floral wall, checking the water levels, pulling and replacing what needed freshening up.

I'd spent the last hour in storage, focused wholly on assembling a display piece made out of a dozen triangles that Tess wanted to plant with ferns and moss. When it was finished, I headed out of storage looking for her.

I found her digging determinedly through the buckets of flowers on one of the tables. Ivy watched her with concern.

Her hair was a little wild, worked loose in tendrils around her face, which was tight, brows furrowed. A huff left her, noisy and impatient as she moved to the next bucket.

"The search is over," I teased, spreading my arms in display.

She didn't even look up, never mind laugh. "There was an orchid in one of these buckets, and I can't find it."

I frowned. "An orchid?"

"Yes, and I need it."

I stepped up to the buckets and dug alongside her. "And what's so urgent that it hinges on this particular orchid?"

"I'm working on the bouquet that I'm going to *pretend* to work on when the editor comes in tomorrow, and I need that orchid!" She dove into the next bucket, too frantic to really see anything. "It's on my list, and I can't move to the next task until I find this orchid and put it where it belongs."

In three steps, I was in front of her, having wedged myself between her and the table.

She glared up at me. "Luke, what are you doing?"

"Getting you out of here," I answered, steering her toward the door.

"But I need that orchid!" she sputtered over her shoulder.

"Ivy will find it. Right, Ivy?"

"On it!" she called after us.

"See? She's on it."

Tess's lips flattened defiantly, digging in her heels like she could stop me, which was adorable. Her feet skipped as I kept walking.

"Luke, if I'm going to get all this done, I need to stay on schedule. I can't leave!"

"Yes, you can."

"No, I can't."

At that, I actually did stop, turning her to face me. "Tess, the world will not grind to a halt if you don't find that orchid."

"But—"

"What'd I tell you about buts?"

"No buts," she grumbled.

"We are leaving here, right now. We are going to get ice cream and walk to the park because you need to remember that a whole world is happening outside of this shop, all day, every day. You know, we have a saying among waiters—*Burgers and fries, nobody dies.*"

That earned me a hint of a smile and the smallest laugh ever known to man.

"This isn't brain surgery, Tess. It's a flower shop. We will get it all done, and it'll get done on time even if we have to stay all night to do it. It's not like we won't be here anyway," I said with a meaningful look.

One that softened her. I felt her relax when she sighed. "Fine. Ice cream and the park, but no lallygagging, okay?"

"Okay," I said with a smirk. "Are you going to come willingly, or do I need to throw you over my shoulder?"

Her eyes flicked to the ceiling, but she laughed. "I'm coming, I'm coming."

We headed out of the store, and though she didn't hesitate, I watched her gaze dart around the room, cataloging things she needed to do.

"Salted butterscotch or mint brownie?" I asked to distract her, pushing the door open.

Her roaming eyes found mine, stilling them so I could get her out of the store. "Hmm … butterscotch. It's too hot for chocolate."

"Is that a thing?"

Her brow rose. "Have you ever seen what happens to chocolate when it's hot?"

"That doesn't apply to ice cream. That's gonna melt whether it's hot out or not."

"It's heavy and thick, too thick for this kind of heat."

"It's ice cream, Tess. Its sole purpose is to cool you off."

But she shrugged. "Butterscotch today, hands down. In a sugar cone. And you're gonna get … dreamsicle. Waffle cone. With white chocolate sprinkles."

I laughed. "Well, that's the first time I've been accused of being predictable."

"Trust me, you're not. I just pay attention to things like that … my brain is full of all kinds of useless information like it. Regarding your ice cream preferences, you like dreamsicle when you're overwhelmed. Cherry chunk when you're happy—sugar cone. Fudge ripple when you're down or stressed."

"Huh. That's true, and I didn't even know it."

"I mean, not that you're down much. But you got fudge ripple with me after my mom died. And the day Wendy came back."

I sobered. "I'm still sorry for that."

"And you still have no reason to be. It's okay, Luke. I trust you. I'm just sorry you have to deal with the uncertainty. That would drive me nuts. I'd probably go looking for a confrontation just to have some sort of resolution."

"Confrontations with Wendy don't typically end well. Broken furniture or stitches maybe, but the fallout usually isn't worth the price paid."

We walked in silence for a moment, the heat beating down on us. It was oppressive, the weight of it. The weight of Wendy between us.

"She's always been like this?"

"As long as I've known her. But she didn't show it until after we were married. And then … well, she was my wife. I wanted to help her, take care of her. It just never got better. She would try for a while, but inevitably, it'd fall apart again. Mom likes to remind me I'm not responsible for her, but that's not how it feels. It feels like I'm the only one who can be responsible for her, including herself. How do you walk away from that? How do you turn your back on someone who can't help themselves, knowing you're the only one who can?"

"I don't know," she answered softly. "I don't know that I could either, not when you put it like that. But … well, at the same time, I hate her for what she did to you. For hurting you."

"Join the crowd. What nobody gets is that she can't help it."

Tess glanced at me.

"I know it sounds naive, but I mean it. I think I'm the only one who knows her. When you live with someone like that for so long, you know what's real and what isn't. Everything she feels, she feels it with all of her. Good or bad, high or low. She loved me, but she slept with another man. And I just couldn't get past that."

"Do you miss her?"

I paused, feeling guilty for knowing the answer was no, not able to lie and say yes. "Wendy isn't who I thought she was when I married her. I love her in the way you love a person for having endured something with them. But the truth is that our relationship wasn't built on trust or respect. It was built on fear and guilt. And that's not the kind of love I want."

"It's not the kind you deserve. You are too generous, too giving for a love that takes so much."

I reached for her hand, smiling down at her. "What happened to me being a lazy, selfish player?"

"I was wrong," she said with adoration on her face and a smile on her lips, a smile that I kissed away before pulling open the door to the ice cream shop.

We ordered our cones and headed back outside, turning for the park. I did my best not to watch her lick her cone like a perv, I swear. I failed miserably.

"Can you believe," she said around licks, "that you've been working at the shop all day, every day for weeks, and you haven't even gotten a rash or broken out in hives or anything?"

I laughed, glad to note that Tess couldn't quit watching my mouth either. "I know. I mean, we'll see how I feel in five months, but it's been good. I think because, even though I'm in the same place, every day is different. There's always something new to do, a new project to work on, a new problem to solve. It hasn't once felt like work, you know? Not like being a bank teller. I lasted one day. One."

"You? A bank teller?"

"It was a little death, Tess. I could feel the years ticking off my life with every second on that big, ugly clock. They put it right in front of you—I assume so you can keep tabs on your mortality."

It was her turn to laugh. "Listen, Ace—I'm pretty sure you could do anything you wanted to, what with being good at literally everything."

"I just said I was a terrible bank teller."

"I doubt you were bad at your job, just bad at staying at your job."

"I think the Santa Monica Bank and Trust would disagree. How about you?" I asked. "Do you want to work at the shop forever?"

"Yes," she answered without hesitation. "I've always wanted to be a permanent fixture at the shop, but …"

"But …" I prompted when she didn't continue.

"Well … I had this dream to publish my own book on floristry. A sort of how-to, basics on flower design, that kind of thing. I've been making notes and outlines for years."

"Why not pursue it?"

She shrugged. "I dunno. What if I fail?"

"You? Fail? Impossible."

A chuckle. "I'll do it someday."

"Promise?"

She bumped me with her arm. "Promise." She licked her ice cream. "Have you ever thought about contracting? You've been so good with our renovations, and you seem to really enjoy it."

I paused, considering it. "I do. It's the same as working in a shop in that every job is different. I would have kept helping out my buddy in California if something better hadn't come along."

We made it to the park, the arch proud and tall, the fountain bubbling. We stopped a ways off, taking in the sight.

"Do you always move on when something better comes along?" she asked quietly.

"Not always. When I commit, I go all in, Tess."

Tess looked up at me, her eyes soft and heart open. "All in?"

I slipped my free hand around her waist, pulling her into me. "All fucking in."

She reached for my face, and I granted her request, bending to press a kiss to her lips.

All in, all the way into my heart she found her way.

And I let her in without thinking twice.

Without thinking at all.

Fixer

TESS

There were few greater joys in life than watching Luke Bennet use power tools.

I'd walked out of my room to grab him and drag him to the shop for the meeting with the magazine editor. But watching him, all my plans—as well as my concept of time—fell out of my head like apples tumbling out of a sack.

He was up on a ladder, installing crown molding, his back rippling and sweating and dotted with sawdust. A pencil rested in the crook of his ear, his big, square hands holding a nail gun. His body jolted with every pop and hiss of the machine, his muscles flexing in sync as he braced for each nail.

A swooning sigh slid out of me, and for a second, I just stood there like a fool, watching him nail a board to a wall even though we were about to be late.

He reached for the corner, displaying his impressive wingspan, and popped the last nail into place before turning to climb down the ladder. He spotted me, smirking when he caught me gawking.

"I'd make a gun-show joke, but it feels too easy," he said, hopping off the last step with a crinkle of the plastic tarp he'd laid out.

"You should have gone for it," I said, smiling up at him as he approached. "Woulda worked on two levels."

He stole a quick kiss. "Time to go?"

I nodded, my smile fading. "I don't want to be late."

"The shop's ready. Everything's going to be perfect—don't worry."

"It's like you don't even know me."

"Or I do, and that's why it's my job to reassure you it's gonna be fine."

I gave him a look, fond and teasing, as I changed the subject. "Are you going to shower or show up shirtless and musky?"

He hooked my neck and brought my nose into his sweaty chest, my squealing and wiggling doing absolutely nothing to ease his grip. It was like trying to fight my way out of a giant's fist.

"You like my musky shirtlessness."

I swatted at him blindly, giggling. "I do, but not for a business meeting."

He kissed the top of my head and let me go. "I'll swing by the house and shower." He met my mighty frown with a sideways smile. "Seriously, don't worry. Give me ten minutes—I'll be ready to roll and musk-free, on time and as promised."

I eyed him. "A ten-minute shower?"

"No, a four-minute shower and six minutes to pick out my outfit."

I followed him toward the door, calling my goodbye at Dad over my shoulder.

When we stepped out, I asked, "How do you take a shower in under five minutes?"

He shrugged, stuffing the hem of his shirt into his back pocket rather than putting it on. "Any longer than that, and you're just masturbating."

A laugh burst past my lips.

We trotted down the stairs, leaving the little elevator for old Mrs. Reynolds upstairs and Dad.

"You nervous?" he asked as we stepped out into the heat.

"Are you kidding? I had a nightmare last night that all the flowers died overnight, and the editor laughed us out of town."

He chuckled. "She's just coming to look around. Don't worry, Tess."

"You keep saying that like it's actually going to make me stop worrying."

Luke grabbed my hand, looking down at me with that smile of his, the one that made it seem like nothing could ever go wrong, nothing in the whole world.

"Do you trust me?" he asked, already knowing the answer.

I sighed. "I do."

"Then let me worry for the both of us."

He squeezed my hand, which was lost somewhere inside of his. And for a second, I did.

We kissed goodbye at his front stoop, and he darted up the stairs and disappeared inside. As for me, well, I headed into the shop and immediately started worrying again. I worried over the installation. I worried over the front display table. I worried over the arrangement I'd started with the full intent of finishing it only once I had an audience. Ivy watched me, teased me a little, but let me fuss.

It just made me feel better. Idle hands and all that.

Twelve minutes later, Luke was downstairs, his black hair damp and rutted from his fingers. When he kissed me, he smelled like soap and tasted like mint, and the combination made me wish he were shirtless again.

But alas, the bell over the door rang. And when we turned, it was to find a woman who seemed only a little older than us, looking smart in a pencil skirt and tailored shirt, assistant at her side.

I followed Luke out into the shop, the two of us giddy and smiling.

She stuck out her hand, smiling broadly back at us. "Good to see you, Luke."

"Natalie. Thanks for coming. This is Tess Monroe, our head of design and production and the mastermind behind the window installations."

I almost laughed—my title sounded so official. "It's nice to meet you, Natalie," I said, offering my hand, which she took and pumped.

"You too. The space is gorgeous. You say it's been in the family since 1849?"

Luke nodded proudly. "A long line of women have passed Longbourne down to their daughters."

"Until now," she said on a chuckle. "Now it would seem the majority shareholders are male."

"The bane of my poor mother's life, I assure you," he teased. "If only she could have bred a pack of girls instead. We'd be easier to marry off, I'm sure."

Another laugh. God, he was charming. A snap of his fingers, a flash of that smile, and the world was at Luke Bennet's feet.

"I'm sure you have no issues getting dates, Mr. Bennet." There was a tone to her voice that made my eyes narrow.

"But few would have the constitution to deal with us long-term. Only the strongest and most willful of women could tame the Bennet brothers." He slipped an arm around my waist, still smiling that million-dollar smile. "Trust me when I say we're all counting the minutes until Tess figures out she's too good for me."

I blushed like a teenager, chuckling up at him. But I wound my arm around his waist and leaned in. He gave my hip a squeeze.

Natalie smiled amiably, a little embarrassed and with the understanding that her place had just been noted. "Well, with talent like she has for flowers, I can see why. Tess, can you tell me about the installation, your process, that sort of thing? And then can I get the tour?"

"Of course," I said, sliding away from Luke to head toward the windows.

I walked her through the concept, how we had come up with it, the work Luke and I had done together. I showed her through the shop, answering the multitude of questions she had. And back into the workspace we went, where she met Ivy and doted on the arrangement I'd been working on, poppies and pods and chrysanthemums in shades of orange. I'd ditched the orchid once I had a little distance and with the visual of Luke making out with a dreamsicle ice cream cone on my mind.

Natalie asked all the right questions. She was knowledgeable and inquisitive, and I found I liked her very much. Luke followed us silently, letting me take the lead like he always did.

When she asked to see the greenhouse, Luke ushered her away, winking at me over his shoulder on the way out. And Ivy and I waved, shooting him a thumbs-up.

This is it, I thought, adding flowers to the vase in front of me without seeing anything.

National recognition. We were about to break out in a way we hadn't in fifty years.

And it was all thanks to Luke.

Everything was.

LUKE

I walked Natalie through the greenhouse, showing her our new setup to accommodate our higher yield. She met Dad and Kash and, last but certainly not least, our matriarch.

She was blissfully charming for the five minutes we'd allotted for her—after that, my mother tended to nervous-talk the ear off of whoever'd stumbled into her.

In five-minute increments, she could rule the world.

Natalie seemed impressed, smiling and engaging and audibly gasping when she walked into the greenhouse. She asked a hundred questions and wandered through the rows of teeming blooms, occasionally bending to bring her nose to a bud.

It'd been a banner meeting, by my estimation.

"So," I started, opening the swinging doors separating the greenhouse from the workspace, "what do you think?"

"I think Floral would love to do a piece on Longbourne," she answered with a smile.

Tess and Ivy perked up from their table, smiling.

Natalie scrolled through her calendar on her phone. "Our next feature spot is for November. Do you think you'd be willing to do a fall window for the shoot?"

I glanced at Tess for confirmation, and she nodded emphatically.

"Absolutely," I said.

"Great," Natalie answered, clicking away at her calendar. "Tomorrow?"

Tess stilled, her smile dropping into an O.

"Tomorrow?" I echoed stupidly.

"I know. It's an insane request. Our planned feature fell through, and I've got to fill the spot now. I have another florist who might be able to do it, but I'd much prefer to feature Longbourne. The history, the fact that you grow your own flowers, the part you play in the neighborhood...it's just such a great story, one I think our readers would really connect with. But I understand if you can't get it done in time. Our next open spot would be ..." She paused, scrolling through her phone. "March."

Tess looked like she'd been electrocuted, but she nodded once.

"We'll do it," I said.

Natalie smiled. "Perfect. I'll be here tomorrow at seven. We've got to get the morning light for the front of the shop." And with that, she was heading for the door to the click of her heels on the concrete.

When I walked her out, I hurried back to Tess, wondering how the fuck we were going to come up with a concept, get supplies, and build an installation in less than twenty-four hours.

Tess did not look any more confident than I felt.

She chewed on her lip, her brows knit together and face scrunched in thought. "A fall window. In August."

"We can't get gourds or anything that will be in season."

"No. It's going to have to be by color. Warm oranges, yellows. Wheat, dried pampas. What if …" she started, brightening up. "What if we took one of the pole frames, like the one we used for the rain and shine display, and hung dried pampas grass by the stalk? Hang them close together, use dyed twine. Maybe in a rust." Her pace picked up, excited. "We can hang them like a wave or at angles. Oh! At angles! Almost to make a triangle if you were standing in front of the shop. Oh—*oh*! We could use different shades of twine from brown to rust to orange to mustard in shades, so it fades from one color to another."

I could see it and smiled. "Yes. And we have almost everything we need. But …" I frowned. "Will it be enough?"

"No." She deflated for a beat before popping up straight, beaming. "Wheat fields."

She grabbed her notebook from the table and doodled. Ivy and I leaned over her shoulder.

"We can make frames, like this." She drew a rectangle. "Chicken wire inside. Take the wheat in bunches and make a field and angle and twist them so it looks like the wind is blowing through in a current. And on the display table—gosh, even under it—we can use the old rain boots and fill them with sunflowers."

"It's genius," Ivy said, grinning ear to ear. "What do we need?"

Tess's mouth quirked as she nibbled on her lip again. "A shitload of wheat. I have a bundle of dried pampas, but I think I'll need some more. And twine. Lots and lots of twine."

I nodded. "I know where to get the grasses and more sunflowers. What about the twine?"

"There's a fiber shop a few blocks from here," Tess said. "I'm positive they'll have what we need."

"All right. I've got to go—if I don't leave now and the supply store doesn't have what I need, I'm gonna have to run around. Are you guys good until I get back?"

Tess nodded, smiling. "This is simple and bold enough, it just might work."

"It will definitely work," I assured her, pulling her into my arms. "I promise."

And I stole a kiss before bounding out the door to make it happen.

It was nearly dark by the time I was heading back to the shop. I'd been on a runaround from hell in the delivery truck, looking for sunflowers that weren't worm-eaten or withering. Thank God we'd closed orders for the day, only selling our stock and taking orders for tomorrow, knowing it would take us all night to get the windows ready and the shop prepared for the shoot.

It was madness, the whole thing. But we would do it. I had no doubt of that.

Tess and I had been in communication all day with updates via text. Jett and Kash had helped her break down the installment and hang the frames I'd built for another installation. The four of them had cut a couple hundred lengths of fiber and tied all the pampas she had, and I was on my way back with the rest while they got the shop ready. And once I was back, we just needed a handful of hours and a whole lot of hands to tie what was left, hang the poles, and stuff the frames I'd build for the wheat.

My phone buzzed in my pocket, and I pulled it out, expecting a dinner order from Tess.

What I found was a text from Wendy.

It was long, too long to read at a glance. I skimmed it at a light, and fear gripped me, cold and merciless. Words jumped out at me: *can't, hurts, alone, how, please.*

I need to see you. I don't know what I'll do if I don't.

I glanced at the time. I was close to her parents' place … I could swing by, though I wondered how quickly I could get back out. I didn't want to go—the dread I felt at engaging was deep and fierce— but if I didn't, I wasn't sure what she'd do. Mix substances and hurt herself. Come to the shop and find me.

I thought through a dozen scenarios, and this was the only one that gave me control. I had to answer the call. I had to go.

I fired off a text to Tess. Gonna be a minute. *You guys good?*

My phone buzzed a second later. *We're good. Got plenty to do. Everything okay?*

I drew a deep, disturbed breath and lied. *Yeah, everything's good. I'll text when I'm on my way.*

All right. See you soon. <3

I tossed my phone in the passenger seat, my jaw ticking and brows drawn.

I'd lied. Because how could I tell her over a text where I was going? How could I have told her at all with everything on her plate tonight?

No. I'd tell her tomorrow when all this was behind us. We could come up with a plan for dealing with Wendy, one we were both comfortable with. Because I couldn't abandon Wendy.

But I would not lose Tess.

By the time I pulled up in front of Wendy's building, a dark cloud had settled over Manhattan with the fall of the sun. The metallic scent of rain hung in the air, charged and ready to unleash. And I hurried up the stairs, not knowing what I'd find.

The meat of my hand thumped the door in three thundering bursts. And I waited.

The door flew open, and Wendy stood in the doorway.

Relief broke over her face, mottled and tearstained and shining. "You came," she breathed, the words hoarse and cracked.

And she threw herself into my arms.

I caught her, my face tight and mind sharp. "What happened?" I asked.

Her hands fisted my shirt, her forehead pressed to my chest. "Nothing. Everything."

Exhausted. Depleted. Stretched out and paper thin was the woman in my arms.

I stepped her inside, closed the door as the rain began to fall in fat splats, pinging the window like hail. A glance into her mother's room informed me she was passed out—half off the bed, clothes twisted around her, her chest rising and falling in that slow rhythm of sleep made slower by booze or pills. Or both.

It was six-thirty.

Wendy crumpled in my arms.

"Whoa there," I muttered, scooping her up to carry her to her bedroom.

The apartment seemed smaller than I remembered, older. Stained and fading. But her room was the same—tiny and bright, the only cheer in this dismal place.

I set her on her sagging bed and knelt at her feet.

"You came." She still beamed as heavy tears rolled down the curve of her cheekbone.

I wondered if she had taken something, wondered how long it had been since she ate.

"Tell me what happened."

"I needed you, and you came. You always do." She chuckled, looking down at her hands. But her smile broke into a sob. "Everything's falling apart, Luke. You're the only one who can put it back together."

"What are you talking about?" I asked gently, knowing this place, this space, this nonsensical circle we'd ride until she came around to it.

She brightened, framing my face with her hands. "Let's run away."

As weak as she seemed, I was surprised at how quickly she'd bounded off the bed to fling open her closet and pull out a suitcase.

I watched, dumbfounded.

"Where do you want to go?" she asked, opening a drawer and scooping an armful of its contents into the suitcase. "We can go anywhere. Seattle maybe. Denver? There's such good hiking there. Think of all the hikes, Luke."

I stood, intercepting her as she brought another load to her suitcase. I clasped her upper arms. "Wendy," I said calmly, "we're not going anywhere."

Her face bent in anger. She unceremoniously dropped the haul of clothes on our feet. "Why not? Luke, you love me. I know you do, that's why you came. And I love you. It's always been you. I know I fucked up. I know I'm crazy, and I hurt you over and over without meaning to. Without understanding why. Why do I do this?" And her anger was gone, replaced by misery.

"I don't know," I said softly.

"But you always know how to make it better. So let me fix this. Let me make it right. Come with me, Luke. Let's start over." Her hands slid up my chest, and she leaned in like she wanted me to kiss her.

I grabbed her hands. "No."

Confusion flickered across her face. "But you love me."

Sadness, guilt. Not for what I'd lost, but for what I was about to do to her. "There's no fixing what's broken between us ... that's not why I'm here. It's because I'm worried about you, not because I love you."

Another tear, heavy enough to fall without touching her face. "But you have to," she whispered.

"I'm in love with someone else."

A gasp shot her back, then into me again, her hands pounding my chest, face wrenched. "No! You can't. You don't."

I grabbed her wrists and locked them in my fists. "I do," I said sternly, lowering my face to look into her eyes. "I've moved on, Wendy. And there's no going back."

"No," she moaned, sinking to the ground, "*no, no, no.*"

There was nothing to do but catch her, hold her to me, let her cry. "I'm sorry," I said, my heart so tight, I thought it would fold in on itself.

Her fingers tightened, twisting my shirt, her forehead pressed to the dip in my chest, her tears soaking the fabric, warm and then cool as she caught her breath.

My hand shifted on her back, my hope emerging that this was it. That it'd been that simple.

And then she spoke two words that shattered my hope like exactly what it was—an illusion.

"I'm pregnant," she whispered into my shirt, into the space just above my heart.

The world shrank to that room, to the trembling woman in my arms, to the screeching of my mind, the thundering of my heart.

"What?" I breathed.

"I'm pregnant." The admission was miserable, broken and frayed.

"I'm pregnant with your baby."

My constricted heart blew open like shrapnel, shredding everything in its path.

"Tell me everything," I said.

And silently, I listened as she decimated my world once more.

Fool

TESS

Laughter rang through the shop in the early morning light, the tired sound of relief and victory from the Bennet brood.

The whole family was in the shop eating donuts from Blanche's, sipping coffee and trying to keep our eyes open. Luke smiled at me from across the room, filling my heart with fluttering whispers.

He'd come back to the shop quiet and withdrawn, heading straight into storage to start on the frames for the wheat fields. Down I went to check on him once, finding him sullen. A hug softened him, a kiss earned me a smile, small though it was. It'd been a long day, he noted, said he'd tell me about it after the editor. But when he said it, his eyes were touched with pain, regret. Fear.

I tried not to let that fear get on me—we had too much to do. And I trusted him. There was no reason not to. He'd tell me everything when this was behind us, and that was enough for me.

So I threw myself back into work.

It had taken us nearly all night to get it done, the lot of us breaking to shower and change.

Luke had brought boxes of donuts and a cardboard crate of coffee from Blanche's like the savior he was. And we were just nibbling, waiting on the editor to arrive with her photographer.

Luke made his way over to where I sat on the register counter, smiling that smile of his. But his eyes were tired, exhausted beyond the lack of sleep. Whatever was troubling him had mellowed enough from last night that he was almost acting himself.

Almost.

From my perch, I was a little taller than him, and when he looked up at me, all I wanted to do was hold his jaw and kiss him. My hands and lips tingled with the desire to, but I stayed still other than the raising of my paper coffee cup.

"We did it." I beamed.

He tapped his lid to mine. "It's beautiful, Tess. Just when I think you can't outdo yourself, you do."

"Funny, I think that every day about you. We're just full of surprises, aren't we?"

His smile faltered, his blue eyes darkening. Something about the motion—the parting of his lips, the draw of his brows, the creases of his face—sent a shock through me. I braced myself for impact.

Before he could speak, the bell over the door rang.

I looked up with a rush of excitement and a bright smile, expecting Natalie. But I found Wendy instead.

She looked like a different woman than the one who had come in here a few weeks ago, fresh and effortless, like she'd stepped out of an ad of a magazine. This Wendy was almost unrecognizable. Her blonde hair was dirty at the roots, dark and tangled up in a bun that looked like it had been slept on. The puff of her lids, the dark circles beneath, made her eyes look sunken and small, but they were bright, feverish, sharp with worry. Somehow, she managed to make a rumpled, oversized white T-shirt and leggings look stylish, but everything about her was frenetic, buzzing, humming, static electricity clinging to her, carrying her.

The shop went silent.

"Luke," she croaked, tears streaming down her face at the sight of him. Her lips were dry. Pale.

My heartbeat doubled.

"Wendy, you can't be here right now," he said as he flew across the room toward her, the words both hard and comforting.

"We need to talk about this," she begged, her face wrenched. "We have to figure this out."

He snagged her by the arm and tried to steer her out. "I told you, we will. But the magazine will be here any minute, and I—"

"Figure what out?" Mrs. Bennet asked in a tone that stopped him dead.

Wendy laid a hand on her stomach, watery smile on her face as she said, "I'm pregnant."

The room was silent again for a protracted moment before every voice in the room exploded.

Every voice but mine.

I folded in on myself, unable to parse what I'd heard. Wendy, hand on her belly and eyes adoring as she gazed up at Luke. My Luke, his eyes locked on mine, the heartbreak and apology on his face unmasked and raw.

Pregnant. She was pregnant. And judging by the look on his face, that baby was his.

Mrs. Bennet had started to cry, her voice high as she fired questions at him like a machine gun. Mr. Bennet had a hold of her arm, lips at her ear. Laney looked like she was about to claw Wendy's eyes out, but Jett stood in front of her as she yelled around his wide shoulders. Marcus's face was drawn, and though his lips were moving, he couldn't be heard over the din. Kash had stepped toward them, but he wasn't yelling at Wendy. He was yelling what seemed to be a string of obscenities at Luke.

Ivy stood at my side, repeating, "Oh my God," on a loop, hands on her face and eyes big as ping-pong balls.

And I was somewhere separate, somewhere other.

A baby. Luke was having a baby with Wendy. She wouldn't go away, wouldn't disappear. He'd never escape her. She'd be a constant presence in his life.

In mine.

"Excuse me!" we heard over the din, and the room fell silent once more.

Natalie glanced around, her face hard from the doorway. Everyone held their breath.

"Is now a bad time?" she asked pointedly.

God bless Ivy Parker, who snapped into action. "No, of course not! Please, come in. Give us just a minute. We have donuts and coffee!" She hurried to Natalie's side to divert her.

Natalie cast a dubious look around the establishment as Luke quietly excused himself and steered Wendy out of the building. I didn't hear anything anyone around me said. Instead, I watched them talk outside the window. Luke's face drawn and haggard, his hands on her shoulders as he tried to talk her down. Wendy looked down, nodding, her chest occasionally hitching with a sob and hands taking turns swiping at her cheeks.

But what broke me completely was when he pulled her into his arms, holding her head to his chest. His eyes closed, tight with pain, his head bowed as if in prayer. And Wendy curled into him like she belonged there.

I didn't realize I was crying, not until Laney touched my leg. Her brows were together, her face tight with concern.

I sniffled, brushing the cool trails of tears from my face.

"He doesn't love her," Laney said.

"I know." And I did.

"I'm not even sure I believe her, Tess. But Luke will figure it out. And if it is true, we'll get through it. He'll make it right."

"I know," I said again. Because he would.

I just didn't know how I fit into that picture. I imagined him shepherding her through her pregnancy, attending all the doctor's visits. The bond they shared would deepen. Would it rekindle their affection? Would they fall in love again?

Would he leave me for her?

It was too much. The room too small. The air too thin. Too many people, too many pressures, all in one room.

"Are you going to be okay?"

I nodded, sliding off the counter, my shoes full of lead. "Let's just get through this."

Laney nodded, taking my hand, squeezing it gently.

I didn't feel anything.

Luke entered the shop, and what little breath I had was sucked into him like a vacuum. He moved across the room to me like we were caught in a tractor beam, my awareness shrinking yet again.

"Tess," he breathed.

He was touching me, I realized absently, the pressure of his hands on my arms distant.

I looked up at him, unseeing.

His eyes searched mine. "Please, say something." Those hands moved from my arms to my face, tilting it up to his. "We'll figure this out," he promised.

"So it's true then."

Fear. I could feel it skating on his fingertips.

"I don't know. There ... there hasn't been time. Please, Tess, let me explain—"

"You've been keeping this from me too, Lucas?" Mrs. Bennet's voice was shrill, her face ruddy.

Natalie glanced over her shoulder at us, but Ivy laughed too loudly, hooking her arm in Natalie's to direct her outside where her photographer was setting up.

Mrs. Bennet's eyes shone with furious tears. "What else have you not told me?"

"Mom, I—"

"A baby. With *her*. Of all the irresponsible, thoughtless things you could do. After all she's done, after you finally were free, and now *this*? You knew she was trouble. You knew it, and you went back. And here we are. She will never let you go, Lucas. Never. You handed her all she needed to take advantage of you forever. *Forever*." Her face bent, her twisted hand pressing to her lips. And she turned away, found her way into Mr. Bennet's arms.

He guided her away to the back with an apologetic, disappointed look on his face.

Luke had let me go, his hands covering his face and fingers pressing into his eyes. And I just stood there, stunned still and silent.

I watched through the front window. Marcus had gone out front to try to smooth things over. Kash trailed after his mother, probably to plead a case for Luke. Jett and Laney were head to head, speaking in hushed whispers in that way twins sometimes did.

It felt like a dream, my body and mind too tired to process the madness of what was happening. All I wanted was to wake up. Or fast-forward. Or go to bed. Or be anywhere but standing in this shop next to Luke Bennet.

I opened my mouth to excuse myself so I could retreat, to find a place where I could catch my breath, quiet my mind.

But before I could speak, a pop shot through the room, followed by a groan, a snap.

A crash.

Our faces snapped to the sound, every person in the room frozen still as everything happened in slow motion. One of the installations came unfastened, the pole the pampas was tied to falling into the wheat with a crunch and a thump, crushing it.

Crushing everything.

We ran toward it as everyone outside ran in. Luke reached it first, inspecting the end of the pole that had fallen, looking up with his brows gathered. Tears pricked my eyes, seized my heart with a squeeze of my ribs.

The rope it had been fastened with was in his hand. "It's wet."

Down the rope his hand moved, to the pole. When he picked it up, my hand flew to my mouth as I took in the carnage.

The dyed fibers had gotten wet, the colors bleeding onto the wheat it had touched. That wheat was crushed, the stalks smashed and bent, with a myriad of color in senseless streaks across the feathery heads.

It was ruined. There would be no salvaging it.

"I can fix this." Luke made another promise he couldn't keep, a frantic, thoughtless promise. He grabbed one of the ladders from behind the counter and popped it open.

"Stop, Luke," I said. "Just … don't touch it."

"I can fix this, Tess," he said, determined.

"No. It can't be fixed. You're just going to break it worse. We need another ladder. We need to move the wheat. We need to—"

"No," he insisted, rope in hand as he climbed the ladder. "Look, there's a leak. Marcus, call the plumber."

Marcus's phone was already in hand.

"If I just screw it in here instead—"

"Just leave it alone," I snapped. "You're not helping, Luke! It's just going to—"

"For fuck's sake, Tess, *I've got it*," he snapped back, glaring at me.

Another groan, a snap. The lot of us yelped and jumped back, narrowly avoiding the other side of the installation falling in a poof of dust and wheat.

We stared silently at the wreckage for a long, breathless moment. Everything we'd worked for, all we'd done…gone.

The installation. My relationship. My heart.

Gone.

In its place rose a wave of frustrated fury, and I leaned into it as I looked up at him.

"I told you not to touch it." The words trembled, quiet and contained. "But you just did whatever you wanted. You didn't listen to anyone but yourself. Just like always."

"I was trying to help. I was trying to make it right. I didn't do this, Tess. I didn't force a leak. I didn't make it fall. I didn't *do* this."

"No, you're right. You're innocent, as always. It's never your fault. Nothing—*nothing*—is ever your fault," I snapped.

Natalie interjected, her voice hard, "It's clear that we're off for today. I know I put a difficult timeframe on you, and you delivered something truly outstanding. But there is no way for me to shoot this, and I'm not certain you can conduct yourselves in a way that we'll be able to photograph you all and the rest of the shop. I need to talk to my team, figure out what to do. We'll be in touch."

Luke hurried down from the ladder. "Natalie, please. Wait."

He hopped down, following her as she hauled ass out of the shop. I watched them talk on the sidewalk—Natalie stern and closed, Luke pleading. With a narrowing of her eyes and a curt nod, they parted.

The second he started for the door, I started for the back.

Because I couldn't. I couldn't face him. I couldn't control my tears. I couldn't understand what had happened with the shoot, with the shop, with Luke. And I couldn't fathom what would come.

All I knew was that I needed to get somewhere safer than this in order to figure it out.

He called after me. I didn't stop. I'd leave through the back. Go home. Pray Dad wasn't awake. I'd climb into my bed and stay there until my tears were dry and I had a plan.

"Tess," Luke called again, closer.

I picked up my pace.

"Tess, *stop*." He hooked his hand in my elbow and pulled me to a stop.

"Let me go." With a whirl and a snap, I removed my arm from his grip, glaring up at him through angry tears.

"Please, let me explain."

"You were with her last night. That's why you came back here so upset."

A sorrowful nod. "I was going to tell you tonight. We had to get the installation done, and—"

"Bullshit, Luke. She's why you were late. You should have told me. If you had told me, I wouldn't have been blindsided. I could have prepared myself for this, but now … now…" My throat closed, choking off the words.

His dark brows came together. "I should have called you in the middle of all this and told you I was going to Wendy's? That I didn't know what she'd do to herself if I didn't? What was I supposed to do, Tess? And then … then she told me … she told me she's…" The words died in his throat.

He couldn't even say it, and in that moment, I wanted to feel sorry for him. I wanted to understand.

But I couldn't. It was too fresh, too raw, and I was too tired to be reasonable or logical.

"I can't do this," I said, my voice broken.

And his face crumpled. "Do this? With me?"

I shook my head. "I can't talk about this right now. I can't. There's nothing I can say, no way I can be rational. I … I need … I need to think and I need to try to understand and I need to get away from you to do that."

He searched my face, took my hands, and I let him, too tired to fight. "This happened before you, before I left LA—"

"Stop," I sobbed, removing my hands from his. "Please. I don't … I don't want to know the details. Not yet, not when I just…"

"Tell me it's going to be all right. Tell me you trust me still."

"I … I can't."

He stilled. "Because you don't?"

"Because I don't know."

Something cracked behind his eyes. "I don't love her, Tess. And she knows I'm in love with someone else."

My eyes widened, locking on his. I was made of stone. "Luke, do not finish that thought. Do not say those words right now." Shaky words. Shaking hands. Knees locked. Feet stuck.

The knot of his throat rose and fell. A nod, small and resigned. His gaze fell to the ground.

And I did the only thing I could.

I turned and ran.

Heart Burn

LUKE

I watched my heart walk out the door.

A space in my chest opened up, empty but for tingling static, sharp with electricity, frenetic and edged with pain. One day ago, my life had been on a different trajectory, one lit with hope and possibility. Twenty-four hours ago, my biggest concern had been a sunflower supplier and the length of time I'd have to endure before I could hold Tess.

Now I'd lost her.

She needed time—unsurprising, as well as I knew Tess—time to get her bearings, to figure out what she thought, how she felt about the succession of bombs that had detonated. But I couldn't shake the feeling that time would not fix this. Time wouldn't reverse the impact. It wouldn't change the fact that Wendy was pregnant.

I couldn't imagine how it'd happened—Wendy'd been on birth control since I'd known her. But the why and how of it didn't matter. Everything had changed with the knowledge, and everything had fallen apart with Wendy's announcement.

And now, Tess was gone. The magazine shot was potentially ruined. My family was upside down. All because of me.

So I'd have to fix it all. Starting with what I could.

I turned, heading numbly into the shop where my siblings were busy disassembling the broken installation with flat lips and drawn brows and far too much silence for the number of Bennets in one room. They glanced up as I entered the room, pausing and gathering around when I stopped. Accusation weighed heavy on their faces.

With a painful swallow, I started with the first and most important thing.

"I'm sorry."

I don't know if it was the sight of me or the tone of those two little words, but their faces softened in unison.

I shook my head, glancing at the ground. "She told me last night. I was going to tell you guys as soon as I talked to Tess and this meeting was done. I thought I had at least that long. Should have known better."

Laney shifted at my side and laid her small hand on my arm. "Luke … how did you get yourself into this mess?"

I tried to swallow the stone in my throat. "We went out before I left LA. She … she's always been on birth control, so I didn't think to…"

Laney and Jett shared a look, but it was Marcus who said what they all seemed to be thinking.

"Do you think she did this on purpose? To trap you?"

"I can't believe you'd even say that," I snapped.

"Come on, Luke," he urged. "It's not an unreasonable assumption. The shop is doing better—"

"That wasn't the case when we slept together."

"Are you sure she's even really pregnant?" Laney asked.

"She wouldn't lie about being pregnant."

"Why not? Fake a miscarriage. Get out from under the lie, but lock you down first," she postulated.

A defensive wind blew through me, hot and bitter. "I know you all think she's conniving and predatory, but it's not the truth, and deep down, you know it. I know you want to protect me, but villainizing her, making up your own story? That doesn't help any of us. I'll be the first to admit that she would use me—trust me, of all of us, it's *me* who has a front row seat to that particular truth. But there are things she would lie about and things she wouldn't. Trust me. Please, trust me."

None of them looked convinced.

"Okay, let's assume she's pregnant then," Kash said. "Are you sure it's yours?" He glanced at our siblings, adding, "She had a boyfriend she conveniently failed to mention until *after* she slept with Luke."

Outrage and hope sparked in the room, a strange, heavy combination of emotions. A couple of curses. Half-smile here and there. A disbelieving, scoffing laugh under someone's breath.

I stood in the center of them, numb.

In the hours I'd spent in solitude last night, I'd worked it all out, knowing it could go either way. Her story made sense, timeline-wise. It explained Wendy's coming back, her insistence to see me. I took that information, applied it to the opposite—maybe it wasn't mine, and she'd made the whole thing up to trap me. And then I'd accepted both possibilities as best I could, packing it away so I could focus on this meeting, the ruins of which lay in crumpled piles in the window.

I scrubbed a hand over my face. Sighed with a breath drawn from the very bottom of my lungs. "It's possible. I don't know when she's due or how far along she is. She was hysterical when she told me, and I had to get back to the shop with supplies. There was no time to get into it. And today ... well, you saw how much was accomplished today."

Marcus's face darkened. "You need to nail this down and get confirmation from a doctor. I know you want to believe her, but—"

"I *don't* want to believe her, Marcus. I don't want this to be true, not with her, not like this. If it is, you know I won't walk away. But I'm under no illusions when it comes to Wendy or her intentions, especially when her back's against the wall. I have something to do with why she's back, and either it's because I'm the father of her child or because she wants me to be."

Laney shook her head. "God, if she lied … Luke, this is so fucked up. And Tess…"

Pain split my chest in two at the mention of her name. "I know."

Jett's brows were drawn. "What about the magazine? Do you think you can patch that up?"

"Not until I hear from them. I'll try to reach out in a few days, but I can't force them to give me another chance any more than I can Tess. Time and space. That's all I've got to work with. And in the meantime, I'll figure out exactly what's going on with Wendy."

"You're gonna have to deal with Mom too," Kash added.

Everyone sighed at that, even Marcus.

"You committed the cardinal sin," Laney noted. "You slept with Wendy, and Mom will see that as a personal betrayal. She's probably wondering what she did wrong when you were a baby that you'd sleep with Wendy after all she's done to you."

"I'll talk to her tonight, after she burns an effigy and cries over my baby pictures."

"And how are you planning on avoiding her *and* Tess?" Marcus asked.

"You act like avoiding things isn't a special skill of mine." A chuckle rolled through them, but I didn't so much as smile. "I'll stay here all day. I've got the installation to figure out, or at least break down. See if I can get another one put together with stuff we have in storage. That should take me all day. I don't suspect anyone will bother me. The only one who wants to talk to me is the one person I don't want to see."

"Wendy. Goddamn her," Laney said with a shake of her head. "How can we help?"

"Just keep the front running so I can salvage what I can, where I can."

We broke the meeting with a plan—Kash and Jett would finish breaking down the installations. Laney would check on Mom. Marcus would get the rest of the store ready to open.

And I would escape to the back.

The second I could, I did, dragging myself to storage. I clicked on the lights to assess our stock, but when I looked around at the space—our space, mine and hers—I felt the last bit of my will crack and shatter. The pieces we'd worked on. The old rocking chair with the blanket slung over the back. The pile of hay.

I lowered myself to sit in the hay, dropping my head to my hands, closing the world out. The familiar scent of this place, like old wood and sweet hay and fragrant florals drifting in from the greenhouse. It wasn't a realization of my mistakes, and it wasn't a marker of loss.

Because I'd known what I had to lose from the start.

And despite how I'd tried to keep her, I might have lost Tess for good.

TESS

I bolted out the back door, blinded by the sun and drowning in the heat. The block I traveled home was navigated through a sheet of tears, my destination in my forethought and a thousand emotions bubbling beneath it.

Just get home. Get home. Get home. When you get home, then you can break.

The stairwell was cool and dark, my composure crumbling with every step. I unlocked the door. Stepped inside.

The one place in the world I needed was home, and the picture of this place was tangible in my mind.

A picture that no longer existed.

The walls were white but for the accent wall of Mom's ugly, old wallpaper. The kitchen, white and pristine, Carrera marble countertops to replace the old pea-soup formica, backed by subway tile.

It was beautiful. But it wasn't home, not anymore.

Everything had changed. And all because of Luke.

Before he'd come back, everything had been perfectly normal, perfectly predictable. But ever since he'd walked through the door of Longbourne again, it had been nothing but chaos. What had once been stable, secure, familiar, was turned upside down, inside out. The shop. My home.

My heart.

I couldn't look at the room. I needed my place, my safe place, the one place I knew hadn't changed.

"Tess?" Dad called from his study. "That you?"

It wasn't me. I didn't know who I even was anymore.

But I followed the sound of his voice to face what I could. When I passed the threshold, his face ran a gamut of emotions—concern, sadness, pain, anger.

"What happened?" he asked.

I drew a shaky breath. "The installation broke. We didn't get the feature."

"Oh, honey. I'm so sorry."

A weak smile touched my lips, forced and aching with falsity. "I … I just need some time. Rest."

He nodded. "All right. Go shower and sleep. I'm here. Okay, Pigeon?"

I nodded, my chin quivering. "Okay, Daddy."

But when I stepped into the hallway, I didn't head to the other side of the apartment for my room.

I turned for Dad's room instead.

This room was the same as it had always been. The book she'd been reading when she died still sat on the nightstand. The bedding had faded and thinned, but it was the same navy-blue and white florals, the bed neatly made with care by Dad every day. But I didn't linger. Instead, I opened the closet, dropping to sit in the small corner, closing the door behind me.

Light snuck in through the slats of the shutters, slashing lines of light on everything inside.

And I laid my head on my knees and cried for all I'd lost.

Empty Spaces

TESS

My exhaustion was complete.

I was a fire that had burned to ash, leaving only dust and dying embers. What had once been solid was now in pieces small enough to be carried away by nothing more than a gentle breeze. But somehow, I found a way to haul myself out of bed that morning. To dress and brush my teeth, bleary-eyed and numb. To exchange a few words of deflection with my father before ducking out the front door. And I went down to the flower shop, not ready to face what awaited me, but without any choice in the matter.

The shop needed me, and so did Mrs. Bennet.

I'd spent a long time in the safety of Mom's closet, exhausting my tears long enough to shower and slide into bed. But as tired as I was, I barely slept, my mind too frantic, too busy fantasizing about all the unhappy endings that could come to pass, all the things I would lose in their wake. It was only between fits of crying and long, silent stretches spent staring at my ceiling that I fell into restless sleep, the kind that exploited exhaustion without relieving it.

Two hours I lasted before I peeled myself out of bed with one objective—distraction.

I cooked two meals from scratch. Watered the plants. Took some photos for Instagram. Played Mario Kart with Dad. Watched a couple of my favorite romcoms—*The Princess Bride* and *Soapdish*. Dove into a new book and stayed up until I couldn't keep my eyes open. But the second I turned out the light and my distractions were gone, my brain woke up and chugged through everything that had come to pass, imagined what would come next.

The first item of business was to try to pin down exactly why I was so upset, and I boiled it down to a few points, which I held on to, repeating them on a loop like Arya Stark and her kill list.

At the surface was the skin-deep wound: we had lost our shot with the magazine, not only by looking like a pack of fools, but incompetent fools. *I* looked incompetent—which on its own hit a deep perfectionist trigger in me—and the responsibility felt like mine, regardless of my knowledge that it wasn't.

The cut that had glanced bone: Luke had gotten his ex-wife pregnant, and she would become a permanent fixture in his life. Which meant she would become a permanent fixture in my life. I didn't blame him for not telling me when he'd found out—he was right in that the timing was garbage. I trusted him with her, I did. I believed him, it was true. But finding out like I did was brutal, shocking and brutal and too fast to follow, leaving me no time to process or even react beyond the knee-jerk desire to get as far away as I could. It was my nightmare—there had been no way to plan around it, no way to prepare, and the trauma had been blunt and forceful, taking me out at the knees.

But the deepest wound of all—the biggest, most impossible reason why I could not seem to stop crying—was because I had fallen in love with Luke Bennet.

It was perhaps the worst of all outcomes.

Not because he made me happy. Not in the way he had earned my trust. Not for the freedom I'd found in him. Luke was full of vitality and possibility, his spark igniting something in me that I hadn't known existed—adventure. Spontaneity. Joy in the unknown.

It wasn't even because he loved me too.

The painful realization that I had let Luke in was a mortal wound. I gave him my heart, day by day, minute by minute, piece by piece. And that was a sacrifice, one I hadn't realized the weight of.

Not until yesterday. Not until I had seen him with her, learned of the bond they would share, and I realized with a brutal drag of the knife that I could lose him.

And when he left, he would take my heart with him.

I would be alone again.

Maybe this was the reason I'd guarded myself all this time, all these years. I'd made excuses—work, my father, etcetera, ad infinitum—because I didn't want to make room for someone. Because when they were gone, the space was still there, empty and whistling with the wind.

The cavernous space left by my mother had never closed, never contracted.

I wondered if the one Luke left would either. Somehow, I doubted it would.

He didn't say he was leaving, I told myself as I trudged down the steaming sidewalk toward Longbourne. *He doesn't want to leave any more than you do.*

But was that desire, that intention, enough to hold us together through the hurricane on the horizon? Because there was another list, one of truths that made up Luke Bennet, truths that had made themselves too known to ignore.

He was irresponsible enough to have slept with his ex-wife, unprotected. He needed constant change, constant action—without it, he would be miserable—and I needed stability. Stillness. Security. For a moment, I'd thought he could be all that I needed him to be. But the chaos of yesterday had pitched me off a cliff and sent me tumbling in a freefall. Everything had changed, and my bearings were lost. I couldn't draw the line between the boy I used to know, the man who'd returned, the man I had fallen in love with, and the man he would become.

Wendy would never stop manipulating him, and he would always let her. It was apparent in the fallout of what she'd said. Two words from Wendy, and our future had been wiped away.

Wiped away but not gone. Like a chalkboard—a smear and swirl of chalk dust, the message beneath it only dimmed by the sweep and residue left by the eraser of those two little words: *I'm pregnant.*

Time. I needed time to catalog and assess the damage. But I would not get it. Not if I knew Luke.

I drew a breath to fortify me as I approached the shop, slowing when I saw the windows, stopping when I realized what was beyond.

Luke had reworked the windows with a concept we'd only discussed. But he had taken the idea and made something beyond my imagination, the message bringing sharp tears to my eyes, setting those embers in my heart aflame.

Giant dandelion heads stood in the window on the left, nearly as tall as me and too big around for my arms to encompass. Foxtails composed the globe of feathery seeds, and the five dandelions were bent toward the door and the right window as if the wind were blowing the seeds away. Across the windows they went, suspended in flight. And in the window on the right, written in daisies and surrounded by flying foxtails, were the words *Make a Wish*.

I wondered if he'd made a wish, wondered what he'd wished for. And then I closed my eyes and made one of my own with my broken heart nicking my ribs.

I swiped my tears away and turned for the door, the cheerful ding of the bell a small blasphemy. The shop was already busy, my tardiness granted by Ivy and fully expended by me, though not to rest and not to find answers. Both had eluded me with expert skill.

Jett offered a small smile and a nod of comfort as I passed, but I was scanning for Luke, heart thudding and breath shallow. But to my relief, I only found Ivy, who rushed me much faster than a woman of her gestation should be able to.

She scooped me into a hug. "Oh, Tess. I'm sorry."

I love him. I gave him my heart, and now, he'll break it. He won't even mean to. I shouldn't have done it. I'd do it again.

"I'm okay," I lied, forcing a smile as I gave her a squeeze and backed away. "How many orders are we working with?"

She worried at her lip, clearly not wanting to talk about work. But she said, "Fourteen. We're behind from yesterday, and a bunch came in this morning."

"Good. I could use something to do with my hands."

A feeble laugh from Ivy. "A whole day off too much for you?"

"You have no idea."

I set up across from Ivy, flipping through the orders, making notes in my mind for what I'd need, grateful for another diversion. Luke had come up with an idea to have a Dealer's Choice custom bouquet option—they would tell us their price range and the recipient's favorite color and flower, if they had one, and I'd make something off the cuff. They had become my favorite bouquets to make simply because each bouquet was different, and I relished in the challenge.

They nudged the edges of my box, encouraging me to get out of it.

It was the Luke Bennet special—getting me out of my box whether I wanted to or not.

For a little while, I lost myself in work. When Brutus wasn't winding his way around my legs or mewling up at me, he stood sentinel at my side, watching the door as intently as I did. Ivy filled the time with idle conversation, and my distraction was almost total. Almost. Luke was suspiciously absent from the shop. Every time the greenhouse doors opened, my heart would stop dead, but it was never him. By lunchtime, I'd convinced myself he wouldn't come in. Maybe he'd been kept busy by the Bennets or Ivy in an effort to do me a solid. Maybe he was tired from working on the window display. Ivy said he'd gone all day yesterday on no sleep, not stopping until they finally forced him to go home.

When the greenhouse doors opened, I didn't look up. But when he cleared the threshold, every nerve in my body reached for him, knowing he was there without my realizing it. When my eyes followed, they met his, held them, said a thousand things, made a hundred apologies.

Ivy slid off her stool, saying quietly as she untied her apron, "I'm going to grab us some sandwiches for lunch. I'll get you the usual."

"Okay," I muttered, my eyes still on Luke.

He was darkness—hair shades of midnight, eyes shadowed by a thundercloud. Lips normally curled with levity were flat and heavy. When he strode toward me, I found my body moving to meet him without permission, as if I belonged in his arms whether I liked it or not, and I wouldn't stop until I was there.

I was almost there when we stopped, too close to be casual, too far apart for comfort.

"Are … are you okay?" he asked, his voice raw.

I shook my head. "You?"

He shook his. "Tess, I ... I'm sorry. I know it doesn't mean much, but I am."

"I know. So am I." A pause, thick with painful silence. "The windows. You made the dandelions."

His smile was brief, thin, just a flick of the corner of his lips. "You like them?"

"They're perfect, Luke."

Another pause as we scrambled for what to say. There was too much, with no way to start.

But Luke found a way. He always did.

"I need..." The knot of his throat bobbed. "Please, Tess. Can I explain?"

I nodded once, bracing myself.

He drew a breath, seeming to do the same. "When I went to her the other night—" He shook his head. "No. Before that." Another breath, a straightening of his spine. "I've never felt more right than since I walked through those doors, Tess. And it's because you were here, waiting for me."

My heart split, the contents spilling out into my chest in a warm pool.

"When she messaged me, the things she said ... they scared me. When she's in that space, bad things happen, and I didn't want my absence to be the reason. I never could have imagined why she wanted me there, what she'd say. And I should have told you then. I'm sorry for that. I'm sorry I got myself into this with her, but I didn't know. I didn't know this would happen."

"That she'd get pregnant?" I asked incredulously.

"No. That I'd find you."

I swallowed my response in a sticky lump.

"She had a boyfriend I didn't know about when we last were together. And when I left LA, I swore I'd never see her again. I moved nearly three thousand miles away to ensure it."

"A boyfriend?" I frowned. "God, Luke. So it really might not be yours?"

"That's the question."

My mind whirred with possibilities and questions and a dozen emotions.

"She has a doctor's appointment in a few days, and I'm going with her. She insists the baby's mine, but ... I don't know. I want to believe she wouldn't lie about this just as much as I hope it isn't true."

I stared at him, feeling his honesty in every word, written in every line of his face. He hadn't known. And Wendy was desperate—I'd seen it for myself when she came here yesterday. But I had no response, no answers. It was all too much to comprehend. But there was one thing I knew for sure.

"I'm so sorry," I said, my chest aching. "I'm sorry you have to go through this, no matter if it's true or not."

"I don't care about that, Tess," he said gently, pleadingly, taking my hands. "None of that matters as long as we're okay. None of it matters if I still have you."

But I couldn't give him the answer he wanted to hear, not because I didn't want to. But because I didn't know if I should.

I'd taken enough risks for a lifetime. The next time I took a chance, I had to be sure.

I withdrew my hands from the confines of his. "This has all been so much, Luke. The drama, the upheaval in the shop, in my home, in my life. It feels like someone reached in and pulled it inside out. I don't know which way is up because there is no one answer. It's not black and white. There is no yes or no, and there's no right or wrong." I watched as his face fell, his eyes sharp with pain.

"But there is. I haven't done anything wrong. I didn't do this to hurt you—it's out of my hands, out of my control. And you don't trust me. After all of this, you still don't trust me."

"I do, Luke," I insisted, my emotion rising in a wave. "But if this has proven anything, it's that Wendy will always manipulate you, and you will always let her. I don't know how I fit into your life, not when it's always in danger of being controlled by her. I need time. And you need to sort things out with Wendy."

"I don't need time for that," he urged, his eyes sparking with desperation and honesty. "I need you, Tess. That's all I need."

"Then you've got to give me time," I said with a shaky breath, taking a step backward I didn't want to take. I wanted less space between us, not more, but if I fell into his arms, I'd never get back out. Too much was unknown to take a leap, and I was all out of faith.

"How much time?"

"I don't know."

His face darkened. "What *do* you know?"

That I love you. That I hate this. That I'm confused and overwhelmed and every choice feels like a mistake, I thought.

But I said, "That right now, Wendy needs you more than I do."

I turned and rushed out of the shop. Because if I'd stayed a second longer, I would have kissed him. I would have promised him everything was going to be okay, not knowing if it would be, and I held on to the mantra that I refused to hurt us even more.

Even if that was its own lie.

Rainbow Road

LUKE

I trudged through the door to my parents' house with the intent to talk to Mom shadowed by the hope that she was already asleep and I wouldn't have to.

It was a day of reckoning, of making things right, and I'd already failed once.

Wendy will always manipulate you, and you'll always let her.

Tess's words, a truth so plain, so blatant. And I'd never seen it, not in those terms.

I just had to decide what to do about it. But first, I had to get through this doctor's appointment, figure out how to determine if this baby was mine. Because if it was, Tess was right. There would be no escaping Wendy.

My life had careened away from me with those two words. And I was no longer in control of anything.

I strode through the first floor, checking the living room, the dining room, the kitchen, finally finding Mom in the library, tucked into the big armchair with a romance novel.

Her eyes were sad when they met mine, but she smiled small, closing her book and resting it in her lap. "Hello, Lucas."

"Hi, Mom." I glanced at my feet, feeling like I was six again. "I … I'm glad you're up."

"Well, I figured you'd come home eventually, and I owe you an apology."

My gaze snapped up to meet hers.

"Come here," she coaxed, waving me toward her as she shifted to move her feet from the footrest.

I took a seat, and she took my hand.

"I shouldn't have said such terrible things, and I shouldn't have lost my temper like I did. I was just so shocked, Lucas. I thought … well, I thought when you separated, you wouldn't see her again. I should have known she wouldn't let you go so easy. And I should have known you wouldn't abandon her. It's a testament to your character, to the fabric of who you are. When you love, you love fiercely. And for that, I'm proud."

"But it was stupid and reckless. I didn't think … didn't realize the stakes."

"No, it's just that the stakes changed when you fell in love with Tess."

I blinked back my surprise. "How did you—"

But she laughed. "I might be old, but I'm not blind. And my children are too easy to fool into believing I'm unaware. Do you really think I haven't seen you two together? You can barely keep your hands off each other."

A chuckle puffed out of me. "So much for secrets."

"Oh, I can't blame you for not telling me—I knew you would when you were ready. And besides, I would have meddled, and we all know it." She squeezed my hand. "How's Tess?"

"Upset. She asked me for time, and I have no choice but to give it to her."

"She doesn't come around quick, but she always comes around. I promise, Lucas. She will."

"I hope you're right. But I can't shake the feeling that it's out of my control. It's in Wendy's."

A shadow passed across her face. "Damn her."

I drew a sigh from the very bottom of my lungs. "Tess said Wendy would always manipulate me, and I'd always let her. And she's right. I just don't know how to untangle myself from her, Mom. I don't know how to let her go because I'm afraid if I do, she'll drown."

"Or she'll swim. But the only way you won't be dragged down by her weight is if you put up boundaries. If this baby is yours—"

"You know about that too?"

She rolled her eyes. "There are no secrets in this family, Lucas. If this baby is yours, get a mediator and sort out custody and rights. Show up and do your duty, nothing more."

"And when she falls apart, threatens to hurt herself and the baby?"

"Then you call the ambulance and go to her. And you fight for full custody. But the child might not be yours. And if that's the case, then you walk away from her once and for all. It's time, son. It's time to move on."

"But I have. I thought I was no longer beholden to her, and then this. Every time I think I've gotten away, I get sucked back in."

"Wendy thinks she still has a chance with you because your actions have never said otherwise. So put your money where your mouth is, Lucas Bennet, and *show* her."

I nodded, hope sparking in my chest. Because showing Wendy just how through we were would not only prove my sincerity.

It would prove my devotion to Tess.

Because above all, that was what I wanted. She was what I wanted.

I only hoped I could win her back.

TESS

My heart thundered as I rounded the last bend of Rainbow Road with Dad hot on my tail. The finish line loomed, and for one second, I thought I might actually beat him.

Should have known better.

A heat-seeking turtle shell blasted me in the rear, and while my car flipped and bounced, Dad flew past and under the banner.

I groaned. "Sneaky bastard."

"Face it, Pigeon. I am the resident champion, and beating me is a pipe dream. Get it? Pipes? Mario?"

"Har-har," I hyucked. "It wouldn't kill you to let me win every once in a while. You know, for my ego?"

He gave me a look. "You'd really want me to throw a game?"

"No," I admitted on a sigh, stretching my back. "Wanna go again?"

"Maybe in a minute. Need to give my trigger fingers a chance to regroup." He held them up, wiggling them for effect. "How'd it go at the shop today?"

"It was…" A sigh slipped out of me. "Dad, I didn't tell you the whole truth."

He smiled sadly. "I figured. What happened?"

"Before the installation broke, Wendy showed up at the shop. She … she's pregnant, and she says the baby is Luke's."

"You … you're kidding."

I shook my head. "We were exhausted—it was chaos. And we got into a fight. No … not a fight. I just couldn't deal with the shock, so I bolted, came home. And yesterday, he came in to talk to me about it. But I can't tell him what he wants to hear, Daddy. I can't tell him everything's fine because it doesn't feel fine. It doesn't feel anywhere close to fine."

"How does it feel?"

"Inside out. Unreal. Scary. I'm afraid," I said softly. "Afraid that everything will change. That he'll leave me. That I'll come second to Wendy, always. That she will manipulate him until the end of time. And I don't know how to manage that fear. I don't know how to take a risk, not when the circumstance is sticky with unknowns."

"Life is full of unknowns. It's scary, and you can't avoid that. You can't plan for it. The happiest and most successful people in the world are flexible, Tess."

"But what if I make a mistake? What if I get hurt? What if I lose?"

"When was the last time you beat me on Rainbow Road?" he asked, the corner of his lips rising.

"Thanksgiving 2012. You had the flu."

"Has that ever stopped you from playing me?"

I rolled my eyes. "It's a video game, Daddy."

He shrugged. "Maybe the stakes are lower, but the feeling is the same. You can't tell me that just now, when you thought you were gonna beat me, your heart wasn't banging and full of hope. What if you'd beaten me? If you hadn't played, you wouldn't have won."

"You beat me," I said on a laugh.

"But what if I hadn't? If you want to play the what-if game, I'm gonna make you consider the good, not just the bad."

"No risk, no reward, right?"

"That's the idea. Listen to me, Pigeon. Don't sacrifice your future just because you're afraid. Sacrifice your fear for hope."

My gaze fell to my hands, emotion tightening my throat.

"Luke makes you happy, and that's not gonna stop just because of Wendy. Deep down, you know that. Don't ignore it just because you're scared. If you need time to come around to the idea, take it.

Luke will wait. I think that boy loves you, and I think you love him too. Don't throw that away, Tess."

I nodded, unable to speak. But he didn't require a response, just reached for my hand. And I found my way into his arms, hoping he was right.

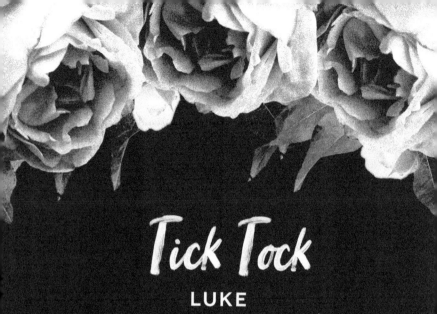

Tick Tock

LUKE

Three days since the bomb had been triggered, and every tick of the clock had brought me to this moment.

Silence crackled in the room, sharp with anticipation as the doctor watched the ultrasound monitor.

My lungs were empty and locked, my pulse loud in my ears. Wendy lay on the exam table, her face tight and eyes bright. She reached for my hand, and I let her, the feeling of her clammy palm against mine sending a shudder of aversion through me.

Everything about this felt wrong.

Wendy's presence. The cold exam room. The static on the monitor. The fluttering sound of a baby's heartbeat. The disbelief that the creator of that heartbeat was me. The sick sensation that I didn't want it to be and the subsequent guilt that it could be. And what a shitty father I was for wishing for something so abhorrent.

The only sound was the bow, bow, bow of a heartbeat and the clicking of the doctor's mouse as she took measurements.

Every second was protracted, unending, the suspense slithering its way through me.

"Well," the doctor said with a smile, "baby's looking great. Strong heartbeat, which is a good sign. Looks like we've got our due date wrong though. You're measuring two to three weeks ahead."

Just like that, my lungs opened up, and I breathed in fire.

Wendy's eyes widened, but she smiled, laughing casually. "No, that can't be right. I know when my last period was. I marked it."

My hand unwound from hers. I took a step back, mind racing.

The doctor chuckled. "Oh, don't worry. There are a lot of reasons it could be off, like when you ovulated, when you conceived. Plus, a lot of the time, we just have the dates wrong. But the good news is, everything's looking like exactly what we'd expect. You're almost in the safe zone."

Shallow sips of air, stoking the emotion stirring in my ribs.

"I don't have the dates wrong," Wendy insisted, her voice sure and light. "Are you sure I'm not just measuring ahead?"

Lied. She lied.

The doctor spun on her stool with a ghost of a frown on her lips. "The margin of error on a pregnancy this early on is only about a week. You're easily two weeks ahead, more like three based on my experience."

Numb hands. A tingle of disbelief. A satisfying sense of rightness, coupled with overwhelming revulsion.

"You should check again." Her voice trembled. She hadn't yet looked at me.

Out. I had to get out. I had to get away.

The doctor's gaze darted to mine in confusion, her frown fully formed. "I can, but the numbers will be the same."

"I know when I conceived!" White ringed her eyes.

"You lied," I breathed.

The doctor's frown flattened, lips pursed as she stood. "The date that you gave me is not the conception date based on the development of your baby." She moved around the table, giving us both a knowing look that lingered on me. I saw an apology in her eyes. "Let me give you the room for a few minutes."

I had backed several feet away from the table, unable to fight, unable to fly. Instead, I froze, staring at her, parsing the truth I'd known in my heart.

"You lied."

She sat, swinging her legs over the edge of the table, her face wild. "I didn't. I swear, Luke."

My head slowly, absently, shook its assent without my telling it to. "It's always the same. The same line, the same story, but with new, painful ways to hurt me. You came back here to trap me, to lie to me. To take advantage of me because you knew I would help you because I always do. I always do. But this time is different. This time, when I walk away, I'm not coming back."

Wendy's face bent, cracked open, and the tears fell. Genuine though they might have been, I had no sympathy.

"Luke, please."

"Please what?" I shot. "Save you? Take on another responsibility that's not mine?"

She shook her head. A sob racked through her as she looked at her hands, resting open in her lap.

"I'm not doing this," I breathed. "I'm not fucking doing it, Wendy. Stay away from me and my family. Stay away from Tess. This is over. *Over.*"

She jumped at the sting of the word, at the jab of my finger in her direction. I turned on my heel, reaching for the doorknob, overwhelmed by the desire to run as hard and fast and far as I could until I collapsed.

I cursed her, cataloged every betrayal, built a wall with every painful memory, not expecting her to speak, not anticipating the depth of honesty in her words when she did.

"I didn't know what else to do," she whispered, the words broken.

My hand stilled.

"When I found out, I-I went to Chad. He told me to have an abortion. Dumped me when I refused. Kicked me out. Blocked my number. But I couldn't. I … I tried, made it to my appointment, and then … I just couldn't do it, Luke. But I don't know how to take care of it either, how to provide. I want to give this baby the life I didn't have. I wanted its parents to love each other, to raise it with love. And I knew you were the only one I could come to. I knew you would take care of me."

I turned, fuming over her as she took my hand.

Her eyes were on our hands as she traced the lines of my fingers. "I thought you still loved me, thought I could get you back for good this time. This baby *should* have been yours. I came to you because you are the only man in the world I want to father my child. And I'm sorry I lied to you—" The words died in a sob. "I d-didn't know what else to do. I love you, Luke. And I f-fucked up. Now … now all I can think about is this baby and how I'm going to take care of it." She pressed her palm to the flat of her stomach, her head bowed. "I have no job. I have no insurance. I have no means and no support. Only you."

My anger ebbed, though my jaw was still clamped shut. Because I understood. I hated that I understood, and I hated that I gave a fuck.

But I did.

"I don't love you," I said in a tone that brooked no argument.

She nodded at her shoes.

"And I can't help you. Not anymore." My heart ached, twisting and tight. "You have to figure this out yourself. And we both need to move on."

Another nod, a sniffle. "I'm sorry, Luke. I'm so sorry."

I fought the urge to soothe her, my mind occupied with imaginings of what she'd do on her own. And even now, even after all this.

"I wish you'd come to me and told me the truth. Because I could have helped you without all this. But you've gone too far. It's all gone too far."

"I thought I could get you back. I … I didn't know you'd moved on."

"Wendy," I said, taking her by the shoulders, waiting for her to meet my eyes. "We will never get back together. Do you understand?"

Sheer and utter sadness touched every angle and plane of her face. "I understand."

And for the first time, I actually believed she did. But this time, I wouldn't wait for proof.

Not with my own life to look forward to.

A Certain Faith

TESS

"I don't know how you've avoided him," Ivy said into a bucket of rhododendrons.

"I don't know either." And it was both a blessing and a curse. I found I didn't want him in the zip code just as desperately as I wanted him to walk through those doors, just so I could breathe his air.

I'd spent the last days looking for answers by avoiding all the questions. I wondered if seeing Luke would jar something loose. If he'd walk through the doors and the clouds would break, shining light on him like a saint in a burst of divine intervention. But I had convinced myself that seeing him, talking to him beyond the few cursory texts we'd exchanged, would only confuse things more.

The last thing I needed was more to be confused about.

"Marcus has been keeping him out of the shop, and Mrs. Bennet too. He's so deep in the doghouse, he'll be making it up to her for years. But I figured he'd find ways to come see you anyway."

"I asked him not to, and he said he wouldn't," I said quietly and with a touch of regret.

Ivy watched me, though her hands moved flowers to a pile on the table. "Have you heard from him?"

A nod, just one. "We've texted some. The … the doctor's appointment is today."

She groaned. "Oh God. No wonder you've been so quiet. Why didn't you tell me?"

I rolled a shoulder. "Because I didn't really want to talk about it."

"Tess, I know it feels safer to board up your shutters and lock yourself away from everyone, but you don't have to go through all this by yourself. You don't have to carry the burden alone."

"I know."

She chose her next words carefully. "I know it's not easy … to be vulnerable. But you're allowed to have feelings. You're allowed to be confused and hurt and angry. However you feel is valid."

But I shook my head. "Every time I'm vulnerable, I get hurt. Every time I love, I lose."

Ivy frowned, pinning me with a look. "You haven't lost me. Mrs. Bennet. Your dad."

"And trusting someone else is dangerous. Because the more I love, the more chances I have to get hurt. The more I open up, the more helpless I am. Why am I not allowed to protect myself against that?"

"Because you're not protecting yourself—you're running away. And those are two very different things."

I had no response to that. My throat squeezed painfully, and I swallowed to open it up.

"I know you think you can plan for danger, but when you're constantly looking for something to go wrong, it inevitably will. You become the master of a self-fulfilling prophecy. And I have a little secret for you." She paused, waiting until I met her eyes. "Uncertainty is part of life. You can't plan for it. You can't brace yourself. There was no way for you to have seen Wendy coming."

Tears bit at my nose. "So what am I supposed to do?" I begged, my voice shaking and tight. "How am I supposed to react? Because I don't know another way."

She reached for my hand, covered it with hers. "You can't run away, and you can't fight it. You can't freeze from indecision and overthink it to death. Sometimes, there's no right answer and there's no wrong one. The only way through it is to have faith."

Faith. Complete trust and confidence, but in what? Life? Luke?

Life had not been kind, but it had given me so much too. My father's words rang in my ears—*sacrifice fear for hope*.

"Whatever happens, Tess, it will work out. Luke wouldn't have it any other way. You have to know that."

I nodded down at our hands. "I do," I said, the truth of it slipping over me, into me, warming my heart and setting a tear on a track down my cheek.

"You have to have faith in him," she urged. "Believe that it will work out despite how much it hurts to get there."

Hope glimmered quietly in me. I pictured myself letting go of my fear. I could see it, my admission of feelings, our reunion. I imagined how it would feel to see him smile, to see the relief on his face, to feel the relief in my heart and the weight of his arms around me. For all my indecision, for all my uncertainty and fear, one truth remained, unflinching.

Luke was all I wanted. There was no choice to be made—there never had been. It was clear and crisp for the first time after days spent wandering through soupy fog.

"I've got to tell him," I said, reaching into my pocket for my phone. "Do you think he'll talk to me?"

Ivy smiled. "Oh, I think he'll talk to you all right."

My bottom lip slipped between my teeth as I wrote out a text.

Hey, if you have a minute, do you think—

I deleted it and started over.

I'm sorry I haven't been in touch—

Are you busy? I wanted to—

Ivy rolled her eyes. "Oh my God, stop overthinking it."

With a laugh, my fingers flew as I reminded myself to have faith in Luke, myself, that everything would be okay. But before I hit send, Ivy drew a sharp breath.

My gaze snapped to her face, but hers was locked behind me. Judging by her expression, I imagined who was there before I looked, my neck turning slowly, deliberately to find Wendy Westham.

She seemed smaller, dimmer than I'd seen her. The fever in her eyes was gone, replaced with a quiet sadness, her hands clasped in front of her. She looked frail. Fragile.

"I … I'm sorry to bother you, Tess. Could we talk for a minute?"

Fear straightened my spine—not of her, but of what she might say. There was news on her tongue, and I found myself certain that no matter what she spoke, things would inevitably change.

Uncertainty is part of life. Have faith.

I tried to smile against my anxiety, wiping my hands on my apron as I stood. "Sure."

Ivy grabbed a couple of vases and headed toward the front. "Let me just take these to Jett for delivery."

A moment later, she was gone, and Wendy and I were alone.

I didn't know how to start, what to say, and it seemed that she didn't either. For a moment, we just stood there with our thoughts whizzing and our mouths firmly closed.

And then she spoke. "I've done a lot of things in my life that I'm not proud of, and almost all of them I've done to Luke." She took a heavy breath and held my eyes. "I love him, I always will, but I just keep hurting him, over and over. And he's always been there, despite it all. Until now." Her throat worked as she swallowed. "The baby's not his."

My lungs contracted, emptied like I'd been kicked in the chest. In that moment, I realized I'd convinced myself that it was his child, that everything he and I had to face, we would have to face it with a child and his ex-wife between us.

Somehow, the knowledge that she had lied about something so serious was a thousand times more shocking.

"Why?" I breathed. "Why would you do this to him? To the Bennets?" *To me?*

She swallowed visibly, her face tight with pain and regret. "Because I didn't know what else to do. You … you have to understand—I know you've seen it for yourself. He is my safe place. No matter what happens, he's always there. The man who fathered this baby doesn't want it and doesn't want me. I … I've never been able to support myself, and now? This baby's future depends on me, and I don't know if I can provide it. So I did the only thing I knew to do—I came to Luke. Because I knew he would take care of this baby and me. I thought maybe he could even love me again. But I was wrong. I didn't know he was in love with you."

My hand had found its way to my lips, my thoughts tripping over themselves.

"I came here to make amends. To tell you the truth. You deserve to know that he didn't do anything wrong, except trust me. As long as I've known him, he's only denied me once before you—when I cheated. When I called, he always came. When I needed him, he was always there. He has been the most steady and true thing in my life, my entire life. But he's not mine, not anymore. He's yours."

She took a step toward me, her eyes bright with pain.

"Please, don't let my mistakes stop you from loving him. Because he deserves to be with someone who will give him what I never could."

My hand fell to my side. "Did he tell you to come here?"

"No. He doesn't know I'm here. But I owe him so much, Tess, more than I can ever make up for. I'm here because I owe it to him to fix what I broke, to clear his name. Luke said I have to do this alone, and he's right. It's time to move on." She laid her palm on her stomach.

Something about the look on her face, the tone of her voice, the gentle honesty written all over her hit me deep in the recesses of my heart. She was alone and afraid, and she'd come to Luke. She'd sought safety, and as much as I hated what had happened and how it had happened, I found I couldn't hate her for it.

She wasn't evil. She was afraid. But not for herself.

For her child.

What she'd done, she'd done for her baby. And that was a truth I could find forgiveness for.

"You won't hear from me again," Wendy promised. "I won't interfere, and as soon as I talk to Mrs. Bennet, I'll be out of both of your lives. Make him happy, Tess. He deserves it." She offered a small smile, bowing her head as she turned and walked away.

My mind reeled.

As long as I'd known Luke Bennet, I'd believed him to be flighty and unpredictable, unreliable and irresponsible. Even through the last few months I'd held on to that kernel of doubt, the old ideology never letting go.

But I was wrong—he was exactly the opposite. He was kind and giving to measures of absolute certainty. He sacrificed himself for others, even when it cost him dearly. He shouldered responsibility for things that were not his to be responsible for. He was steady and sure in ways I never thought he could be, in ways that had brought Wendy across the country strictly to seek safety in him. If the baby had been his, he would have done anything, everything to provide. Even now, even having endured what she'd put him through, I believed he would try to help her, do what he could to ensure her security.

And if I gave him the chance, he would do the same for me. More, if I let him.

I wanted to let him. And I wanted to give him everything he had given to me.

Ivy rushed to the back, wide-eyed and back stiff, but before she could ask any questions, I grabbed her hands, smiling.

"I need your help."

"Anything," she said with a sputter.

"Help me tell Luke I love him."

And her own smile spread. "I thought you'd never ask."

Moments

LUKE

The entire Bennet clan was squirrely.

The Bennet penchant for gossip—regarding Wendy, I assumed—was the cause. Every time I walked into a room, it was to whispers that burst into overly loud chatter. I was being systematically guided through my day in an effort to keep me out of the shop. My siblings disappeared at intervals. My mother led me around by the nose, citing my promise to make up my transgressions, an especially fresh bruise after Wendy had come by to talk to her. They'd said goodbye with a tearful hug, and afterward, I'd been surprised the Bennets didn't bust out a preordered cake and pour the good scotch to commemorate the occasion. Instead, Mom had wrapped her arms around my waist, burying her face in my chest while she cried. Partly from relief, I was sure. But her words only spoke of her pride in me.

That, and her desire for me to make things right with Tess.

But that was the thing. The only thing for me to do was wait, and it was driving me to the edge of insanity. I'd asked to see her, but she'd blown me off. I wanted her to hear the news about Wendy from me, but not over text. I needed to see her.

But I'd lost the right. And by this point, she'd probably heard from one of my siblings. No chance that news wouldn't spread like wildfire.

That night, I lay in the top bunk with Kash snoring below, phone in hand and Tess's messages pulled up. There were so many things I wanted to say. But I couldn't say any of them. Not if I wanted her back.

And I wanted her back. I wanted her back so badly but had no control. The thought of losing her was white-hot pain in my chest, the knowledge that it was largely out of my hands crippling.

But I knew what she needed. I could be patient. I could give her space. Because I believed in my love for her, and I had faith that she'd come back to me. So instead of typing out all the words of my heart, I clicked off my phone and tried to sleep.

When I woke, it was with that same solid sense of hope I'd gone to sleep with, alive and tangible in my chest. In fact, it was stronger, more vital than it had been since everything came unraveled. Maybe it was because I was no longer beholden to Wendy, or maybe because my name had been cleared.

Or it could be the hope set in motion by Natalie's agreement to come to the shop to talk to me about potentially working with the magazine again. That was, if I could convince her, which I felt certain that I could.

But today, I could sense a shift. I only hoped it was in the direction I wanted.

Kash was already gone for the day, and I pulled on clothes and padded downstairs, breaking up another Bennet whisper session. My mother, Laney, and Jett popped apart with comically wide smiles on their faces.

I folded my arms and gave them a lazy smile. "What are you

whispering about?"

"Nothing! Nothing at all, Lucas," Mom said, floating across the room with a flush smudging her cheeks. "Did you sleep well? Are you hungry? Laney, get the donuts. We have Blanche's. Would you like Blanche's?"

I eyed her as I baited, "No time. Going down to the shop."

Her face snapped open like I'd known it would. "Oh, no—you have to have breakfast first! They don't need you down there, no, not yet." She hooked her small hand in my elbow and tugged me toward the table.

It was like the time they'd tried to throw me a surprise party. The Bennets sucked at secrets—everyone except Marcus and Dad at least.

"Not hungry, but thanks, Mom." I dislodged her hand in the same motion that I kissed the top of her head. "Natalie's coming to the shop to talk about the feature, and I need to meet her soon. Want to make sure everything's looking good down there before she gets here."

The three of them exchanged a worried glance.

Mom grabbed my arm again as Laney pulled out her phone and scooted into the kitchen.

"Well, if you have to go, I'll come with you," Mom insisted. "Just let me get my shoes on."

The next fifteen minutes were spent being stalled by my mother. First with a case of missing shoes—her favorites for her outfit, she insisted. Then, it was a hunt for a sweater even though it was almost ninety degrees out. Whoops, look at that, she had forgotten to take her medicine, which killed another five minutes. A bathroom stop, a brief phone call, and a question Laney needed an urgent answer for in the kitchen, and we were finally walking out the door.

"Subtle, Mom," I said with a smile as I opened the door.

She smiled slyly up at me as I passed. "It's unlike you to be suspicious, Lucas."

"You would make the world's worst spy, you know that?"

With a laugh, she said, "It's true. Never did have a taste for firearms."

And then it was my turn to laugh as we descended the stairs to the sidewalk, turning for the shop. I looked up, not sure what to expect.

That was when I saw her.

Tess stood in front of the turquoise door, sunlight gleaming on her auburn hair, casting a shine on it like a new penny. Her velvety eyes were alight with hope and apology as she stood before me, waiting for me.

"Hear her out, Lucas. And tell her how you feel," Mom said gently, squeezing my arm before letting it go.

I drifted toward Tess with a confession, a profession, an admission on my lips, but before I reached her, she stepped toward me to grab my hand and tow me to the window, turning me to face it.

My lips parted in awe as I took in the display—I'd only seen Tess until just then.

Written across both windows in flowers were the words *Love happens in moments.* And I stepped closer, distantly noting that her hand fell away.

In each window were three vignettes, marked by signs held by scrolling frames. Moments, moments we'd lived, moments I'd lived with her, moments I'd loved her. The first was a small pile of hay with our blanket tossed over it, a whiskey bottle and two glasses on display next to a sign that said, *When you first kissed me.* The ladder she'd fallen from: *When you saved my life.* The swing I'd made for her: *When you stole my heart.* Numb feet walked me to the other window where three of our succulent crates were strung. *Sometimes, things work out,* its sign said, and next to it was a piece of our broken installation. *And sometimes, they don't.*

At the end was a mirror, its elaborate gilded frame carved in whorls and waves. In the curves of the scrolls, ranunculus in creams and peaches over leaves of green.

I glanced at my reflection, then at the sign under the mirror.

But as long as I have you, nothing else matters.

Tess moved to my side, and for a long moment, I memorized the sight of us in the mirror, the vision framed by flowers, the rightness of it staggering.

She turned. I met her. Looked into the face I loved so well, and all the things I wanted to say boiled down to one.

"I love you," I said, my hands framing her face, tilting it up to mine.

A laugh slipped out of her, her eyes shining with tears. "Wait, that was my line."

But I smiled without an ounce of regret. "You did all this for me?"

"Because I love you, Luke Bennet," she said, smiling as she spoke the words that would forever change me. "Can you forgive me for my fear if I promise to always have faith?"

I drew a breath that drew her into me, and I answered her with a kiss, pressing my lips to hers in a delicate crush of decision and affirmation. And I kissed her with every corner of my heart and soul open in offering.

She melted into me, her body pressed against mine, the space between us gone, even when I broke the kiss.

"I am so sorry, Luke. I was so afraid—afraid for our future, afraid I'd lose you—and I can't … I don't want…" Her voice broke.

I thumbed her cheek, the space under her palm on my chest aching. "Shh. Please, don't apologize," I whispered.

"You told me nothing matters, not as long as we have each other, and you were right. Losing you would leave a wound that would never heal. Nothing matters, not as long as I have you."

With a breath, I made a promise. And with a kiss, I sealed it.

"I'm yours," I said against her lips before taking them.

Forever was written in that kiss.

When it finally broke, I gazed down at her, brushing her hair from her face with a smile on mine. "I knew they were keeping me from something, but I had no idea you'd done all this."

Tess laughed. "We hatched the plan yesterday." Her smile faded. "I'm sorry. For what you've been through the last few days. I should have been there for you."

But I shook my head. "I didn't know how to handle it either, and I don't blame you for needing time."

She gazed up at me in wonder. "Anyone else would have been furious with me for pushing them away like I did."

A chuckle. "Four days we were apart. Granted, they were four of the longest days of my life, but you needed a couple of days to process my ex-wife telling a room full of people she was pregnant with my baby. You weren't being unreasonable, and you have nothing to apologize for. And Wendy won't bother us again. You were right, Tess. She would have always manipulated me, and I would've let her. But not anymore. I promise you that."

A sheepish expression touched her face, brightened her cheeks. "Wendy came here yesterday. She told me everything, and after talking to your mom … well, we thought maybe there was a way we could help her after all. We need an extra set of hands, and she needs a stable job with insurance and an employer who understands her situation, who can be flexible if she needs to take a few days off. We want to give her a chance, if you feel the same."

I searched her face. "Is that really what you want?"

"It is. I believe her. And I want to help her."

"Then I'm in."

"All in?" she asked with a sidelong smile.

"All fucking in." My eyes traced every plane and angle of her face. "I can't believe you're here. I can't believe you came back to me."

"Oh, I didn't go far," she said on a laugh. "I love you, Luke Bennet. And I'm not going anywhere."

She tightened her arms around my neck, and I leaned in, knowing exactly what would happen before it did. I knew the moment our lips would meet, knew the way she would taste. I knew the softness of her lips and the familiar curves of her face, fitted in my palm. I knew her. And in that moment, I realized she always would come back, and I always would be waiting.

Because the way I loved her would never fade. And as safe as she was in my arms, I was safe in hers.

We wound together, a tangle of arms, bodies flush and kiss deepening. God, how I'd missed her. And for a moment, I gave myself over to the joy of finding what I'd thought I'd lost.

Cheering was what broke the kiss with a shocked pop. Whooping, whistling and clapping came from beside us, our surprised faces swiveling to the entirety of the Bennet clan, Tess's dad, Ivy under Dean's massive arm, everyone watching us with watery eyes and flushed cheeks. Blushing, we turned to them, though she was still tucked into my side. I couldn't let her go, didn't want a millimeter between us. Tess laughed, leaning into me, the weight of her hand on my chest like an anchor, tethering me to the earth as I took in the happy faces of those who loved us.

When I reached the end of the line, I realized with no small amount of shock that Natalie stood at the edge of the brood, and a photographer stood next to her. I couldn't see the girl's face though—her camera was pointed at us, shutter flashing.

Tess saw her too and sucked in a breath. "Is that—"

"I forgot she was coming the second I saw you. It was supposed to be a surprise."

"Well," she said, straightening her spine, "let's go see if we've got a shot."

Before we could talk to Natalie, we were rushed by our family and friends. Mom was crying and blubbering and taking turns holding our faces and hugging us. Dad just smiled proudly from the back of the crowd, his eyes deep with emotion and hands in his pockets. My brothers and sister making jokes and laughing and hugging and clapping shoulders, as was our way. Tess hugging her dad, kissing the top of his head. His grip was iron, his smile sideways, his blessing plain.

And the second I could, I laid a hand on the small of Tess's back and nodded to Natalie.

She stood, smiling on the sidewalk, as the photographer snapped pictures of the front of the shop. When we approached, she offered a hand and a smile.

"Well, we didn't quite expect all of this, but what a pleasant surprise," she said, gesturing to the windows.

"I know just how you feel." I glanced at the photographer. "I didn't think you'd be shooting though."

"It was too perfect not to. We haven't filled the spot, so I was hoping we could still do the piece, if you're interested. I know after the other day you might not want to—"

"We'll do it," I interrupted. "But this isn't the installation you asked for."

"It's not, but this story is even better. The Bennet family comes together to save the family legacy. How Luke Bennet and Tess Monroe brought the failing flower shop back from the dead and found love somewhere along the way. I'd like to feature you, the two of you, as the center of the article. What do you think?"

I glanced down at Tess, deferring to her, sure she'd decline such a public exposure.

But to my utter shock, she smiled broadly and said, "I think it sounds brilliant." She looked up at me, full of hope and love. "What do you think?"

"Tess, I want to tell the whole world how much I love you, and this seems as good a medium as any."

And she laughed up at me as long as she could before I kissed her.

Make a Wish

TESS

The day was a whirlwind.

The Bennets rallied, taking care of the shop while the photographer followed Luke and me around as we toured a typical day in the life of Longbourne. Luke and I clipped flowers, buckets and armfuls. I made a few arrangements as the shutter clicked. We went to storage and pretended to work on things, which mostly consisted of Luke using power tools without purpose and the two of us fiddling with some of the old installations like they were new. While we stuffed our faces with pizza, the photographer shot the rest of the Bennets in their natural habitats—Mr. Bennet and Kash in the greenhouse, Mrs. Bennet in the front with Jett, Laney taking pictures with her phone and ribbing Marcus, who looked both wildly out of place and perfectly himself in a suit black as midnight.

Everyone seemed equally pleased and exhausted by the time we were finished in the early afternoon. Mrs. Bennet retired to rest, and the rest of the brood dispersed. I jumped into work with Ivy, and I thought Luke would leave to run deliveries. But he didn't seem to want to be parted from me, and for that, I was ecstatic.

Four days without him had been too long.

We closed the shop at dusk, said goodbye to everyone, the last ones there, as we always were.

And when we were alone, it was as if no time had passed, as if nothing had changed. Except everything had, and in the best way.

I sighed blissfully as he locked the grate and the front door. The possession I felt for him ran bone deep as I measured the breadth of his back, marked the flashes of his jaw. The care he took, the love he gave to this shop, to his family, to me. In this man was a heart too big to contain, with patience and love beyond the bounds of comprehension. And he was mine.

Never had I felt so fortunate. Not in my entire life.

When he stood, he turned to me with that smile on his face, the one that had once infuriated me simply because I thought it could never be mine. The one that now lit me up like a pyre, dedicated to my love for him.

He took my hand and stepped into me. My chin rose so I could hold his eyes.

"I love you," I said.

"Good, because I love you too."

The brush of his lips against mine were too tender, too achingly adoring.

"Come on," he said, towing me toward the back.

I chuckled, trotting to keep up. "We can go to my place, you know."

"I know. But this … this is our place."

The simplicity of the words didn't undermine their weight. And I followed him through the moonlit greenhouse, carried on a cloud of perfume and hopes and starlight.

Storage was dark, but he knew the way. My hand was lost inside his, his free hand reaching for the outlet. When the golden fairy lights illuminated the space, it felt like we were standing in a dream. The dandelions he'd made surrounded us among the familiar furniture and frames, baskets and crates. And there in the middle was our hay pile, the home of my happiness and joy.

This. This was where I had fallen in love. This was where I'd learned to let go. This was where I'd found myself and where I'd found the man who changed my life.

When he kissed me again, it wasn't a brush or a flutter. It was a claiming. He captured me with his arms, his lips. With his hands, so strong as he laid me down. With his hips, so insistent. It wasn't slow, though it was deliberate—the way he undressed me, the way he touched me. The way he kissed me whispered a word to me, and my heart echoed another back.

Mine, his body said.

Yours, mine replied.

And he took the offering I gave with a declaration of heart, a promise of self, one I knew was forever.

Forever. I knew without knowing that he was my forever.

And I wouldn't waste a minute.

Not one.

Imagine That

LUKE

Tess chuckled against my chest, and I pulled her a little closer, as close as we could get without tripping and eating sidewalk.

"Seriously, as much as I love the hay pile, can we please sleep at my place tonight?" she asked. "I'm going to be picking hay out of my hair for a week after sleeping there last night."

"You say that like it's something new."

"I know, but now we actually have another option. My room is on the other side of the apartment, and Dad not only sleeps like a rock, but he has a white-noise machine. Please?" She was almost whining. "Just think—clean sheets and pillows and a nice, soft bed that doesn't make us itchy."

"You sure your dad is okay with that?"

"He says he is. I'm sure he's not thinking about it in much detail."

I laughed. "God, I hope not."

"Honestly, I think he's just so happy about the prospect of us and of me not ending up a spinster, he'd agree to just about anything."

I kissed the top of her head. "All right, we'll sleep at your place, but if I wake up with a rifle pointed at me, I'm out like disco."

That earned me a laugh and a squeeze of her arms around my waist. "I'll lock up his bullets at least."

"Preciate' that."

We turned the corner toward the shop and my parents' place where dinner with my family awaited. The last thirty-six hours, Tess and I had only been apart for a forty-five-minute stretch, so we could shower and deal with our families. Well, I'd dealt with mine and rushed off to her place as quick as I could.

Part of me worried it was all a trick of the mind, that I'd knock on her door and she'd be gone or we'd be kicked back to a few days ago when everything was suspended midair, when we were waiting to see what would happen when the chips fell. But she'd answered the door, flushed and smiling, hair damp and smelling of flowers.

It was as if she were composed of flowers. Roses, red and thorny, delicate and dangerous. And somehow, I'd eased my way through the brambles to lose myself in the velvety beauty of her.

We climbed the steps and walked through the door to the sound of the chaos that was my family. They were seated at the table, their faces swinging to us when we entered, followed by a chorus of cheering. Dinner was freshly on the table, and so we hurried to sit, somehow managing to simultaneously greet six people in the process.

"Well, I must say," started my mother, "the sight of you two together warms my old, rickety heart. I can't imagine why you kept it from me all this time."

Kash snorted a laugh, shoveling a mouthful of potatoes into his mouth. "Sure, because you would have been so hands-off and kept completely to yourself, right?"

Mom made a derisive noise. "Don't talk with your mouth full, Kassius. And I would have been the very picture of restraint."

Laney laughed. "Your first item of business would have been nailing down a wedding date."

Mom gave her a look. "One day, you will have a brood of children, and then you'll understand. Can you blame a mother for wanting her children to be happy and find love?"

"Only if she's incessantly nosy and makes you go on dates with Jenny Arnold," Marcus deadpanned.

With a wave of her hand in his direction, Mom said, "Jenny Arnold is a sweet girl. Don't you worry—I'll see you all happily in love and on your way down the aisle sooner than later. If you didn't think I had Tess saved for one of you, you don't know me at all." She met my eyes, flashing a wink I don't think anyone else saw.

Tess smiled from beside me, reaching for my hand.

"Now, I wonder which of you will be next?" Mom said, smiling sidelong as she scanned the table.

"Not it," Kash said around a mouthful of dinner roll.

Echoing not-its made the rounds. Pretty sure Jett was last simply for the look of warning he shot at Mom, which we all knew was as useful as an umbrella in a hurricane.

But I held Tess's hand and met her eyes. Her smile pressed a kiss to my heart.

And forever began.

Epilogue

TESS

The pop of champagne sounded with a yelp and a chorus of whoops as we stood on the sidewalk outside Longbourne, the lot of us smiling up at the brand new sign.

The last six weeks had been a heady whirlwind of action along with a settling in of routine. And this—the raising of the new sign—seemed to mark the end as well as it marked a beginning.

Mrs. Bennet raised her glass. "To Longbourne and all the people who love and care for her. May she bloom eternal."

Hear, hear! we cheered and took our sips of solidarity.

I leaned into Luke, his arm around my waist and a smile on his face. I smiled back up at him.

"Show her," I said quietly.

With a nod and the briefest of kisses, he let me go to reach into his back pocket. "Mom, I've got something you might want to see."

She looked down at his hands as he unfurled the latest edition of Floral magazine. One gasp, and she was crying, passing her champagne to Mr. Bennet with her eyes locked on the cover.

Longbourne stood tall and proud with that pop of vibrant blue that Luke had painted the door jumping off the page. The installation sang on the cover, the words *Love happens in moments* across the windows framed the top of the page perfectly. And in the middle stood me and Luke, my arms around his waist and his around my shoulders. We were laughing, as we often were, the candid moment setting my heart skipping in my chest.

Mrs. Bennet couldn't speak, overwhelmed as she flipped through the pages to the spread for the shop. The article was titled "Coming Up Roses," next to a full-page picture of Luke and me in the greenhouse, arms full of flowers and smiles boundless.

This was the point when she burst into tears.

Luke pulled her into his side as she turned page after page. The last page of the spread was the entire Bennet family with Mrs. Bennet in the middle, holding a bouquet of roses in shades of fuchsia. At this, she turned into Luke's chest and cried openly and without an ounce of shame.

The article recounted the history of Longbourne, starting from its establishment and its legacy. Its decline and its resurgence. The work we had all done, the window displays and the innovative arrangements. And at the heart of it all was a theme no one could deny.

Love.

A family's love. A love of growing and creation. The love Luke and I had found together, our partnership sparking change that tore through Longbourne like wildfire.

The Bennets watched their matriarch, their faces bent with emotion. Ivy and Dean stood off to the side, watching as I did, because the Bennets were their own entity, their own animal, their bond so strong and certain that everything else was left outside without intent. But we watched them with the love in our hearts as fierce as theirs.

And just beyond Ivy was Wendy, eyes shining and smile soft.

We'd had to work to convince her to come work at the shop. I won't lie—I'd been more than a little worried about having her there. But she had been not only kind and brimming with deference, but eager and excited to learn. The extra set of hands left me more time to design the windows and come up with specialty seasonal bouquets, which had in turn blown up our deliveries.

My gaze moved back to Luke, my pride in him lighting me up from the inside. In a few weeks, he'd start trade school in the first step to getting his contractor's license. He could learn new things, which was his favorite itch to scratch. And the second he'd decided, he'd thrown himself into a remodel of my bathroom in order to connect it to my bedroom, not even pretending like it wasn't for his own benefit.

The second time my dad had busted him in a towel in the hallway was the last straw.

And as for me? Well, I'd proposed my book idea to Natalie, and she'd made me an offer last week—their parent company was interested in publishing a book on floral arrangements, and they wanted me to write it. It was my dream realized.

Things were coming up roses all right. And we all felt the effervescent joy and hope that came along with the success.

The Bennets converged around Mrs. Bennet, wrapping her up in a huddle of dark hair and brilliant smiles. And when they broke, Mrs. Bennet was in the center, swiping at her cheeks.

"I'm beginning to think you all enjoy watching me cry," she said on a laugh.

Mr. Bennet smiled down at her. "Only when it's with this much joy."

She leaned into him, pressing her cheek to his chest as he kissed the top of her head.

Everyone began to chatter, the cluster breaking to head back inside. Everyone but me and Luke.

He snagged the last two of his boxes from just inside the shop, kissing his mom on the cheek as we passed. I wrapped her up in a hug of my own.

"Take care of him, Tess," she whispered.

"Always and forever," I promised.

And with a smile of understanding, we parted ways.

He carried the boxes like they were nothing, but I could tell by the hard bulges of his biceps that they were heavy.

"I think she liked it," I said as if it wasn't obvious.

"I don't know, I couldn't be sure. On the Mrs. Bennet scale, those waterworks were lackluster at best."

A laugh slipped out of me. "Really, a poor showing if I ever saw one. I told you you should have proposed."

He shot me a crooked smile. "Don't tempt me, Tess."

My heart and my stomach switched places, my smile wide and cheeks hot. "Luke Bennet, if I didn't know better, I'd think you had plans."

The look he gave me liquified my insides. "Oh, I have plans all right. And when I implement them, you'll know. But first, move-in day. I've got to make sure you can handle Luke who leaves his socks lying around and doesn't close drawers."

"You act like we haven't spent the last six weeks joined at the hip."

"Joined at the something, definitely in the vicinity of the hip." He waggled his brows as we reached the door to my building and headed inside. "Anyway, now you're gonna get the real deal. The unabridged, unadulterated Luke Bennet. The one who never hangs up hand towels and puts dishes next to the sink instead of in it."

I smirked at him as we climbed the stairs. "Are you trying to scare me off?"

"Nah, but full disclosure—I will leave laundry in the basket for a month if it means I don't have to fold anything."

"You're impossible."

"I know. What are you even doing with me?"

"I ask myself that every day."

He pouted next to me while I unlocked the front door.

But I smiled, clarifying, "If I could figure out one reason why you're with me, I'd be satisfied."

"Oh, I'll give you a hundred, Tess Monroe."

The way he said it was a promise or a warning—I couldn't be sure. Either way, I wanted every one.

"A hundred, huh?" I turned for my room with him on my heels, hoping at least a few of them involved kissing.

"Mmhmm," he hummed, kicking the door closed and setting the boxes down. He stepped into me with a predatory look on his face that hit me in every soft spot of my body. "For starters, your lips are the sweetest thing I've tasted. Your devotion to what you love inspires me. Forever used to feel like a cage, a trap, but then you taught me that forever is an adventure, and I want to spend every minute of it with you."

I wanted to tell him all the reasons I loved him too, but he kissed me before I could. Laid me down in the bed we would share, in the room where we'd spend our honeymoon and where we'd conceive our own Bennet brood. I had a glimmer of it then, a tingle of hope, and a rush of possibility for a future that would come true.

I'd live every moment with joy.

And I'd love him with every heartbeat, to my very last breath.

thank you

Every book we write is its own ride. Down a rocky hillside. On a bike with square tires. It's a fun ride, but a difficult one nonetheless. And as such, there are always a lot of people to thank for enduring that journey with us.

At the top of my list is always my husband, Jeff. The man with the plan who always anticipates what I need, usually before I even realize I need it. You are my forever hero. Thank you for always believing in me.

The second person in my list is always Kandi Steiner. She's the first person I say good morning to (as Jeff rises long before me in a feat of willpower I will never possess), and she's the last person I speak to at night. She is privy to every little bump, every little scrape. Every high, and every low, she is always there, my Polly Pocket and best friend. I love you, babe. Thank you for holding my hand always.

I am fortunate—*so* fortunate—to have a tribe of women who are always kind, generous, and loving with their time and hearts and souls. Karla Sorensen, who is always willing to listen, always eager to help, unflinching and prepared for anything. Everything. Abbey Byers, who spends countless hours plotting with me, deconstructing characters, discussing the minutia of every scene, every moment between these people who aren't people, but are. Kerrigan Byrne, my love and mentor, my guru whose imagination is bigger than the known universe, who is always prepared for a long string of what ifs and a blooming of a story into something epic. Sasha Erramouspe, who is always the first to offer to read the story *just one more time,* ad infinitum.

There's Kyla Linde, my villain litmus. Jacqueline Mellow, who is always prepped to help this Texan girl bring New York to life. BB Easton's always waiting to remind me that none of this matters and we're all gonna die (burgers and fries, nobody dies. Aka, Frankie Says Relax). Tina Lynne is at the ready, just waiting to help however she can, usually by helping me run the insanity that is book signings and social media and book mailing and swag, forever and ever, amen. Carrie Ann Ryan always has words of encouragement to spare, even when she's spread thin—though you'd never, ever know she was. She's simply that kind.

My betas never let me down. When I make Kris Duplantier cry, it's the equivalent of winning a major award. Sarah Green always tells me the truth, even when it stings, following it up with all the ways she believes in me. Danielle Legasse forever makes me feel like a queen, even when I'm certain I'm pond scum. Heather Monroe gives the most sound, vital feedback, and has made this book so much better for it.

To my production crew—Jenn Watson and Sarah Ferguson at Social Butterfly, Jovana Shirley at Unforeseen Editing, Ellie McLove at Gray Ink, Nadège Richards at Inkstain Design Studio, and Najla Qamber for putting together promotional resources. Every single one of you is vital to me, and I can't tell you how much I appreciate you. Thank you, so much.

To all of my bloggers—you make the book world go 'round. Thank you so much for all your hard work, dedication, and the joy of books that you bring to the world.

And readers—Thank you. Thank you for reading, for spending your time in my brain and heart, for loving books. Thank you, thank you, thank you.

about staci

Staci has been a lot of things up to this point in her life: a graphic designer, an entrepreneur, a seamstress, a clothing and handbag designer, a waitress. Can't forget that. She's also been a mom to three little girls who are sure to grow up to break a number of hearts. She's been a wife, even though she's certainly not the cleanest, or the best cook. She's also super, duper fun at a party, especially if she's been drinking whiskey, and her favorite word starts with f, ends with k.

From roots in Houston, to a seven year stint in Southern California, Staci and her family ended up settling somewhere in between and equally north, in Denver. They are new enough that snow is still magical. When she's not writing, she's gaming, cleaning, or designing graphics.

FOLLOW STACI HART:

Website: Stacihartnovels.com
Facebook: Facebook.com/stacihartnovels
Twitter: Twitter.com/imaquirkybird
Pinterest: pinterest.com/imaquirkybird

CPSIA information can be obtained
at www.ICGtesting.com
Printed in the USA
LVHW012319161121
703493LV00004B/762